Welcome to *Hello and Goodbye*: two dark tales from two deceased narrators – bottled-lightning treats that will make you gasp, gurn, shiver and squirm.

Please read on for *Hello Mr Bones*, in which an evil puppet master and his flotilla of fiends reacquaint two reformed souls with the demons they thought they had defeated.

First published in Great Britain in 2013 by

Quercus
55 Baker Street
7th Floor, South Block
London
W1U 8EW


Balloon artwork by Nicola Budd



A CIP catalogue record for this book is available from the British Library

ISBN 978 1 78206 013 0 (HB)
ISBN 978 1 78206 014 7 (TPB)
ISBN 978 1 78206 015 4 (EBOOK)



10 9 8 7 6 5 4 3 2 1

Typeset by Ellipsis Digital Limited, Glasgow

Printed and bound in Great Britain by Clays Ltd, St Ives plc

# Hello Mr Bones

Patrick McCabe

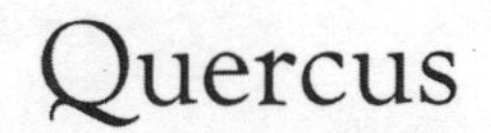

For Richard

# 1

Impairment, intellectual or otherwise, I tend to approach with the equanimity I do all other human failings – extending to the disadvantaged the civility which is their due. And in this respect little Faisal Taylor was no different to anyone else.

Chris Taylor had given birth to her son Faisal in the autumn of 1975, the unfortunate consequence of a brief and ill-fated liaison with a fellow student in training college.

Embittered though she had been by her abandonment – her former partner had returned to Palestine and was never seen again – Chris Taylor had rallied impressively. It was their 'bubble of love', she declared – her and her son against the world.

Thus affairs had proceeded – until Valentine Shannon had appeared, arriving into their private emotional fiefdom in the spring of 1987, having being appointed to the staff in Tower Hamlets – and placed in charge of Class 6M.

A development which had been the occasion of much rejoicing for the former Christian Brother Valentine Shannon – who, having immigrated from Ireland at the end of the previous summer, had all but given up hope of securing employment, regular or otherwise.

And now, even though at the age of forty-two he was still a virgin – was there anyone in London who would have credited such a thing? – he had found himself also deeply involved with a woman whom he loved.

His appreciation of his good fortune knew no bounds. Which was a fact he daily acknowledged. For, whatever his trials might have been in his former school of Glassdrummond College, they had not succeeded in breaching the walls of his faith. No, in the secret city of Valentine Shannon's heart, his faith in the Godhead remained unassailable.

Which was why, to the bewilderment of his beloved Chris, he continued to insist that when the time came to seal their union, it would have to be within the bosom of the Catholic Church.

That was his wish, what he desired, he had informed her many times – and she respected that.

---

In Chris Taylor's youth, as an ardent feminist, she would promptly have scorned such antediluvian orthodoxies – brazenly welcomed the opportunity of doing so, indeed.

But the appearance of Valentine Shannon had altered all that. As indeed had the cold procession of nights in her Cricklewood flat – where the relentless polemicism of the past now only affronted her with its unyielding certitudes, as did the memory of the routine collegiate defiance of those years, when her absurdly healthy, quite indomitable coterie of humanities students assembled on the university quad cobblestones for yet another march – against student fees or some comparable grievance. Now seeming as significant as some anonymously humdrum suburban family photograph.

*

She liked Valentine principally on account of his lack of deviousness. In that respect he resembled her progeny – that is to say, her partially deaf boy he had nicknamed 'Wee Fysie'.

—You love him, don't you? she would say to her son as she combed his hair, you love your new daddy. Because he's so dependable – you just know he will always be there. Isn't that right, Faisal?

And her son would agree because he didn't know any better. Except that Valentine Shannon was anything but free of deviousness. As I, to my cost, have known for some time. Just as Christine will – and soon.

Or my name isn't Balthazar Bowen.

# 2

In the past, in spite of his relative youth, Valentine Shannon had been considered something of a traditionalist, and was respected for it, imperiously patrolling the halls of Glassdrummond College like some latter-day 'Mr Chips' – a text which, coincidentally, had been set for his pupils during the current academic year. And which he missed no opportunity to deride, casting his head back haughtily as, yet again, he found himself pouring scorn upon it, mocking its sentiments – rather badly, it has to be said – in an exaggerated public school accent:

—Yes, boys, the years for Mr Chipping seemed now to pass like 'lazy cattle' moving across a landscape.

As he himself, like some old sea captain, who still measured time by the signals of the past, listened anew for the faint cries of alumni – Pettider, Pollett, McKenna, McCartan . . .

Alumni – well-respected traditionalist or not – that he himself most certainly would never be likely to encounter again. As he came to realise when news of the 'Glassdrummond Scandal' finally broke. That is to say, when details of 'The Martin Boan Affair' began to seep out. And Valentine Shannon was forced to leave his place of employment in disgrace, banned forever from Glassdrummond College.

---

That was some years ago now, of course. Not that it was on his mind, sifting through some more essays on the subject of that very same 'bagatelle', a description he insisted on applying to the Hilton novel, which he claimed to be of so little worth that, far from being 'the classic novel of school life', represented nothing but a waste of both his and his pupils' valuable time. He had even, fleetingly, considered a class viewing of the 1930s Robert Donat film for the purpose of ridiculing it even further. Even going so far as to contemptuously dismiss the very *notion* of 'boarding school' as a way of life. Although one wonders why such a simple and innocuous account of a now almost vanished way of life ought to have assumed such a degree of importance in his mind. After all, if it was of so little consequence, why did it seem to irritate him so?

It was a question, however, which I knew he would never ask – and I didn't expect him to. As he continued to lift those copybooks from a pile, one evening in October – it was actually the 16th – in Class 6M. Before becoming momentarily distracted – he could have sworn he heard a rumble, like the faintest tentative roll of far-distant thunder. He leaned forward, listening attentively – no, it had been nothing. The air outside was still and clear.

Giving himself once more to fond thoughts of Chris – who was waiting at home in Barnet along with Faisal.

Yes, this was the behaviour of the man named Valentine Shannon, as I observed him intently, listening to his intermittent sighs as he absently tugged at the sleeves of his plaid jacket. Which was of the 'sports' variety, complete with the obligatory pedagogical leather elbow patches.

—There's a phone call for you, the young boy announced, poking his head around the door.

At which point the custodian of Class 6M arose from his chair and, with impressive purpose, came striding along the main corridor of John Briory School.

An innocent indeed, I mused with some considerable bitterness. Asking myself why had I not heeded my brother's constant and insistent warnings? My beloved twin Bailey they could call remote and even cruel – but in truth my dear relative, certainly in the grander scheme of things, rarely ever got things wrong. He would stand by the window and upbraid me, remorselessly:

—You're much too tolerant, Balthazar, can't you see? You ought not ever to have invited that boy Shannon up here to The Manor. It will, all of it, come to a bad end yet – believe me.

Mother had lived in the house with us until long after Father's death. We had never gotten along – it might have been better if she had hunted me from the place – for that, in her heart, is what she secretly desired.

—You'll never be anything – nothing compared to Bailey! I used to hear her complain with bitter regularity – at least that's what I *think* she was saying. It's what I remember – over and over, flouncing in and out of rooms.

—Do you realise that? she would carp in that deadening drone of hers, routinely commending his stern moral principle and clipped, reserved bearing at the expense of my purported dissolute emotionalism. Until the day came when I could endure it no longer. I distinctly remember the *episode*, if you could call it that – it was as if my brain was splitting – ultimately, however, parting so cleanly it might have been a satsuma. As a cascade of tears came flowing down my cheeks.

But, whatever she may have said over the years, I bear my brother no grudge for having been her favourite.

For it could get lonely up there in The Manor, particularly being confined to one small corner of the building which, like so many of its kind in the modern age, was no longer financially viable. Only for his company I don't know what I'd have done – my stern and remote twin brother I mean.

Not Shannon. Oh, no.

May the curse of seven kingdoms light upon him.

---

We had been in Rosses Point, I remember, one day – Valentine Shannon and I. I kept my yacht *The Morning Star* moored there six months of the year. I had just treated him to a fabulous slap-up meal, and he had practically cleared the plate, as I recall. Had quite an appetite, this young chappie from the terraces. Yes, displayed quite a voracious enthusiasm indeed, throughout what was to be our last meal together. Not that I could possibly have been aware of that. After all, he had neglected to inform me that he had more or less decided to pay a visit to the local police station. No, I hadn't as yet been acquainted of that regrettable fact.

# 3

Now, if you don't mind, Valentine Shannon actually found himself singing as he came along the corridor, jauntily approaching the staffroom door. Which gives some indication of how confident and self-assured he had become. Why, it was as if the college scandal had never even happened. Once upon a time, believe me, the announcement of something as innocuous as a telephone call would have been enough to pitch him into a state of the most profound distress and apprehension. Not now, evidently.

—Chris Taylor, I love you, he heard himself murmur as he pushed the door of the staffroom open.

—The forecast is good for this evening, I'm happy to say, remarked the school principal, looking up from his desk – according to the BBC, at any rate – and our old reliable weatherman, the ubiquitous Michael Fish!

—Yes indeed, Valentine replied, which is good news for me for I don't see myself leaving here until well after six this evening.

—Not long now until half-term, Mr Shannon! laughed the principal. It doesn't take long for the backlog to pile up!

—It certainly doesn't, Valentine agreed, as the headmaster nodded towards the receiver on his desk.

—Thank you, he said, and reached over to pick it up.

The headmaster excused himself, exiting the room.

---

It was hard to believe, Valentine thought, that they had met at Camden Market, Chris and he – a place to which he had been only twice in his life. Chris had mounted a stall there, selling various trinkets and knick-knacks – leather goods, bead necklaces and assorted items of oriental jewellery. She and Faisal were well-known there – all the traders greeted them by name.

He would never in his wildest dreams have expected them to have anything in common – which, as it transpired, they didn't. In her blouson leather jacket and heavy lace-up boots, not to mention her constant deployment of roll-up cigarettes, her attitude and lifestyle seemed light years away from his own. But they'd gone for a coffee and, surprisingly, had discovered that a kind of comfort existed between them.

—I like your accent, she had said to him, I like its sound.

That was all she had said that day. In the Golden Spoon café in Camden Town. As Faisal, quite oblivious to the racket he was making, stirred some melted ice cream in a glass, with his jet-black hair hanging down across his face. Valentine couldn't, for the life of him, believe it was happening. Her comments regarding his voice – he had actually blushed upon hearing the words.

---

But already that day belonged to a somewhat remote time. Almost, in its way, as distant as those last few miserable weeks in

Glassdrummond College. He was a new man now – composed, with an inner resolve. All thanks to Chris and her lovely son Faisal. He smiled and cleared his throat, drumming his fingers on the padded surface of the principal's office desk.

As he raised the telephone receiver to his ear, he imagined it was probably Chris who was calling – most likely wondering would he be home late this evening. Because of course she knew that his half-term reviews were coming up. He smiled to himself as he thought of her sitting there at home – with Faisal beside her, legs up, lying on the rug – wholly absorbed, as usual, in his jigsaws.

—Play with me, Mr Valentine! the boy would cry.

Shannon spoke deliberately into the mouthpiece:

—Hello, is that you, Chris?

There was no reply.

—Hello? he repeated.

Still nothing – which was odd. Not that he was worried. It was just inconvenient.

---

As he thought of her tucked up there on the settee with her boots off, turning the pages of one of her magazines – the *New Statesman*, most likely. And was on the verge of smiling. But just at that moment the muscles in his neck stiffened and he became aware of a face at the window, staring directly at him. It was that of a boy – in fact he looked quite hideous, pressing his face grotesquely against the glass. He held this unmistakably repugnant pose before, quite dramatically, with a shrieking laugh – inexplicably disappearing again. A draught was blowing some papers across the desk. Valentine Shannon gripped the receiver tightly.

—Is that you, Chris? he continued – with some considerable impatience.

There was a hiss of static, then silence once more.

—Is that you, Faisal? If that's you, Faisal—!

He was suitably agitated now, and I primed myself for a telling whisper.

—It's not Chris, I said, it's not her. It's me – Mr Bones. Say hello, dear Valentine. Please will you say hello?

I was rewarded with a dumbstruck silence.

---

Then, just at that moment, the principal returned, brushing past with some files and other papers, before retrieving a forgotten item from his desk. As, with equal brusqueness, he disappeared once more.

—Hello? repeated Shannon, tapping the receiver.

But no sound was to come. Even the static had dissolved into silence.

# 4

In the light of what happened, at least as far as the caretaker's wife was concerned, the fact that John Briory School had been playing an important second-round league match was not important. She had been insulted by the Class 6M teacher, she claimed.

—Took the face off me in front of everyone, she explained vehemently, just who on earth does he think he is?

Prevailed upon by the headmaster, Valentine Shannon had, with some reluctance, eventually consented to apologise.

What had happened was this: he had been in the middle of correcting some of the essays on his desk when he had found his concentration broken by what he had later described as an 'unholy riot' taking place outside the classroom.

—Perhaps if I'd never received that bloody telephone call, he later considered.

Then he might not have found himself, with scant appreciation of what he was doing, rushing headlong out into the playground in order to confront the boys concerned – and coming very close to actually striking one of his pupils. Demanding hoarsely:

—In the name of Christ, what do youse think you're doing? Don't you know I'm trying to do my half-term reviews?

Any manifestation of blasphemy was deeply fro
John Briory school – and certainly from a member of
A number of youthful faces regarded him perplexedl
dawned on the teacher what it was he had just done.

Having returned to his classroom, a flush of deep embarrassment was seen to colour his countenance. The shrill cries once more had also returned to the playing field, as if – at least that was his impression – with the intention of humiliating him. A bitter taste was forming in the schoolmaster's mouth. As, facing him, a single blurred line seemed to compound the felony:

—Authority must depend for its legitimacy on formal rules and established laws.

All of sudden he felt quite disquieted. Before a small item on the desk caught his eye. It was approximately three inches in length – shaped like a pearl-white, narrow scallop. He was on the point of picking it up when an abrupt knock sounded on the door. Without realising it, he had already turned around:

—Yes, for heaven's sake – what is it now? Isn't it possible to get a minute's fucking peace?

Before realising he was confronting Mrs Beggs, the caretaker's wife. Who was responding to this new and quite unanticipated outburst by glaring back sullenly and resentfully towards him. Later he would come to accept that this display of tetchiness on his part had been both unnecessary and unacceptable. Which was why he went down to the kitchens in order to deliver a full apology to Mrs Beggs. But the caretaker's wife was nowhere to be seen. And when he returned to his classroom, he was ashamed to discover that the item he'd assumed to be a bone – a bone, for heaven's sake! What had gone and made him think that? – turned out to be nothing more unusual or remarkable than a child's plastic hairgrip, presumably mislaid by one of his students.

# 5

The woman on the upper deck of the bus had been staring at Chris Taylor for some time but Faisal's mother had continued to remain quite unaware of the fact. And it was only when she eventually snapped out of her reverie that she came to appreciate the source of the lady's concern – and how unnecessarily protective she was being of her son, whose limp, fleshy hand was lying prostrate in her lap.

—That hurt me, Mummy! Faisal cried.

Without thinking, Chris had been clutching it ever so forcefully – something of which she was now deeply ashamed. Because it wasn't the first time, as she well knew. From her bag she produced a packet of Emerald caramels – a present from Valentine, confectionery which Faisal absolutely adored.

—He's happy now, said the woman sitting opposite, settling her own hands on her lap with relief.

Chris Taylor smiled – but still remained uncomfortable. Once upon a time, she knew, she would brazenly have confronted her fellow passenger – demanding to know what business it was of hers. But, over the years, Chris Taylor had mellowed considerably, for a variety of reasons. And now such sallies into battle were reserved solely for issues she considered to be of major importance. Gone were the late-night debates on the subjects of abortion and rape and the inhospitability of the streets for women – which had taken up so much of her time when she'd been employed in the Hackney Women's Centre. Supplanted now by issues of a much more trenchant nature – ones which directly affected marginalised children, such as Faisal. On whose behalf she'd been labouring tirelessly – in an effort to ensure him a place in Kingsbury Senior. Because very soon the time would come when he would have to leave Coles Green Special School. She had been experiencing nothing but resistance in this regard, however. A fact which contributed considerably to this tendency towards over-protectiveness, not to mention the anxiety attacks which she had been experiencing recently. Which, being a rationalist, she found difficult to comprehend. In general, she attributed the episodes to nothing more dramatic than simple everyday overwork – it just came with the job, she persuaded herself. But sometimes these attacks could become so overwhelming as to almost debilitate her in the most alarming fashion. And which I have to confess tended to make me laugh – one time I watched her actually stumbling in the street, as though afraid that someone was pursuing her. There was another occasion when she became convinced that Faisal had sustained the most terrible accident. All of which turned out to be in her head. But had nonetheless seemed so vivid and real at the time. She had even been sure she'd heard him call her name. Then there was the so-called incident with the band-saw – when she had become obsessed by this idea that he'd had the most terrible accident at his carpentry in the sheltered workshop. In which his thumb had been severed – nothing could seem to put her mind at rest. Except that when she arrived, in quite a state, at the workshop, the first person to meet her was, in fact, her son Faisal. Standing waving in his tracksuit, with his rich black hair obscuring his face.

Before wrapping his arms around her neck, and as he did so ostentatiously displaying what might be described as nothing less than the healthiest complement of thumbs, if that's not a little flippant and unfair. Which isn't my intention – at least, not yet.

---

Simply because my plans for Chris Taylor are much more ambitious, really, than that – as they are for her partner Mr Shannon. Plans not unconnected with a report in the *Evening Standard*, concerning the most horrific murder of a similarly disadvantaged boy – in this case Down's syndrome – in Florida, USA.

From the very moment I read it, I became taken with the idea that it was a fate more than appropriate to Chris's credulous prodigy. To her darling little boy who means so much to the dear lady. A matter to which, inevitably, I would sedulously attend, just as soon as I had finished with Valentine Shannon. Or to be more precise, whenever I considered his collapse complete. Having recruited for that precise and specific purpose a certain personage who is waiting dutifully in the wings – what you might describe as a veritable angel in her white Fiat Uno, and who in the fullness of time shall be dispatched to deliver him to those happy fields – pious cherub with care upon her cheek – dearest Ronnie Clegg.

Of course there will be those who will protest, perhaps with some measure of justification, that Chris Taylor and her son deserve no such retribution. Oh, please! is all I can say – while calming them, generously, with my unique little trademark ditty – in uncoiling falsetto:

*—Say hello to Bonio*
*Always on his ownio*
*Never will he moanio*
*Because he's your best friend!*
*Collywobbles!*

---

There had been a number of disappearances, apparently – in the South Beach area of Miami, the paper said. But it had been only in more recent times that any link had been made to the children's parties. In particular, those which had been conducted by a clown whose professional name, apparently, was 'Bonio'. Which, as you can imagine, tickled me immensely – so reminiscent, certainly nomenclaturally, of one's long-standing sympathetic associate, Mr Bones.

—My boy was just waving at the pink flamingoes, his mother had been heard to helplessly protest, and then when I turned around he was gone! Like, had, literally, vanished from the earth!

The reality of the murder, as is so often the case, was infinitely more grisly than anything detailed in print. There had been nothing at all immediately evident in the bedroom suite of the International Hotel. It was to be in the Frigidaire that their unimaginable fears were to be realised. Where, lying in a dish, they discovered three pearly, crimson-stained baby teeth. There had been no wounds on the boy's body. Those are my words, I should mention, not the detective's; who would likely have employed more professional and neutral terms – kinder, and for good reason, in the circumstances. There were no marks of teeth to be found on the body of the deceased, male, 12. Possibly that's how he would have put it. It soon emerged that the clown Bonio had a predilection for those who were physically or mentally subnormal. Or just simply impaired in one way or another.

—That will suit young Faisal just fine, I remember smiling as I closed the *Evening Standard*, and to which I will give my full attention, just as soon as I've finished with little Master Shannon, twinkling Judas, villainous perjurer.

# 6

To many it would seem that events in this world just simply occur, take place randomly without even being perimetrically connected. That, however, is simply not the case. One is much more meticulous than that. Having spent a significant proportion of her twenties denying the existence of the maternal impulse, there was no one more surprised than Chris Taylor when she discovered that very same tendency asserting itself spectacularly some time after meeting Valentine Shannon. There was something so appealing, so guileless in his eyes, that it routinely breached her sturdy defences. Their partnership exerted a remarkable effect on the normally fractious Shannon also – one which did not go unremarked in certain quarters. In the classroom, in particular, he had become noticeably calmer, much less prone to quick-tempered outbursts. A development which would have seen his old colleagues in the minor seminary of Glassdrummond College, where he had served as dean for some years, reacting in an extremely bemused fashion. Although among his colleagues there were those who ascribed this nervous tendency to his former association with people such as myself. Or 'those awful Bowen people' as people were wont to refer to my dear brother Bailey and myself – and particularly when the embers of the scandal were still warm.

Such assertions, of course, as I have already pointed out, having no basis at all in fact – simply none. The actual truth being that, if anything, Bailey and I, we actually spoiled the little terrace urchin. It is far more likely that his highly strung nature was a consequence of his father's untimely death when Valentine was ten – after which his mother couldn't cope, poor thing. Who else in the village could possibly have guided him? There was no one else from whom the boy could derive his standards, no one at all to look up to, bar the Bowens.

—It's not his fault but it's preordained, Balthazar. He'll use you and dupe you, then in the end he'll turn on you, like them all. It's the way they see us landed gentry.

That was his view, my beloved Bailey. I only wish I had listened to him. But, like he said, I was always too much a softie – far too easily led by my emotions. No wonder Mother preferred him, looking at me in that way that she did. As if to say:

—There's something *wrong* with you. There are times, Lord knows it, when I ask myself why did I even *have* you?

One day I confronted her – stamped my foot and screamed until I became hoarse. It was the worst thing I could possibly have done in the circumstances. When Father came home he found her sobbing and took me aside to give me the thrashing of my life. Then he flung me underneath the stairs. Which I liked, in a way, there in the dark with the smell of paraffin, playing with my doll, the eminent Mr Bones. It was a little toy skeleton I'd found amongst the lumber. I used to wish I was Bailey in those days – disciplined, dispassionate, more than capable of subjugating his strong nature to his will.

—They'll eat you alive, consume you every inch, he used to warn me.

And oh, how right did my twin brother turn out to be!

---

Which doesn't matter now – for all that is in the past. But of *course* it is – with the adult Valentine Shannon having found himself contented and in love in the arms of Christine Taylor. Oh, of course he has no need of such dilapidated aristocracy, of the likes of Balthazar or grim, austere Bailey Bowen. Or, as he might term us himself, that pair of 'eccentric perverts'.

For, at last, Valentine Shannon has become a proper man.

Yes, he had become a man now, he would repeat to himself during those early days when he was first going to meet her. Gone now, he would muse, were the nights of cold anticipation and dread, when apprehension and anxiety would leave the poor fellow quite worn out. Departed also were the days when even the slightest of sounds – a sudden footfall, perhaps, or the simple closing of a door – would see him, boy and adolescent, turn grimly pale, quite worn-out by emotion and irresolution. For these developments he was inordinately grateful.

---

Even in the aftermath of that regrettable incident with Mrs Beggs the caretaker's wife, he was still now feeling that. That so often he found himself in complete command of things, more than capable of subordinating his will and emotions. And, sitting alone there in the hushed classroom, this was what he repeated to himself, as he applied a damp handkerchief to his forehead – that he had nothing at all to worry about.

He was convinced he hadn't. Which of course made me glad, for it was a cast of mind which suited my purposes admirably, as might be imagined. He looked out the window. Everyone had gone. It was just after six o'clock.

—Is that the time? he asked himself. I'd be as well to start making tracks. Chris and Faisal will be home before me.

I followed in his wake all the way to his car. Without so much as uttering a word, not even bothering to ply him with the slightest suggestion. All of that would come in good time. And I have plenty of that.

Why, Mr Shannon, I think I may have forever.

# 7

In the aftermath of her break-up with Faisal's father Salib Toyeh, in midsummer 1976, Chris's friend Mo Rogers had proved herself to be of invaluable assistance – throughout what had been a terrible time. But it had to be admitted, what with Mo having no children of her own, there could often be issues which would prove quite beyond her. Issues which would find her resorting to inappropriate responses of the most platitudinous kind. Such as, for example:

—Do you think perhaps it's just a phase he's going through?

Or:

—Do you think Faisal's getting enough physical activity?

There were even times when – Mo Rogers and Ronnie Clegg in particular – emboldened by their political convictions, they would emotionally castigate the hopeless inadequacies of the British educational system, or chastise individual teachers, whom they accused of not being sympathetic to those in the category of 'special needs'.

But, deep in her heart, Chris Taylor knew they were deceiving themselves and that certain combative responses on her part had been prompted by something closer to panic. She had even apologised to a class teacher in this regard – classifying her own aggressive behaviour as 'unforgivable' – which was laudable, really, it has to be acknowledged.

She had accused the teacher of 'making too many demands' on Faisal – insisting that he, 'quite unnecessarily', conform.

—Every child is different, partially deaf or not! she had snapped at the classroom door. Their own individual expression must be allowed to remain that – their own!

---

Now, over eight years later, somewhat older and wiser due to experience, or maybe because Valentine Shannon had entered her life – or perhaps a combination of both – Chris Taylor tended to view things in an entirely different light.

Yes, those mornings when she would wake up anticipating yet another 'small disaster' almost as a matter of course, in the classroom or supermarket or wherever it might be, seemed nothing more than regrettable times which had been inexplicably visited upon some faint, scarcely remembered acquaintance.

Once, when Chris had been attending a women's conference in Leeds – Val had taken Faisal to Chessington Zoo – she had found herself alone after a few drinks in the hotel bedroom, and an awful night which lay buried in her memory had returned to defiantly plague her, on her own. It was that time when Faisal had appeared out of nowhere on the landing – standing in the doorway with his little voice quivering.

—Look, Mummy, it's *the man*! he had moaned pitifully – with his finger pointing.

There was nothing at all to be seen, of course. But what had horrified Chris, at the time, most of all was the impulse which she had experienced to physically – and violently – strike her son. Where had that come from? she asked herself.

It seemed as though the suggestion had been planted, slyly inserted through a gap in her defences.

—I told you before! There is no *man*! she had bawled at him hysterically.

But already she knew how Faisal would describe him. It would be just like the figure he had drawn in art class – and which his teacher had suggested gave cause for some concern. In its sheer obsessiveness, she had explained.

He would fearfully describe the man and 'his hat'. The hat with the feather which he always wore while he was watching him. With the piercing eyes and the smile that said: 'Fysie.'

—Mr Bones! Faisal would shriek, with tears and mucus intermingling on his face. Mr Bones – no!

In her heart she would have preferred tapered fingers and matted hair. A graven image – hideous, repellent.

But 'the man' possessed no such characteristics. In his feathered trilby he looked every inch the unremarkable suburban gent. There was something so familiar about him that she did not want to name or utter it.

There had been another similar incident, which she could not bear recalling. When they had been driving along the M1 motorway and, quite without warning, her son loudly burst into tears.

—*The man! The man!* he continued to cry out.

So upset had Chris Taylor become on that occasion that she'd had actually no choice but to pull the Polo in. Before rounding on her son with an unforgivable ferocity, which later would return to shame her.

—Stop it, do you hear? There is no man! You will have to stop, Faisal, now I'm warning you!

But neither reason nor reprimand could seem to persuade him. As he continued to point towards the side window with quivering forefinger, as the streams of traffic roared past in blissful ignorance.

Over the course of that year she had lost almost two stone. Such episodes, however, were now – hopefully – concluding. Thanks, certainly in some measure, to the solidarity and comfort provided by one or two close friends. But, more than anyone, it was Valentine who had helped her to 'believe again'.

Lately he had started bringing Faisal to football. To cheer on Arsenal, his favourite team.

—Yeah! The Gunners! he would heartily cry – proudly attired in white and red.

And as time marched on, relaxing into one another's company, it did indeed begin to seem as if all of her troubles belonged in the past. With Faisal sleeping like a top every night. And from the man in the trilby, why, there hadn't been so much as a word in ages.

---

Making her way across the road from the car park in Camden, out of nowhere Chris Taylor found herself getting the most amazing idea. Deciding out of nowhere that it would be the most wonderful thing for her to arrive home to Barnet with tickets in her bag for a fabulous, surprise holiday!

—Where could we possibly go? she asked herself, searching in her bag for her credit card and purse.

The assistant behind the travel agent's desk could not have been more helpful.

—What about here? I've just been! she suggested, passing the glossy brochure across the counter.

—Miami, Florida, USA, mused Chris, abstractedly turning the sumptuously coloured pages, where a foamy wave was breaking massively upon a powdery, dreamy-blue shore.

—There are special deals for kids with disabilities! This looks like the one for me! Fantastic! I must be crazy but no – I think I'm going to go for it! announced Chris.

Quite literally amazed by the impulsiveness of her response. For it really wasn't like Chris at all. What had made her behave in that way? she wondered. Maybe it was Valentine Shannon, she chuckled, not without giving a shiver of delicious delight.

Or maybe it was something else, I murmured. But not to Christine. Oh no, we couldn't do that.

---

Making her way back across the road towards the market, she thought to herself how this – her going and doing an impulsive thing like that, she meant – was yet another indication of just how transformed her life had become. Talk about leaving the past behind!

Then she turned the key in the rolling wooden door, sliding it back to reveal her inner sanctuary – her own private emporium, with its boxes of Asian clothes and various accumulated knick-knacks, all there ready and waiting to be sorted. And which she set to straight away, hardly having begun when – to her astonishment and, indeed, no end of amusement – what did she find? Only a small, jangling skeleton, a little toy, which became illuminated in the dark, with a little band around its hat forming the name 'Mr Bones'. A chance discovery which had the effect, what with her being in such good humour already, of sending her into paroxysms of laughter, as she popped the toy, for Faisal, into her bag. As she gave herself once more to thoughts of their forthcoming vacation in Miami. Where, if she'd but known it, Bonio would be waiting. Bonio, that is, who was fond of extracting teeth. But where would be the advantage in letting her know that? Why, then, for heaven's sake, she might never have gone!

# 8

You and that Bones, my brother used to say. You're almost as superstitious as these God-awful peasants. But if he had such powers as you claim he has, why doesn't he predict the awful end that's in store for you? Scooting about the village in your boater – you look a fool, thank God our mother's not alive to see it. Driving around the place in your Trojan, honking your horn and acting every inch the benevolent gentleman. She'd have you back under the stairs in a flash, my dear deluded, maddening brother. She'd have claimed, like she always did, that you simply weren't 'right'. That she knew in the womb there was something very much the matter with you.

It can hardly be argued that my brother was incorrect. For I had indeed, as he had predicted, set myself up for a fall.

—Stay away from that boy Shannon. I implore you as I have done in the past. It can but come to a bad end, Balthazar.

In those days, of course, he was simply wasting his words – I was a fool. I didn't listen.

It may well have been that Valentine Shannon had planned the whole thing – to dupe me for favours and then inform the police. To this very day, being honest, I really cannot be certain. I cannot say. All I know is – he broke my heart and consummately fractured my soul. And for that, believe me, he is going to pay. For the vengeance I propose to exact – it will be without precedent. (Well, almost – ha ha!)

---

Of course, I ought not to have let it, as Bailey had insisted, come to this. But, try as I might, somehow I just could not apprehend the guile in Valentine Shannon. Not, at least, in the beginning, when he'd come up to The Manor after school.

—I love Pinky and Perky, he used to say.

I always made sure to give him plenty of cake. Mrs Thornton's best home-made marble, mixed with the creamiest milk and eggs. Which I always made it my business to purchase. Even Bailey couldn't resist it, and no matter how he might protest to the contrary, there were plenty of times when he came down to join us at our entertainments in the boatshed. Where I'd erected a screen and put in a projector, a Bell & Howell I'd bought in London. As we all laughed our heads off, enjoying *Betty Boop*.

---

Then there would be other nights, when I returned from the village, when I'd find my brother sitting there, dark and brooding. Squatting all alone in the parlour, with his features white and restrained, his words distinct in their forced composure:

—You're not to let him ever come here again!

It's only a matter of time now, he'd say.

And how right he was. The sergeant arrived exactly one month later.

—Valentine Shannon has made these accusations, he said, he says you interfered with him . . . is this true?

---

—There is only one thing you can do now, my brother.

I can remember them so well – Bailey's parting words. As he turned his back, and in that wry and deeply regretful way that he had, said:

—Goodbye, old friend. Whatever else you might be, you'll always be my twin brother.

With a weary heart, I assented and left.

---

Father had purchased the cherry-red Trojan convertible in Germany. It was a beautiful machine – a four-seater convertible with solid rubber tyres and hinged flaps to either side that lifted to reveal the motor. Without further deliberation, I placed my foot firmly on the acceleration pad and, overtaken by the most extraordinary tranquillity, plunged headlong into the greenish waters, sinking to the bottom with but one single thought remaining in my mind.

—Rest assured, you will pay. You will pay for what you have done this day, Valentine Shannon. Of that be certain – and that I will not rest until retribution has been made, until untold terror has taken up residence – come permanently to reside inside your cruel, disloyal heart.

# 9

*Disabled Action* read the heading on the leaflet in Chris Taylor's lap as she waited for Faisal outside the psychotherapy room in Coles Green. As so often before, she chastised herself for having arrived early. Which was pointless, really – for she did it every time.

Very shortly now her son would appear – tumbling along, hopelessly uncoordinated, jet-black hair hanging, crying happily:

—Mummy! Chris! Yeah!

In the beginning, she was not about to deny it, these flamboyant displays had tended to embarrass her. But then, for so long she had been bitterly confused – a hair trigger, really, if the truth be told.

Many of her friends had expressed deep concern. But contented themselves with the conclusion that the noticeable change in her personality was an inevitable consequence of her parting with the Palestinian Salib Toyeh. With whom they, of course, had been friendly also, having spent three years in Strawberry Hill together.

Nonetheless, however, they professed themselves surprised that she had not considered a termination – but decided in the end that they had no right to judge – certainly no automatic entitlement. For, at the end of the day, it was Chris's personal decision – as a person, a woman in her own right.

—I'll get through this on my own, she defiantly announced – almost as a matter of routine.

However, her inner tension and apprehension were manifest. It wasn't going to be easy – and they all knew it.

During their first year as practising teachers, they arranged to meet every weekend at a North London pub. But after a period of time had elapsed, when the somewhat forced conviviality had ultimately run its course, these meetings eventually came to an end, as everyone committed themselves to the task of building practical new lives – severing the umbilical cord that continued to bind them to the college.

This, however, was by no means easy – and Chris Taylor found herself experiencing enormous difficulty. The main reason for this was that, no matter how she might endeavour to persuade herself otherwise, she still missed Salib. In this respect her psychiatrist, Dr Freeland, was to prove indispensable.

—It's a testimony to your strength that you didn't go under back then, her shrink would often muse, much later on.

Dr Freeland, at least as far as Chris Taylor was concerned – was the author of the feminist mother's bible. Had it not been for that volume, Chris remained convinced, she simply could not have endured. She would have given up the fight – why, long before. And most certainly would never have confronted another particularly unhelpful teacher – that principal, the cow – who, initially, had resisted Faisal's integration.

That conflict had represented one of the greatest traumas of Chris Taylor's life.

But she had come through in the end, had seen it through to its bitter and traumatic conclusion.

⋆

Like so many things, though, it was over now – and that was where it would remain, in the past. This was what she told herself as she waited there patiently in the polished school corridor of Coles Green. She could hear Faisal's chuckles behind the psychotherapy-room door. Which, of course, as always, made her smile as she light-heartedly returned to her magazine. Whose pages now, to her surprise, reported no facts concerning research and practice in the world of those with special needs, for the simple reason that she had picked up an entirely different publication. The pages she was leafing through told her all about Florida, the hotels, the entertainments, the powdery white beaches. A twenty-foot breaker surged high above the towers of Miami and it almost made her swoon. It was hard to believe but this holiday in South Beach would, in fact, be just her second holiday with Faisal. As well as being her first with Valentine her partner – soon, she privately hoped, to be her husband. She smiled as she thought of his open, innocent face – that red hair, those boyish freckles. That twinkly Irish expression that she loved – his sheer handsomeness!

She thought of what Ronnie Clegg had said (Ah! My sweet chosen angel!) after meeting him for the first time:

—Quite extraordinary – who would have dreamt that you two would make partners? An English atheist and an Irish Catholic clergyman!

She thought of them both now on a veranda in Miami – knocking back cocktails, right in front of the hotel. With Faisal modelling a big straw hat. Boy, were they gonna be happy or what! she laughed.

—Faisal Taylor the king of Florida! she heard herself calling – as her son in his flip-flops waved from the water's edge.

—Faisal Taylor is the king! she cried.

As Valentine tugged his baseball bill down – and smiled in that sparkling way she'd grown to love.

---

The only other holiday she'd had with Faisal had been in County Sligo in midsummer 1976, when she had boarded the B&I ferry for Dublin, making her first and only trip to Ireland – moved to travel there for no reason that, even yet, she could understand, and finding herself in a country where she didn't know a single soul.

—It was such an odd time, she said to herself, I wasn't myself at all. I could have ended up anywhere, I guess.

She had booked into the Yeats Country Hotel in Rosses Point and almost immediately wished she had not. It was the most distressing thing – that nagging feeling of constantly being observed. It seemed to be everywhere. Which indeed it was – for, from the moment she arrived, I never once took my eyes off her.

Then of course there had been the small matter of little Faisal, dear heart – why, he seemed to have been crying from the moment they'd landed. How miserable she had felt – chastising herself for having made such a mistake. And it didn't help things when she discovered a framed print on her bedroom wall – containing the well-known line from 'The Ancient Mariner':

*A frightful fiend doth close behind him tread.*

It wasn't perhaps surprising that it had induced an involuntary shiver as she stood there, reading it. Not that she had any need to worry, not then. I was only having a little bit of fun. No, no harm at all was going to befall Christine Taylor. At least, not yet. It simply wasn't the time.

However, her memories of that night were to remain ever so vivid. She hadn't been able to settle after reading the print. All through the night she had been tossing and turning, before getting up to stand by the window, unsettled by indeterminate misgivings as she gazed out across the bay and the stark upright concrete tower – along the pale expanse of sand whose smooth pattern was broken at regular intervals by black wooden groynes. And close by, the dim, ever-present, murmuring sea.

Where could it possibly be coming from, she asked herself, this intense physical fear, this profound mental loathing?

But no amount of reasoning could dispel the throbbing feeling of uncertainty and discomfort. She attempted to draw on the tried and trusted strategy of routine antipathy directed towards her former partner. But even that proved insufficient. As a broad flood of moonlight seeped in through the massive panes. And then they arrived, as if expressly to ridicule her tremors, the first few drops of cold perspiration, standing out starkly upon her forehead.

---

Such had been the fragility of her temperament the following evening that it would have been foolhardy not to avail of the opportunity it presented. Christine had done her best to look unperturbed – seeming indeed casual, after the fashion of the time. As she waited in the foyer in her maxi-length milkmaid-style paisley dress and knee boots, carrying the wicker Moses basket which contained her son. No trace of the perspiration remained on her forehead. She was feeling perfectly fine, she told herself – absolutely and perfectly fine. But why had she been feeling so terrible since she arrived? As a result of these private interrogations, wild quarrels erupted now within the confines of her imagination – succeeded by wilder, even more fruitless reconciliations. She began to consider that some sly deceit was being practised on her. As a figure, out of nowhere, suddenly appeared – so unexpectedly he might have emerged through a recess in the wall. For his part, however, it seemed he hadn't even noticed Christine at all. As he proceeded jauntily in the direction of the main desk. He was attired, somewhat oddly considering the hot weather, in a plain brown raincoat and a hat with a feather.

—My name is Mr Bohan, she heard him say, with impressive good manners.

A refined gentleman, of the Anglo-Irish type, she concluded. She had read about them in the guidebook that morning. There were quite a few of them, apparently, in the Sligo area.

Apparently there had been some problem with his key.

—I'll attend to that straight away, Mr Bohan, the receptionist assured him, smiling.

---

The dreams had returned the following night – were even, in fact, more troubling than before. She could see herself plainly, moving precariously amongst the groynes, with that now familiar sense of being closely observed. She could hear Faisal's cries but could not seem to find him anywhere. The tower and the clubhouse – she could see them up ahead. The lights were still on so that, at least, was a relief. But then, almost immediately, they were sharply extinguished. And she could see the figure of the man in the raincoat, the guest with the hat who had so unexpectedly appeared earlier – standing on the cliff-edge, staring fixedly out to sea – as though oblivious of the world and its inhabitants.

# 10

I must acknowledge, though, being profoundly impressed by her strength of will. Indeed, her control at that time was equal to that which one might have expected from someone of an almost military cast of mind – an ascetic, even. No, there could be no doubt about it, as far as I was concerned – at the age of twenty-three, Christine Taylor was a force to be reckoned with, a young woman in possession of a fierce and quiet code of her own. Which, inevitably of course, made the challenge all the more exciting.

But on this particular morning in Rosses Point, it has to be accepted that these considerable resources deserted her. What happened was this. She had called Mr Bohan's name and waved to him where she saw him below her, strolling casually along the shore. Across the slopes of the links a few desultory figures were moving towards the clubhouse.

—Can you see me, Mr Bohan? I'm up here! she had called.

But in spite of her call he had neglected to turn. After which she decided to go down to him – he seemed such a gentle, companionable type – and was obviously on holiday, same as herself. Now he was standing, stock-still, shading his eyes. Though she did not admit it, some irrational force was compelling her to talk to him. But she was not worried. For there was something so open, she continued to feel, about his face. Something which she had almost instantly perceived about him, when he had stood there smiling at the receptionist, drumming his fingers. What could it be, she asked herself, this kindness she felt from him? Never daring to admit that it might be some aspect of her father he was suggesting to her. At least what might be called the 'happy father' – the one she had once known, as a very young girl. Before the time of the 'bad thing', as it were. Her feminist friends would never, she knew, have approved of such supplicant thoughts. Especially Mo. The truth was, however, that Christine couldn't help herself. Which was why, once more, a cry came thrusting towards her lips:

—Mr Bohan!

She had left Faisal with one of the hotel babysitters – it was a service that they provided. The girl had taken his hand and beamed. Saying it would be a pleasure to be permitted.

—To be allowed to look after the 'little dote'.

—Mr Bohan! Hello there! Christine called behind her cupped hand.

He wasn't a big man – in fact he was rather thin and angular – clearly liking to keep his own company. But for his open and inviting face, Christine might have found it difficult to approach him – much less trust him, for she was now instinctively suspicious of any man.

As she proceeded along the narrow winding path that led from the cliff towards the shore, her footfalls gave out a strange hollow sound. But she remained confident – for the more she thought about him the more he began to seem like some kind of genial uncle. Then she indulged herself a little – musing on the subject of the legendary hospitability of the Irish nation. And found herself thinking about the concept of the 'kind and lively Irish face'.

—I'll look after your daughter! she heard him say, indulging herself, again somewhat inexplicably.

For she could not have imagined permitting such thoughts to enter her mind before. Entertain such considerations regarding a male? It would have been unthinkable. But there could be no denying she now found it pleasant – comforting and reassuring. It was as though she needed it, whether she admitted as much or not. She raised her hand and called out again. But no reply came. He remained standing motionless there by the hushing shoreline.

—Mr Bohan! she repeated.

To nothing but the indifferent, dim murmuring sea.

---

We have all experienced what a presentiment is – and there are few amongst us who do not instinctively know the intuition along with which the faculty of observation can sometimes be inordinately heightened. And Christine Taylor, in Rosses Point in 1976 – she seemed to know that better than anyone. For now she found she would start anew at even the slightest of sounds – a car horn, even the soft clinking of copper curtain rings. Trying not to think of her father as she lay there in the solitude of her room. Endeavouring gallantly not to hear him speak any words, those ones especially where he would turn and smile and address her once again:

—You were my princess. That's what you were. Why did you let me down, my queen? You were my princess and you went against my wishes.

She took out a photograph and, in spite of herself, continued to be compelled by the image it depicted – that of a girl who could have been no more than ten, standing in a garden on a warm day in June. A broad straw hat was hanging from her shoulders

– decorated profusely with flowers, with a trickling pink ribbon suspended on either side. She felt so unmoored as she stood there staring at it, lost and longing to be anchored to the earth. Her father's loving arms used to have that effect – before the time of the bad thing went and happened.

There was a book which Salib kept with him all the way through their college years – it was Robert Heinlein's *Stranger in a Strange Land*.

That was what it had been called, she remembered, and it expressed exactly what she was feeling now. Which was why a cry of anguish rose to her lips.

—Daddy, where were you when I needed you?

She could imagine only too well the extent of her friends' disapproval as the fragile plea escaped her lips – Ronnie and Mo would be united in their derision. In the face of what they would read as a surprising and disappointing capitulation to the dismal and discredited orthodoxies of the patriarchy. Tears stung her eyes, as uncharacteristic defences made themselves heard. She did not care, she told herself, and anyway how would they ever know? Any more than they might become acquainted of the illogical impulses she had experienced earlier and which had led her to call out to a complete stranger. 'Mr Bohan', in other words, who – just at that precise moment, with infinite grace and patience, it seemed, went gliding past her bedroom window, with the gravel crunching softly beneath his feet – the tweed trilby, as ever, tilted slightly on his head, with a little green feather tucked neatly into the band.

# 11

Even as a child in Manchester, Chris had thought the northern city over-invasive, excessively and unproductively over-familiar in its ways. But in Rosses Point that summer in July, it had ceased to seem anything like that. And Chris began to consider just how wrong she had been – and how positively cosmopolitan her birthplace now seemed, when she compared it to a place like this. Why, she fumed inwardly, did these people assume that they had some God-given right to coerce you into a conversation whenever they felt like it? She prepared herself. For, once again, the over-earnest university student whom she had the misfortune to be sitting beside and who had stimulated this inner debate was rallying impressively and coming up for air. Before launching yet again into yet another semi-articulate, bleary-eyed tirade.

—I was watching you earlier on in the foyer, he told her, and if you don't mind me saying, I see you have a deaf son. Also I see that you're reading *Hibernia*. It's an interesting magazine. What's your view of the North of Ireland? And don't tell me the violence is indefensible. You've got to take sides. What other revolution . . .

She looked up from the magazine to which he had referred, an Irish political/social journal. Much of whose content meant little to her. But its broadly left-wing editorial stand was somewhat reassuring – enabling her, at least, to feel somewhat intellectually rooted in what increasingly seemed a remorselessly inchoate atmosphere.

**HAVOC AND RUIN:**
JOHN SHAW AND GEOFFREY EVANS –
CAMPAIGN OF BARBARISM UNPRECEDENTED

The article she had been preoccupied with before the student's ill-mannered interruption reported details of an ongoing manhunt. It carried photos of two men, both menacing and heavy-jowled, looking aggressively away from the camera. She had been startled to read that one of them hailed from Lancashire – which, of course, was where she had been born. It had been their intention, she read from the chilling account, to sexually assault and thereafter dispatch at least 'one girl a week'. To be plucked indiscriminately from the rural backroads and smalltown streets of Ireland.

She turned away from the beaded black eyes and the sullen, pendulous, near-canine jaws. Then she looked up and, somewhat alarmed, for no reason that she was aware of, descried Mr Bohan standing alone at the end of the bar. He was ordering an orange juice and unfolding a paper. She made her excuses and left the student, who was clearly astonished that such a thing could be possible.

—Excuse me, she said, wondering, as she did so, where her courage had come from, I was wondering if maybe I could have a word?

As it turned out, Mr Bohan could not have been more accommodating. A ripple of the quietest pleasure ran through Christine.

—I was trying to catch your attention yesterday, she explained, when I was calling to you from the top of the cliff. You were down on the shore, staring out to sea.

—Oh, but I'm sure you must be mistaken, he smiled, I wasn't out at all yesterday. Why, I hardly left my room all day. Sad to say, I have a touch of sciatica.

—Oh. Are you sure? she replied, more than a little taken aback, although doing her best to give no indication.

—So how are you enjoying your holidays, my dear? he asked.

And was full of enquiries regarding Faisal's welfare. He had seen them together so many times, he told her – and he seemed so happy.

—Yes he is, Christine told him, at least that's something.

—Oh, don't be like that, Mr Bohan said, cheer up, my girl.

—Do you know what? You're right, Christine replied – feeling more than a little embarrassed.

—I'm sure the sun is doing him good, he continued, a power of good I'm sure it's doing him. On these balmy days which the weather reports tell us are set to continue right through till September.

She was delighted to find herself so relaxed in his company – however that had happened. Perhaps because it turned out he was such a wonderful talker. He was a founding member of the Sligo Yeats Society, he informed her.

—It is one of the greatest pleasures of my life, taking tourists around the area. I do these little tours – my 'Yeats Walks'. An old retired fellow like me. It gives me something to do, I suppose. But tell me – why are you not enjoying yourself more? You seem somewhat ill at ease. A little out of sorts. Would I be correct in saying that? Please forgive me if I'm being presumptuous.

—It's just that Ireland takes some getting used to, I suppose, she went on as he nodded in sympathy, I mean there's just no getting away from it – the people are different. And this thing in the North of Ireland – it seems to keep coming up. Even during the most innocuous of conversations, it tends to rear its ugly head. I tend to feel so inadequate whenever it's mentioned. It's just, I suppose, that we're not informed over there – of the sheer gravity and depth of the conflict. To be perfectly honest, I know more about South Africa than I do about the political situation in Ulster. And that's odd. With Ireland being so near – you somehow just don't think of it in that way.

—Too much blather, that's more the problem, Mr Bohan smiled, tipping back his feathered hat, too many people who want to hear themselves talk.

Then his attention was drawn to the grainy images in *Hibernia*. The hirsute sociopaths, I suppose one might call them.

—Now those two gentlemen, he began, are they a type of 'freedom fighter' too? Self-styled anarchists of a type – perhaps? – that seem so fashionable in this day and age.

A wave of apprehension swept through her and, inexplicably, she felt guilty about coming from Gorton. Mr Bohan rubbed his forehead.

—One a week they planned to kill. They weighted the girl's body and threw her into a lake. That was a fine day's work, don't you think.

For the briefest of moments Christine could have sworn that a smile had crossed his face. But she surely must have been mistaken, she told herself. She must have been.

—Imagine doing that to another human being, he sighed wearily.

Without warning, Christine Taylor felt icy all over. Not because of the smile which she was now convinced she had just imagined but due to the sheer enormity and extent of the evil which such an act would require of a human being. She resisted the impulse as best she could – but it got the better of her. Why had her daddy betrayed her?

---

Ha ha ha like she was going to worry about a thing like that no I'm afraid not, she thought, and already after one, two, three drinks, Chris had already snapped out of any inclination towards self-indulgence of such a negative and undermining nature – and now seemed positively exuberant. Declaring that what she wanted more than anything was entertainment.

—But where am I going to start, Mr Bohan? – I have three days left and I want them all to be exciting. I want them to be memorable for myself and my son.

She prevailed upon her companion for any suggestions he might have. The affection in his eyes was so encouraging, so indisputably uplifting – it was just what she needed. At least that was how she perceived the situation. For my part, however, I have to confess to being thoroughly bored. I mean, I knew how mercurial and unpredictable she could be. And in which appraisal I was proven correct, literally within minutes. For, whether she was aware of the fact or not, her mood again had already begun to change. For some reason the little chimes on her bracelet could unsettle her whenever they tinkled. I say 'for some reason' – but of course I was more than aware. After all, it's my business. Yes, those little 'tinkles' had the effect of annoying her considerably at times. Which seemed odd to Mr Bohan – understandably.

—Are you all right dear? Mr Bohan was now saying. For quite unexpectedly you seem a little pale. Maybe your boy is keeping you up late, is he? Perhaps it might be an idea for you to get a little rest. You can have all the entertainment you want back in England.

Chris swallowed and thought perhaps that he was right.

—I don't know what I was thinking of, she said – unconsciously covering the charm bracelet with her hand.

Mr Bohan was smiling again – with an avuncularity which, without a doubt, would have fooled anyone. As, in the smoothest and most kindly of tones, she heard him begin anew:

—You know, my dear, when you were joking earlier . . . ?

Chris smiled and twisted a dangling charm – a silver twining ballerina, in fact.

—When I was joking? What do you mean, when I was joking?

—I mean when you said that you called to me from the cliff . . .

—But what do you mean? I wasn't joking when I said that. Why on earth would I joke about a thing like that?

All of a sudden Mr Bohan went quiet. A queue of elderly ladies was making its way across the tarmac towards a touring coach. A single wire rattled on a basketball hoop as a knot of idling teenagers tossed stones, to little purpose.

Then he turned again towards Christine, checking his watch and pushing back his trilby.

—It's just that it's strange – me gazing out to sea.

—Tell me the truth, do you really have sciatica?

—My dear, as God is my judge, I didn't leave my room all day. Are you sure you're all right? Maybe you're getting too much heat. I mean it really can be very warm at times. Such a heatwave . . . !

Christine Taylor winced, feeling sickly – dismayingly so.

—Are you all right, my dear? she heard him say again, as he touched her wrist with a large, matted hand.

—It's nothing, she said, perhaps you are right. It might be better if I went and lay down. Faisal will probably be waking up anyway.

—That's right, my dear. You go and lay down, she heard him say, trembling a little as he pressed her soft hand tenderly to his cheek.

Which had the effect of, momentarily, making her feel relieved – and quite ridiculous for having been so concerned.

---

She sat by the window with her hand resting against the railings of Faisal's cot – thinking back on her training college days. It had always been one of the most hotly debated subjects during her time there, the benefits that the practice of 'hothousing' might bring the learning-disabled. The shrillness of those late-night arguments returned with some vitality, invigorating her in that old familiar way as her Faisal continued to sleep – ever so soundly, thank heaven.

The moon's light spilt on the small figures on her charm bracelet and she thought of the day she'd been given it by Daddy. No, by Papa – which was the name she preferred to call him. Not that he was soft, like a Geppetto or Mr Bumble. No, Papa Taylor was more like a column of the sturdiest granite – but happily soft at the centre, always nurturing a special place in his heart for 'The Princess'.

—My Princess of Gorton, he would heartily cry, and in a broad flood of West of Ireland light she was back there with her father as he opened the door of their three-bedroomed Manchester suburban house and came striding in gallantly with his massive arms outspread. But, as girls will always do, she knew straight away that he was up to something.

—I bought you this. There's a free gift with it, Princess.

How well she remembered it – that lovely day! That glorious day when he had bought her her first comic. Indeed it was the very first time she had even seen the *Bunty*. The charm bracelet was Sellotaped to the front page, visible through the cellophane of a small square packet. She squealed with joy, pressing her hands to her face – just like Faisal was destined to do, much later.

She had taken, in her adulthood, to wearing the bracelet again. She liked to use it to stimulate Faisal. Who at that very minute had suddenly woken up.

—Look, she said to him, flicking a single bauble with her finger, do you see it, Faisal, this little one here that I'm jingling is a dice. You know what a dice is, don't you, Faisal?

And when he demonstrated no sign of response – as perhaps he never would – that old familiar gloom began enveloping her again. As that dissenting voice from those 'Educating the Disadvantaged' debates again returned.

—This latest craze of saturation learning, or of 'hothousing' as they call it – it's just another American fad, a complete waste of time, it insisted, and it really does the learning-disabled no favours at all. What they need is time and patience – infinite patience. All this hothousing does is provide false hope. It's illusory, in the end, self-defeating, really.

The common room had been full of smoke that night, with loud rock music thumping from the corner.

—*Turn that damned thing down!* Salib Toyeh had shouted, before rounding, somewhat tipsily, on her.

—A feminist like you – wearing a bloody bracelet – it's absurd!

But after a few tokes, the whole thing had been forgotten. And, lying there on the beanbag, he had passionately pressed his tongue inside her mouth.

—You sure are a puzzle, that's all I can say, Chris Taylor, he had grinned, mischievously plinking one of the little figurines.

The very same one that Chris was turning now abstractedly as she lay there on the verge of sleep – concentrating at first on the small silver dice, before moving on to the silver crescent moon. As her eyes began closing and then she heard it coming, completely out of nowhere – floating softly across the room. It was her father's voice. Or was it? For if it was, why was his face drawn into a hard, unnatural smile as he stood in a shaft of moonlight by the window? And why did he say:

—You were my Gorton princess, weren't you, Christine? Of course you were. You were my one and only Gorton queen.

As he lifted his face to show a single transparent tear weaving down his cheek.

—I'm sorry, Christine.

That was all he said. And when she looked again – he was gone.

---

The following morning Chris Taylor had completely forgotten everything – indeed was feeling absolutely terrific. And as for Faisal, he was in as good a humour as ever she had seen him. With the result that she could barely contain herself from right there and then making her way down to her fellow guest's hotel room to set the record straight by eagerly declaring:

—What must I have been thinking yesterday, Mr Bohan! But of course I didn't see you staring out to sea, much less call to you from the top of the cliffs! Why, as a matter of fact I wasn't there at all!

As it transpired, there wasn't any need – for she met him quite unexpectedly on the front terrace, after breakfast. He invited her to join him and they sat there together, having another little chat. It really was turning out to be the most wonderful morning, she found herself thinking. And already the Rosses Point brass band were setting up on the lawn, looking resplendent in their gold-braided navy uniforms.

—The things you can get into your head, she had laughed, like you said yesterday, it must be the sun! Do you think that perhaps it's the sun, Mr Bohan?

With characteristic graciousness, he had made light of her apologies.

—An old codger like me, he chuckled, why we're ten a penny in resorts such as this. It's hardly any surprise that you might mistake me for someone else.

She quietly reprimanded herself for ever having entertained suspicions, however cautious, with regard to Mr Bohan – who looked so harmless, sitting there puffing his pipe. It felt so good to be in his company – with no talk whatsoever of trouble or death – in the North of Ireland, or anywhere else. A transcendent calm had descended upon her. The only regret she had – and in this again she surprised herself – was that her former partner Salib was not there to enjoy it with her. But almost immediately she countered this unproductive feeling, drawing on the resources of past.

—Didn't think I'd be able to make it on my own, did you, Salib? Well that's where you were wrong, so wrong, my friend. We women possess resources that most of you men can only dream of.

She absent-mindedly rocked her son in his pushchair.

—I suppose you'll be taking him to the circus in Sligo, said Mr Bohan, lowering his pipe, now that you've had yourself a decent bit of rest.

Christine nodded, with her new-found strength at last now apparent.

Not giving so much as a thought now to tears or to moonlight, whatever she had been thinking about them for, as she rested her hand on the handle of Faisal's pushchair. With no end of distractions, in any case, to occupy them both – her and Faisal. For a start the Rosses Point carnival parade had already assembled, with its serpentine column of blazing colour already beginning to make its way along the seafront, much to her delight, and Mr Bohan's. Before, all of a sudden – he scared the life out of her – a grinning clown came leaping out of nowhere, to the delight of all the toddlers around her.

—*Collywobbles!* squealed the funny fellow. Collywobbles jinglebobs! I'm Bonio the clown and I'm here to make you laugh! Oh, I'll make you laugh – don't worry, for sure! Look at you, my little friend! I'll be seeing you again – you have my word! You hear that, Mummy?

Christine laughed – as indeed did Mr Bohan – as the pirouetting jester went off about his business, curtsying exaggeratedly as he did so, doffing his conical hat with the bobbins. As a big bass drum continued pounding furiously, and an excited terrier yapped hysterically, attacking a wastebasket. Christine turned to Mr Bohan and said:

—And here I was, looking for entertainment, Mr Bohan!

Only to find herself quite taken aback as she realised that her fellow guest's chair was, in fact, empty. She found herself curiously puzzled. In fact, as it turned out, it was the last time she was to see him. A turn of events which she considered quite strange, not unreasonably it has to be said. As, now, quite baffled, she returned inside.

Where a few pale-faced pensioners were obstinately avoiding the sun – staring absently at the television. Which was relaying some grim footage of a search party standing alongside a squaring of police incident tape on a windswept street somewhere in the West of Ireland. The by-now familiar images of the two main suspects, John Shaw and Geoffrey Evans, consummate authors of havoc and deadly ruin, were once more flashed onto the screen – looking more repulsive than ever, she thought – with their unwashed hair, those malevolent eyes.

Mr Bohan continued, however, to remain doggedly on her mind. She felt certain he couldn't be far away. And that she would encounter him at some point, perhaps later on. But she didn't. She went down to the sing-song in the back bar at eight o'clock, in the hope that he'd be there. He wasn't, and she had left after twenty minutes. In any case, the level of noise had deafened her – the sheer intensity of the sentimental passion, the self-serving bald aggression.

—*Northmen, Southmen, comrades all! Dublin, Belfast, Cork and Donegal!*

She felt cowed as she slunk out. What on earth was wrong with her, she kept wondering – Christine Taylor, who had been the star of the students' union, debater par excellence, the firebrand intellectual of 1974? Throughout the night she remained confused – and didn't sleep a wink all night, her vigilant eyes flickering, illogically, as she well knew. Waiting for a certain figure to materialise in the shaft of moonlight. Waiting and waiting – until she fell asleep. In her dreams to dream of:

—Sooty and Sweep.

—I'm sorry, she heard her father say, I'm sorry I ever asked you to play that game. For, as God is my judge, I hate Sooty and Sweep.

And then it came again – the single, strolling, transparent tear.

# 12

The glissando facility with which he now could seemingly effortlessly transport himself – and had been doing ever since meeting Christine Taylor – had become a source of both comfort and reassurance to Valentine Shannon. It was as though she had enabled him, among other things, to find it within himself to, at last, confront the past. Something which, and for so long, he had signally been unable to do. Was it any wonder he was smiling, as he turned the car into Aldgate High Street, setting off on his journey homeward – to their modest but comfortable dwelling in Barnet? His amusement in no way diminished by thoughts of the popular weatherman Michael Fish, whose plumpish innocent countenance he had glimpsed while on his way past a Radio Rentals window, repeating his assertion that there was absolutely no need for anyone to be concerned this evening and that any rumours there might have been regarding possibly approaching inclement weather were entirely ill-founded.

—We don't get hurricanes in England! he had announced, with an impressive almost schoolboyish conviction.

Valentine smiled – having suspected as much. There had been some talk in the staffroom about possible storms. But he had not seriously considered it – and now it turns out he was right. Which was why he was giving serious consideration to possibly taking Faisal to the zoo. To Chessington Park, perhaps. What a wonderful life. Was it any wonder he was happy? Enabled, as he had become in recent times, to comfortably confront the past – any time he so wished. He was a new man and no mistake. But then of course why – why unless he had to – would he have bothered returning to such an establishment – a minor seminary which now seemed quite unremarkable, quite grey and featureless, if the truth be told? Why, if he was honest, during his entire time there, there had been but one exception to the humdrum predictability of the routine, and it never failed to bring a smile to his face. This was the incident he referred to as the 'Top Hat' affair.

The top hat had belonged to one of the students – Martin Boan. Who was a very unusual type of boy for Glassdrummond. In that he could have been described as an extremely individual and principled kind of fellow. Valentine knew this because he had taught him drama – directed him, in fact, in a recent production of *Oliver!*. In which he had played the part of the Artful Dodger. This, of course, was where the top hat had come from. The one which they had just been booting, in something approaching a drunken hysteria, along the corridor.

There had been another use for it, however – as Brother Valentine had discovered when the show concluded. Yes, Martin Boan had found another use for the hat. Wearing it, in other words, while pretending to be a certain type of pop star. One who, now in the year 1981, was currently popular, it transpired, and who appeared to be partial to such theatrical items. The pop star in question was named Adam Ant. And he wasn't just partial to eccentric headgear. He liked to dress up like a pirate, it transpired. In flounces and braids and swallowtail coats. One day in class Martin Boan had arrived dressed in comparable fashion. Which was troubling. Because as the senior college dean, it would have to be Brother Valentine's responsibility to discipline the boy – point out to him that this was a flagrant disobedience of the rules, a form of 'silent insubordination', as it would have been perceived. He would have to insist that the like of this never happened again. He carried out his duties to the letter of the law. Promptness of decision and equally of execution – those were his trademarks as dean in Glassdrummond. It was a matter of discipline, he had discreetly informed the student.

But Martin Boan had simply shrugged, saying nothing. And had arrived the following morning, attired again in exactly the same manner. This regrettable development had seen the beginning of the difficulties between the dean and his student. It was now so unlike the way things had used to be between them, he would ruefully reflect – when they had been such friends. When he'd been so proud of the boy's performance in *Oliver!* – when he'd taken everyone's breath away, outshining everyone, without exception, in the cast.

Over a period, it began to seem to Brother Valentine as though Martin Boan's personality had somehow been mysteriously and inexplicably altered – he seemed inordinately preoccupied now with impressing his peers at all costs. Invariably, or so it seemed, at the expense of Brother Valentine. The boy would now release the weariest of truculent sighs when prevailed upon to perform the most innocuous of tasks. There being no doubt that he made dubious remarks whenever the dean of discipline went past.

There could be no mistaking these furtive asides – the slow drip of his veiled provocations. In the end, finding his authority flagrantly being challenged, Brother Valentine was left with no choice. One night after prayer he summoned Martin Boan to his study. Even yet, however, he continued to hope that this rather unfortunate difficulty could be resolved. And these remained his thoughts as he approached along the corridor, striding through the door, in front of the student. Who appeared resolutely nonplussed, as he stood there before him. To begin with, the dean rubbed his knuckles, somewhat thoughtfully, before lowering his eyes. Then he said:

—I see you're not wearing your top hat this evening, Martin.

Boan had shrugged sullenly, not even bothering to dignify the situation with a reply. Which was why, restraining himself as best he could, the dean contented himself with once more repeating, in a glum monotone:

—Like I said, you're not wearing your top hat tonight, Martin.

—No, replied the boy smugly, twisting his thumbs absent-mindedly, rocking evenly back and forth on his heels.

As Brother Valentine's hand closed around the paperweight, smashing it into the young boy's astonished face.

# 13

Puda Bones was a Mancunian local – an old Gorton neighbour visited on a regular basis by Chris, back in those smokily remembered childhood days in Greater Manchester. That she might have been the epitome of wickedness, as some were known to attest, was not something which ever entered the child's open mind, as she sat there quietly in that dimly lit Gorton kitchen, at ten years of age. No, the little girl. who had been given the responsibility of running errands for this ageing pensioner intimated no presence of malignity or ill-intent, descried no Abaddon squatting on a kitchen throne. Saw nothing in her neighbour but kindness and vulnerability, in fact – one incapable of any hazard or bad thought. This, however, whether Christine noticed it or not, was emphatically not the case whenever the subject of men became the topic. Who, she declared, crouching forward in the chimney corner, were 'incarnate evil' – all of them. With a dark passion that would transfix the young schoolgirl as she shrank instinctively from the harsh accusations, the vindictive silence which succeeded them broken intermittently by the emission of an icily heartless, unjoyous laugh.

At such times, the strangest of sensations would begin to take possession of Christine Taylor's ten-year-old mind. A fact of which

Puda Bones was evidently more than aware, picking obsessively at the upholstery with coarse and leathery ringless fingers.

—They're all the same, she would hoarsely whisper, and anyone who has anything to do with them deserves any punishment as they get. Vileness incarnate is what men are, without exception. Pay heed, my dear, to the utterances of the one they call Puda Bones. For she is the one that knows you, poppet, and the only one maybe who now can protect you. Stay close to Puda – Oh Puda, Puda, Puda! Hee hee, they're afraid of me – for they know as I know them!

The interior of the house seemed ancient, with cobwebs descending from the ceiling like strips of rotting lace. The old woman shivered, her limbs making sudden startling movements in the heavy, pregnant air.

—This one from Gorton, Ian Brady, they'll tell you is different – he being a murderer that does in children. But he isn't, my dear. He's no different at all from the rest of them. In his belted grey coat, he's just the same as them all. That's what they're all like – I mean, in their hearts.

The lips of Puda Bones slowly extended as she smiled, leaning forward to part the ashes with her stick.

—Just like someone close to you, Christine Little. Oh, them as is closest, oh, them's the ones most of all to watch.

As she watched that grey eye glitter with pale light, turning from the hearth over which she had been crouched, Christine would often wonder – that perhaps, all along, her neighbours had been right.

—Abaddon the evil one, they'd whisper, the Star of the Morning returned as a woman.

---

Because that was what she used to call her, she thought – Christine Little.

—Christine Little, that's exactly what she used to call me, Faisal, murmured Christine to herself as she took her ten-year-old son by the hand and led him though the turnstile into Wembley Arena. She released Faisal's hand and pulled her anorak tight. Sitting there in her bucket seat, hoping that the meeting would begin without much delay. Which, in her experience, was unlikely. Union meetings were notoriously haphazard. She didn't want to think about Puda Bones, didn't even know why she had done so in the first place. Shifting on the edge of her seat now, she looked up and was relieved to see some movement in front of her – it looked like the meeting was about to begin. A bearded colleague was adjusting the microphone. He thanked everyone for coming along. Then he began:

—This government asserts its good offices with tedious monotony. If Kenneth Clarke is serious – then let him come down and meet us here in Wembley! Let him face the teachers on the ground. Why hide behind statistics in the corridors of power? I hereby issue a call on behalf of the National Union of Teachers – get down here and confront us – come down here and explain yourself, Kenneth Clarke!

Chris's mind was again drifting, as it always tended to do at these meetings – and now she was wondering why it was that Puda Bones would demonstrate such an interest in someone like Ian Brady, whose child-murder trial had been ongoing at that time. She recalled her saying, out of nowhere:

—Tell me about your daddy, dearie. Tell Puda Bones what he calls his baba angel. Hmm?

She saw herself then, dressing up in her bedroom – Christine Little getting all dressed up. Just as her father arrived in unexpectedly.

—Why there you are, my princess! she heard him cry – approaching her across the floor with arms outspread.

In such an assortment of make-up and her mother's clothes, she could easily have passed for a miniature Diana Dors. With her hair piled up and her bracelets all a-jingle, the spotlight could have been picking out a sumptuously made-up starlet.

—Princess Christine at Daddy's service! she had giggled, pressing her fingers up to her face.

As Papa Taylor gave his daughter a swing.

—Mama's gone to Gorton, he said, casting a furtive glance towards the window.

---

These bucket seats are so uncomfortable, thought Christine – releasing a soft moan as she manoeuvred her buttocks. On the platform, the speaker was incensed even further:

—Let me give you some facts now, colleagues! Facts which I am afraid you will not find in the least appealing . . . !

The assembled teachers shifted as one. As Christine caressed her son's fine hair. He was lying, as he often did, with his head on her shoulder. It was so special and relaxing whenever he did that, she thought. But what was making her think about Puda Bones? Why did the old crone, even fleetingly, come into her mind? There was no reason for it. But she kept on doing it.

Of course she did – I have to have my fun. And, after all, however tangential she might appear, she was an essential part of the overall choreography. So I ordained it that she remain in Chris's mind, floating to and fro – as I preferred it.

# 14

It hadn't been in any way planned – it was simply an accident that Chris happened to meet the Panja twins outside the garage. Amit and Anup were classmates of Faisal's. She had been surprised and pleased to see them both, however – inconvenient as their father's request for a lift might be. They wanted to get to Vale Farm Sports Centre, he told her, but their car had broken down.

—My wife, she is abroad, you understand, he said, and my car it has come to a standstill virtually outside the door, Miss Taylor. Most fortunate we should chance upon you.

She found herself amused by his use of old-fashioned English. Mr Panja was a Sikh – not that she knew him that well, however. But Faisal and the twins were inseparable. And when they saw their friend wearing his *Masters of the Universe* mask – well, they were ecstatic. For they, like her son, were avid fans of the popular children's television series.

Which Christine barely tolerated – its luridly animated and quite unnecessary level of aggression was highly dubious, in her view. But her purchase of the grotesque mask had been a form of restitution to Faisal, knowing the unfortunate boy had literally been bored to distraction at the NUT meeting.

—Of course! she replied to Mr Panja.

She would be more than delighted to give them a lift, she assured him – in any case, Vale Farm was very close by.

—Come along, boys! she cried, taking their hands. As they awkwardly climbed into the back seat of the Polo, Mr Panja loudly professing himself pleased with the weather.

—Up until now, he offered, there have been certain rumours circulating regarding the likelihood of a possible and likely dramatic change in conditions. If a number of parties were to be believed, Miss Taylor, right at this moment we should have anticipated whirling slates; indeed there was a suggestion of coming high winds. Of refuse bins hurled with an almighty vigour. But now, as we can see, all of that has been so much nonsense. There is no sign whatever of planks being torn from their moorings, trees writhing in the fiercest of tempests. Nothing whatsoever will be borne aloft – it was really all so much mere speculation. A hurricane, I understand, was specifically mooted – a lot of falsehood, quite quite – as we can see. This weatherman, the one they call Michael Fish – he is the one who scotched this lot of rumour. We do not have hurricanes in England – this is what he said, yes?

—By all accounts that is correct, grinned Chris, unconsciously mimicking the arcane semi-official vernacular, as she clunk-clicked her seat belt, switching on the ignition.

—I think I do remember hearing something to that effect, she added.

Mr Panja smiled in approval, reclining reflectively as he checked on the children in the back. The twins continued to laugh with Faisal – shrieking uninhibitedly as they leaned across to once more feel his mask.

—Masters of the Universe! they screeched piercingly, rocking back and forth.

Faisal was indeed behaving like a master of the universe – every inch the man in charge – as Chris motored along, feeling himself privileged to be so envied by his school pals. But thinking about the mask had made his mother feel guilty again – with regard to her unfortunate outburst earlier on in the day. Which had been quite unjustifiable, and she knew it. How could she not? She did her best to dispel the fluctuating waves of recrimination and embarrassment which were encroaching upon her. But it was no use – the feelings of guilt and self-loathing held fast. She swallowed now as both her cheeks burned crimson.

—What on earth do you think you are doing, Faisal! she had snapped. Get away from that man! I didn't give you permission to talk to him! Do you hear me? Get away!

The garage mechanic in question, with infinite patience, slowly turned to face her, forensically scrutinising her through narrow, squinted eyes. Wiping his hands on his blue overalls, he had said – ever so considerately, it seemed (but she could read the mocking subtext it contained):

—I'm sorry, Miss – but am I missing something here perhaps?

It was then she apprehended the humanoid alien, leaning out through the Polo's open window. It was Faisal, of course – flaunting his fearsomely cubist visage.

—I'm the Master of the Universe!

Surprisingly or otherwise, the simple fact is that this simple misunderstanding happened quite by accident – I had, genuinely, no hand in it at all. Or, indeed, in the subsequent change in relations between Faisal and his mother. It just happened, really. But then Christine Taylor had been in such a state – to the extent of exuding an almost electrical aura. Thanks, almost exclusively, to her union meeting in Wembley Arena. Thanks, more or less, to the National Union of Teachers and their grievances. Yes, even before she had taken issue with the mechanic – who had simply been playing quite harmlessly with Faisal – Christine Taylor had found herself in a state of high dudgeon. It may not be easy to comprehend how a single, relatively innocuous word – a single word, for heaven's sake – could possibly have exerted such a powerful influence on a young and, in so many ways, unusually intelligent woman. But these are the facts. That was what, in fact, had happened. And not only that – but the very moment after the single offending word had been spoken, Chris Taylor came to realise that she had just pinched her forearm with such vehemence, the impress of three pale crescents remained visible on her skin. Her son at this point had also become alerted to a quite dramatic change of mood on her part. And it was directly after that that she had, alarmingly, without warning, raised her voice to her son.

—*Can't you leave those things alone for five damned minutes!! Five minutes, that's all I ask!*

Which he had, in fact, done his best to do – averting his eyes as he haphazardly gathered up his scattered bundle of trading cards.

---

How could she have become so uptight – and so *suddenly*? Chris Taylor wondered. What on earth could be wrong with her?

She considered for just a moment the possibility that she was somehow being manipulated – influenced, cleverly, in some awful way. Which of course was ridiculous, she decided. She had simply been upset by something which the speaker, inadvertently, had said. What was most embarrassing and confusing was how disarmingly innocent the actual word was – for it was the word *dolphin*.

How could it be – that such a word could induce such a degree of such sickening dread? She replayed the incident, almost obsessively, now in her head.

—Margaret Thatcher, the union official had continued, waving his fist in a belligerent manner, has just about the intelligence of the average dolphin! The intelligence of the average dolphin, I'm telling you!

Reluctantly, Chris began to accept that this specific choice of metaphor (how the approving crowds on the terraces had cheered!) had in some way stimulated repressed anxieties within herself – breathed life into shadowy, elusive and ill-defined forms, facilitating entrance to bolted apartments in her mind. And in doing so had disturbed her considerably – had come close to terrifying her, in fact. For somewhere in the dusty corners of those long-secured apartments were the apprehensions and anxieties which Puda Bones had known so well. Her voice returning now, seeming direful – quite atrocious.

—I know, and you know it, Christine Little. It is I alone know you, and the evil of which they all are capable – even the one you love most of all! Which is why, in the privacy of your bathroom, you so often dreamed of being a boy, on the back of a dolphin like the boy in the magazine, steering your own gleaming fish of the imagination as you sailed away into the freedom of blue. Didn't you, Christine? Don't you look away from Puda!

---

As she drove onward towards Vale Farm, Chris Taylor, in spite of herself remained just ten years of age. Who, right at that very moment, might once more have been immersed in her weekly *Bunty* comic, compelled by the tale of the hideous 'Saboteur'. Who, in his cowled black duffel coat had tracked the ballet company all the way to the snows of Russia – where he stood alone, staring at them – like a figure that might have been sculpted out of ash. Only when The Saboteur died would the curse on Lorna Drake's ballet company be lifted. She had known in her heart that the dreaded curse would never be lifted. Shuffling-shuffling menacingly in his awful cowl, committed to treachery and perdition's expansion. Sometimes, she recalled, she would think of her own mother as The Saboteur's accomplice – and see her standing there in the kitchen, on the verge of turning with some new accusation.

Christine liked it when her mother went to Belle Vue – to stay the weekend with her friend, she always told her. Whenever that happened, Christine Taylor would feel free. It soon got to the stage where she would delight in that longed-for moment. When her mother would don her Saboteur's duffel, and her emotionless voice would come drifting down the hallway:

—I'll be back on Monday. I've left money with your father.

On such Saturday afternoons all of Gorton would seem purified – somehow reborn. And Princess Christine would become its lady-in-waiting, soon to be crowned its undisputed queen. But one particular Saturday, it didn't happen quite like that. The Saboteur had certainly gone, but the predatory shadows had not departed in her wake.

---

Christine had been reading her *Bunty* in her bedroom at the time – when, all of a sudden, she heard the sound of the front door closing downstairs. And her dad calling up:

—Is my princess at home?

She never did find out the name of his companion. But, for a laugh, they suggested that his name could be Stewart Granger, the famous matinee idol from the 1950s and early '60s, the handsome debonair star of *Swordsman of Siena* and many other pictures from that time. All she could remember were his silver-tinged sidelocks. A thin line of brown ran along his lower lip and there had been a funny, alerted look in his eyes. She could see the golden cap of a bottle in his jacket pocket.

—Take off those little socks of yours, will you? Take off your socks, like a good girl – because Papa wants to play Sooty and Sweep.

It hadn't seemed right. It didn't seem to be Papa at all.

However:

—Take them off, he had repeated more forcibly, there's my nice princess. I want to show Stewart our little game.

—He isn't Stewart. That's not his name. That isn't Stewart Granger, she wanted to say.

His companion stared. As, trembling, she peeled off each sock.

—They have to go in the wash anyway, her father said, but first we have to put on our play.

Sooty and Sweep were two puppets from the TV.

—Here, Sooty, there's a good fellow. Give Sweep a great big kiss.

Covering his hands with the socks, he sucked in a great big inverted raspberry.

—Let's pretend that the sock is the most beautiful of nylon stockings, her father laughed, one that maybe might belong to Liz Taylor.

Stewart Granger exploded – as her father gave Sooty another great big kiss.

—This is great fun, isn't it, Christine?, he said.

But it wasn't. It was a play she hadn't liked for some time.

—I want to go, she heard herself reply – in a voice that might have been made of stone.

Then she repeated it:

—Papa, didn't you hear me? I want to go.

Only to realise that her father's mood had sharply altered. Now he was wearing that hard, unnatural smile. As Stewart Granger looked away, distantly.

—I have to leave now, Christine told her father.

—Certainly, my dear – when the show is over. Isn't that right, Sooty? Isn't that right, Sweep?

Sweep made a stupid rubber-duck noise. Which was supposed to mean 'Yes'.

By now the so-called Stewart Granger was shielding his eyes. As her father sat down on the bed beside Christine. Elevating the hideous hand-puppet as his brown eyes twinkled.

*—Now, little Sooty. Let's chat with Christine. Come on, dearie – let's have a smile. That's it! That's better! Tee hee! Such fun as we're having!*

Even to this day, Christine thought, leaning forward to give the windscreen a wipe, she couldn't really remember anything much about the neighbour whose name was 'Stewart Granger'.

All she could recall was the flicker of that golden cap – and the fact that, afterwards, he had smoked long slim Panatella cigars. Which trembled between his fingers when he tried to smoke them. Looking at her in what she thought of as 'in that way', out of the corner of his eye, as the washing machine roared in the utility room downstairs, where her father was scolding and throwing things around. She would never be able to look at Sooty and Sweep on the television again, she instinctively felt, as she covered herself with a blanket, staring at her pale bare feet.

And she never was.

---

The night after they had 'put on the play', Christine kept thinking about Puda Bones and her warning. The same Puda Bones who, she now knew, would be the only friend she'd ever have. Because somehow they would all know – they would get to find out. They would know it and smell it and when she approached she would hear them all say:

—Look who's coming! Here she comes now!

So all she had was Puda, with her crouched shape. But at least one friend was better than none. As she lay there sobbing underneath the bedclothes, thinking about what she'd done that day – eaten how many, one two three four flies, or was it five? Which had, nonetheless, made her feel better because when she had done it, the pain wasn't hers. And would never be again because from now on, now that she'd discovered it, it was the flies who would be pleading. Yes, it was them who would be crying, in little flecks of voices that seemed to issue from across the wastes of space:

—Please don't hurt me, will you, Christine!

Those same flies who were sadly without any friends – not like Christine Taylor, aged ten, whose bestest friend in the world was Puda Bones, the wisest woman in the world, because she knew all the bad things that could happen to you, for no reason.

---

Christine eased the Polo up alongside the kerb, directly outside Vale Farm Sports Centre, becoming momentarily distracted by the excessively profuse protestations of gratitude on the part of Mr Panja as he climbed from the car – then she noticed something at her feet, gleaming from between the ridges of the tattered rubber mat. It was coloured silver.

—Goodbye, Miss Taylor. We are eternally in your debt, called

Mr Panja as he closed the door, with Faisal pressing his *Masters of the Universe* face up against the glass.

As his mother examined the small silver dice she was now holding between her finger and thumb – it was exactly the same as the tiny bright cube with the dots, the one belonging to the charm bracelet which came free with the *Bunty*, all those many long years ago. And which her father had bought for her as a present. But not only that – she vividly recalled plying the dice, and along with it the little silver crescent moon, in her room in the early hours in that hotel in the Yeats Country Hotel, in Rosses Point, where she had encountered Mr Bohan all those years ago. Simultaneously, she found herself alarmed and bewildered – but how on earth had it come to be there? Then, suddenly – she *jumped*! – as she saw Mr Panja rapping on the glass. His eyes were wild and his face was contorted in a kind of hysterical grimace.

—Michael Fish say no need to worry! he yelped, with his shoulders shaking.

As a litterbin at the side of the road clanged loudly, falling before rolling erratically on down the hill. But by then, Mr Panja had already gone, and Faisal in the back was quiet and still. Then suddenly he screeched:

—*Me go in!*

# 15

It came as no surprise to Chris Taylor, none at all, that the Vale Farm swimming instructor – 'Mr Bean', as they called him, after a television comedian he apparently resembled – ought to have made such a comment. For to her he was nothing more than a cretin – that was how she perceived the man. Whose arrogance – his laughable narcissism was nothing short of pathetic, really. Especially when he looked like that – with his googly eyes and not a pick on him. He looked pathetic. Not that it bothered Mr Bean. As he stood there by the edge of the pool, confronting her brazenly – with his arm proprietorially around her little boy's shoulder. It was Faisal's affection for the cretin, of course, which compromised her more than anything – preventing her from doing what she dearly longed to do – give the skinny wretch a bloody great mouthful. Now what was he doing? Pretending they were both Masters of the Universe. Jumping around in that idiotic way of his, Mr Bean presents kiddies' morning television. Contriving a gurning, humanoid aspect now as he lumbered foolishly up and down the wet tiles – extending his arms, apelike, doing his Mr Bean face. As Faisal cried, waving his arms excitedly:

—*We are the Masters of the Universe! Yes!*

—I have come here today to take Faisal away! boomed Mr Bean, exaggerating his bulging eyes.

Which really, I must say, had an extraordinary effect on his mother. Who practically lunged at the instructor – who, really and truly, was quite bewildered.

—*Just what the hell do you think you're doing to my son! How dare you give him that! Faisal!*

She tore the slice of cake violently out of her son's hand, leaving the boy completely flummoxed. As Mr Bean provocatively pressed his tongue against his cheek, elevating a sardonic eyebrow. And this really did amuse me – in the exact same way that my own mother used to, whenever emotion would get the better of her. Which was quite often, of course, what with me not possessing the required control. Not like Bailey – her preferred first-born – even if only by a few short seconds – her sober muscular son. Solid, austere, I suppose you might call him. Not like me – invertebrate incontinent, running around the place with my only friend – clickety-clack, Mr Bones. Regularly chuckling to myself under the stairs. How I so loved it – just squatting at peace there, alone in the dark.

But, back at the swimming pool, now it was the turn of Googly-Eyes to bridle. His cheeks had attained quite a high colour.

—Why – does he not like Thornton's? now he was demanding. I can't think why. After all, it's made from the finest milk and eggs. I bought it specially for him myself. Because I know how much he likes it!

Even if I say it myself, I have to insist upon the excellence of 'that touch', I suppose you might call it. For it really did drive poor Christine mad. High colour? The poor instructor wasn't even in the running.

—Don't you fucking dare try to patronise me!

But, with a clinical coolness that Bailey would have been proud of, I had already arranged that he would simply turn and walk away, lighting a cigarette as he muttered under his breath:

—A simple slice of cake, I ask you. Political correctness gone mad, ha ha.

Perhaps it's unfortunate that he never met Valentine Shannon. Maybe he might have knocked some sense into him – dissuaded him from running to the authorities whenever he took the notion, recruiting the forces of the state quite unnecessarily. Might have suggested that he loosen up a little.

# 16

Now cruising steadily at fifty along the Westway, with the Sports Centre already far behind her, Christine Taylor tried to force herself to keep her eyes on the road. But the moors kept forcing her back towards consideration of their sinister omnipresent contours. Had she lost the facility to master her own will? The thought drew her close to tears. She gripped the steering wheel and glanced back to look at Faisal. He seemed to be fine. What was wrong with thinking about her childhood, or the moors for that matter? They could only have power over her if she colluded with them – which she firmly resolved not to do.

---

—Ah, poor old Christine, doughty old feminist, 'brave', 'inspiring' modern mother – what can one do but doff one's hat? Especially when you consider what's in store for the poor little thing. And to which she is actually looking forward, which is wonderful! It's going to be great, checking into the hotel. This is what she thinks. Well, she would, of course, wouldn't she, for her lovely little progeny, he has always loved hotels. What excitement there was going to be, bouncing up and down on the bed, and then off like two kids to play with Valentine on Miami Beach, watching the breakers – staring at the flamingoes! It was going to be the greatest, most enjoyable holiday ever! There were even babysitters for the kids, the girl had told her. She could just see him laughing, as the flocks of pink flamingoes went flapping by – before she left him off at the party with the clowns. Which the travel agent had informed her 'came at no extra cost at all!'

There was literally nothing you couldn't get in Miami. It was the best decision she had ever made, she decided. And it cheered her up. Quite immensely, it has to be said. Thinking about the great big plane lifting off. As they sailed away across the clouds to Florida.

What fun! What larks!

It really was going to be such terrific fun!

So – not acting on impulse? That's really a load of collywobbles, she might have said.

---

The closer we came to their home in Barnet, the colder I'm afraid my fury became. And if that's, like my brother so often said, emotional and spurious, well then I'm sorry, darling Bailey, but that, I'm sorry to say, is just the way it is. Simply the way it has to be. And represents yet another instance of the essential difference between the 'two Bowens', I suppose you could call us. That is to say, the one who said 'Hello, Mr Bones' and the other who might say 'How I loathe Mr Bones!'

Making little effort, as he did so, to disguise his contempt for what he has always regarded as my own unrestrained, impatient, essentially effeminate nature.

Bailey, of course, has always been essentially masculine – with a muscular intellect, consummately detached in his appraisal of situations.

But, even to this day, I marvel at the majesty with which he conducted himself, especially during those first few weeks, before I finally plunged my convertible into the lake. Throughout the whole distressing affair, he had somehow managed to sustain a Herculean calm.

---

Bailey had warned me incessantly, as I have acknowledged. I remember him actually physically tearing Mr Bones from my grasp, railing as he threatened – and this really is true! – to destroy the 'accursed' thing, rip it to pieces. 'Once and for all,' he had seethed at me, breathlessly.

—Trinket! he had continued. Trembling, as I recall – unusual for him.

And which had ended with me breaking down – collapsing, as usual, into tears. A response of which I am, indeed as ought to be the case, quite ashamed. But, in the end, it has to be said, and to his credit, my brother gave me back my 'precious doll', as he described it. Snapping gruffly, impatiently, as he stood there by the south-facing mullioned window, gazing out over the damp huddled roofs of the unprepossessing village:

—Play with it then, God damn you, if you must!

Literally flinging it at me, right across the floor of the room.

Before going on to say that he was not in the least surprised by what had transpired, or that Valentine Shannon had finally betrayed me.

—Why, dissimulation was bound to come naturally to the boy, he insisted, why ought he be any different to the others of his tribe, these indigenous Irish Catholics to whom deception is a veritable art form? Don't you realise how much we are resented, deep down – did you never ask yourself that, my dear twin? What else could we be, other than 'The Ascendancy' – appreciated with an almost intolerable envy, all the time waiting for the opportunity that might present itself? The opportunity for vengeance, sweet dearest Balthazar, and which – credulous fool that you are, you went out of your way to hand to them on a plate. I wept copiously through a cage of my fingers:

—But, Bailey – why can't you admit it – you did it too!

Only to find myself frozen in mid-sentence by the calm elevation of an authoritative, unyielding hand.

—Quiet, he whispered, what's done is done.

As I bade him goodnight and proceeded to the far wing, where as always I slept alone, but for Mr Bones, who of course, ever since Mother's death, has been my sole consolation and constant companion.

To this day, I really don't know what I'd have done without him. Stroking his hard little plastic head, whispering softly into his ear as his hollow eyes regarded me with a softness and sympathy quite uncharacteristic:

—Hello, Mr Bones. I'm afraid the end is nigh, old friend. And it seems to me there is only one thing left that I can do. Thanks to Valentine, I'm left with no option.

# 17

During the course of her stay in the Yeats Country Hotel in 1976, Chris Taylor had found herself quite horrified by the level of violence in Northern Ireland – the effects of which were far-reaching, even if one was not experiencing it first hand. The country she had discovered was a truly baffling place. Death in general appeared to be everywhere – with the Provisional IRA continuing to be extremely active. Within days of her arrival, the British Ambassador had been blown to pieces outside Dublin.

From my own point of view, however, it is a summer I recall with a great deal of fondness – as I ventured west with a firm sense of purpose. Finding myself sitting on a counter stool next to Christine – a fact of which, with blithe innocence, she continued to remain oblivious.

As was my custom, during the days when Valentine and I used to summer in Rosses Point – when I cheerfully told everyone we were related – 'my sister's boy', I used to tell them – I would wear a light-blue short-sleeved nylon shirt, with casual slacks and latticed leather sandals. I looked every inch the retired professional – perhaps even a priest, one observes – not without a little amusement, considering the present circumstances.

They knew my boat, of course, the locals – an eighteen-foot cruiser – *The Morning Star.* Not a name, as I'm sure you understand, which had been selected at random.

—I'm here with my nephew, was the story I remember telling Christine.

Certainly not to do you any harm, or with the intention of marking your card, I might have added.

*Sotto voce.*

—My dear little doughty, and vulnerable, Christine.

---

Valentine's duties on the *Star* had included the cooking of meals, the cleaning of the brasses and the holystoning of the deck. And which, I will admit, he performed with a reasonable degree of competence. As I spent my days, on the clifftops, watching Christine carefully. After all, it isn't as if I didn't know what was coming.

Nephew indeed. Manipulative little Judas-in-waiting.

Even yet, in sharp detail, I can see Christine alone there in the hotel bar, quite oblivious of the fate I had in store for her, leafing through *Hibernia* in her Liberty-print maxi dress, with one brown Wrangler boot crossed over the other.

—Why, I'm so sturdy that I might in fact be made of steel, she was thinking. And do you know why that is? Because I've taken the responsibility of raising my boy alone. He's learning-disabled you know. Look at me – don't you just wish you were me? Such courage in a hostile world – a world unsympathetic to the fundamental rights I possess as a woman.

I sat there, just observing her. The magazine headline read: 'NY's NEW SENSATION. COPPOLA TAKES ON THE STUDIOS'.

No sooner than I had decided to make my departure, she knew immediately that something was wrong. She had even returned to the bar to check, sensing that she'd been invaded in some way. But how exactly?

I wasn't there, of course. I had toyed with the idea of leaving her a little note. Bearing a short, clear message.

*See you in ten or eleven years' time, Christine.*

Something like that. For her instincts, of course, had been absolutely correct.

She was right to be trepidatious, even terrified of the future.

But don't blame me.

Blame Shannon.

# 18

*Yuletide Fun with Betty Boop* was not a film that preoccupied the mind of the former Christian Brother Valentine Shannon, kneeling there now in the front pew of the Catholic church in Spitalfields with his head lowered devoutly. But then, of course, why ought it be – when one considers that for many years past, he had insisted on denying its very existence? In so doing, of course, comprehensively absolving himself of any enjoyment he may have derived from it or associated confections down through the years. Why on earth would he want to watch such rubbish? But of course he didn't – it was I who forced him, quite against his will.

—It was the Bowens, he told the sergeant, I had no choice at all in the matter. They made me do it. You see, I was afraid. I would have watched any film they wanted. It was a terrifying time for me, you see.

But of course it was – having to watch Betty Boop doing her shopping at Christmas. But not only that, going to fashion shows and the seaside, God help us!

There were other films too, and of course the sergeant heard all about them. There was *Carry On Sergeant*, and one that Bailey and I, sentimentalists that we are, and in the circumstances providing a neat ironical twist, one for which we have always entertained a particular fondness – the old Robert Donat version of *Goodbye Mr Chips*. Bailey always bought them in a theatrical shop in London – he had quite a selection of 8mm gems.

The sergeant detained me for three whole hours. Why, there seemed no end to Master Shannon's mendacious assertions. But then, as Bailey had always cautioned, what on earth did I expect?

But what galls me most – as if all of that hadn't been enough – what happens less than two years later? The devious little rascal announces he's decided to devote his life to God! Having been accepted – *mirabile dictu*! – by a drab little minor seminary in Carlow!

His mother – a certain Mrs Dowdy Cabbage, as my brother, so amusingly and precisely, had christened her – of course professed herself delighted. Like all defeated slum-presiding matriarchs of the time, basking in the traditional unblemished glow.

—To have a clergyman in the family – such an honour!

Oh, how the neighbours would seethe with envy, she thought. Perhaps not surprisingly, at least according to Bailey, there ensued a number of routinely remarkable 'visions' on her part.

—I saw you mounted on a white mule, she informed her son, clothed in the most magnificent magenta mantle. There was a golden coach, Valentine, drawn by six horses – and as you passed them by, all the citizens of the town fell at once to their knees. Lord be praised and thanks to my angel!

Angel, indeed. Manipulative little Catholic cur.

I'll soon show him what an 'angel' is.

---

Word got around regarding our 'secret' projections of *Chips* and *Betty Boop*. The chorus of disapproval, of course, was unanimous – but then it was a backward little village. And Valentine had given a consummate performance – making sure that his account was not short on colourful embellishments, innuendoes and exaggerations. By all accounts there were copious tears – and, of course, the stammer. I had always noticed that whenever he got excited.

—He used to make me say I luh-loved Buh-Betty. But I didn't, Sergeant – I hated them all!

—The apostasy of ingrates, Bailey used to seethe, tapping his lapels as he stood by the window, I knew in the end it would come to this.

If only I'd listened, instead of pulling up to the Shannon door in my Trojan convertible – smiling underneath my Panama hat as I leaned out the window, enquiring as to whether the boy wonder might *perchance* be at home?

—Indeed and he is, Mr Balthazar, sir! a clearly delighted Mrs Cabbage would peal – quite beside herself with excitement, it was evident, savouring yet again the seething, inevitable envy of her neighbours.

—I'll be with you just in a moment, Uncle Balthazar! Valentine's shrill cry would echo, wafting through the leaking gas and boiled cabbage of the dreary cottages.

---

Betty Boop's laughter was so impossibly fey. But, in a way, the communal obloquy it provoked was not at all difficult to comprehend. I mean, she *was* erotic. To begin with, there was her garter – a frilly little item which she lost no opportunity to ply, as she batted her lashes and touched her bosom, giving this extraordinary little sinuous wiggle.

—*My sweetie Mr Santa Claus!* she would squeal, draped across his ample lap – pressing coy little sausage fingers to her lips.

---

What's most odd, of course, is that somehow I don't seem to remember any tears that day when we screened it. Indeed as far as I remember, Valentine Shannon was rocking with glee – issuing little whoops of delight. And what tears they were – ones of enjoyment, certainly not of abuse – which was a word that came into fashion much later on. Or ill-treatment of any kind, indeed – either by myself or my brother Bailey. Oh, how we laughed at dear old Mr Chipping, sitting by his fire with the autumn gales rattling his windows, dreaming yet again of all those vanished boys. Where had they all gone to? he often pondered, nodding by the fire in his gown and white hair, with his steel-rimmed spectacles slipping down his nose, murmuring:

— *'I remember the first bicycle. I remember when there was no gas or electric light and we used to have a member of staff called a lamp boy. And now as the tall clock ticks and the smells of ink and varnish fade, I see the last blood-red rays of sun slanting in through the stained-glass windows . . . in Brookfield School where we were so happy.'*

Just as we, in our way, my brother and I, had been in Manor House. Back in those innocent days of 1963. When there was no political trouble of any kind, when people even seemed to like the Protestant Ascendancy of which we had always been a part – or at the very least, respected it.

But, in the end, perhaps, that was all illusory too – a cruel chimera, as Bailey had suggested.

—You'll see that, when your little friend gives you up, with a smile not dissimilar to the Bible's invidious apostle.

How right he had been.

# 19

In the Catholic church at Spitalfields where he was still praying, Valentine Shannon was already considering the season of Christmas. However, not the one he associated with Betty Boop – most definitely not. For, as he insisted, such unwanted memories had been erased from his mind, long since. As far as he was concerned, *Yuletide Fun with Betty Boop* – it had never happened. With the scenes already gathering in his mind of an entirely more amenable and pleasurable nature. Comprising, in the main, domestic episodes featuring – almost exclusively – his partner Chris Taylor and her big-hearted son Faisal – two people who had brought him undreamt-of happiness. A long way, he reflected vindictively, from those days he had spent in The Manor, after school.

—In the company of that repugnant wretch, he sighed.

Charming.

—That loathsome bastard, Bowen the degenerate.

Not that I mind a great deal what he calls me. But I do object to him slandering my brother. Why, I could happily strike him down as he kneels there in the front pew. However, as Bailey always maintained, with his impeccable scientific logic:

—*Revenge is a dish best served cold.*

I admired that so much – that quality I have referred to – dispassion, I suppose. I'll never forget that very first time he apprehended me. It was in the bedroom, as I recall, and I was occupying myself in dialogue with Mr Bones. I had never before been privy to such incandescent rage.

—You milksop! You chicken-heart! I remember him rumbling. He threatened again to smash it into pieces.

I wept like an infant. But he was not yet finished. As he paced the room vehemently, looking taut and spectral.

—Do you not understand, Balthazar? he went on, if anyone finds this out, that this is what you're actually like deep down – you'll be destroyed without mercy!

I knew in my heart my twin brother was right. So I concealed Mr Bones in an old box of shoes. And only retrieved him on special occasions, playing beneath the stairs when there was no one around. I have to say that it helped me, though. For I hadn't been well since Mother passed away. And it could often be so very lonely up in The Manor – particularly if Bailey and I didn't happen to be getting along. Which was unusual, admittedly – but he was potentially explosive. He actually threatened to annihilate me once.

---

In the front pew in Spitalfields church, Valentine Shannon was giving profuse thanks. As he promised never to take Chris and Faisal's affections for granted. How they helped to erase those unwanted memories – and not just those of The Manor either. Even more upsetting, on occasion, were those dark recollections of his final few months in Glassdrummond, in the aftermath of what had happened with Martin Boan. It was clear he was going to be relieved of his post – not only that, but driven from the college – dismissed in disgrace. But what continued to plague him was the persistent probing question – what had made him strike the boy? He couldn't understand. Had something made him do it? He would probably never know, he decided – but for a long time now, he had had his suspicions. That, through a gap in his defences, he had somehow been *influenced*.

He lowered his head and voiced an appeal for advocacy. Realising that he was becoming anxious again, and that the comfort of solidarity would be a strength and a boon to him. However, his gathering consternation did not readily dissipate. In fact, a film of perspiration now shone on his brow as he resigned himself to the prospect of a forthcoming engagement. Across from him, alone in the side aisle, an old man coughed lightly before falling to his knees – venerating an icon with a rain of tears upon his cheeks. Valentine prayed that this disabling moment would pass – and remained convinced that it would. In which assumption, at last, he found himself proved right. As the face of his partner appeared, lovingly, in his mind's eye.

---

Just as it did – yet again, in the Spitalfields church car park. And which saw him smiling as he searched for his keys – just before finding himself distracted by an inexplicable sound. One which, I have to say, amused me no end. Being as it was – can you believe it? – the lonesome wail of a foghorn, in a location literally miles from the sea – and certainly a very long distance indeed from Rosses Point. As a stray aside uttered by some passers-by succeeded in alerting him further, with their footsteps scraping past.

—They can say what they like about Michael Fish but he knows what he's talking about. Look around you – do you see any sign of any storm, much less a hurricane? Of course you don't – it's all a lot of balls. For Michael Fish knows. There's a weatherman the public can trust.

The air was stirless as Valentine Shannon climbed into his car and he switched on the ignition. But then – well, he froze.

—*Daddy*, he heard the young boy's voice pleading on the radio, *the man is going to take out my teeth. He says that little Arab boys are the best*.

There could be no mistaking Faisal's voice.

—*Please can you help me? Can anyone help me? I'm all alone*.

Why did he have to hear that? he asked himself. He would have given anything not to have heard it. To have heard nothing at all, especially the sound of a grown man's laughter. It took four attempts to start the car. He succeeded eventually, with a great show of defiance – but deep in his heart already palsied with fear, somehow having become, he sensed, the instrument of a stranger.

# 20

Whether Shannon and Taylor would ever have met without my express intervention is a moot point. But there can be little doubt that it must have seemed that way – in any case, it proved fortuitous. For both, I might add. For the *lovebirds*, happy to say, turned out to have a great deal in common. Certainly a lot more than might have been anticipated. For example, there were their regular bouts of what one might term their somewhat *convenient amnesia*, to coin a phrase.

A representative indication of this shared tendency was Chris Taylor's routine assertion that any reservations she harboured regarding the male gender were in no way prompted by any experiences she might have had in the past. And most certainly had nothing to do with her father – with whom she had experienced *no problems* at all. Who, in fact, was *tender* and her *rock*, in so many ways. Oh, but of course he was.

Valentine Shannon, as I say, was not dissimilar – especially when it came to erasing large sections of his past. Why, hardly had he turned the Renault out of the Spitalfields churchyard on his way to Piccadilly Circus than even the tiniest recollection of the *so-called voice* as he was already thinking of it, had been comprehensively removed from his memory. Yes, subtly compartmentalised in a receptacle marked *empty* – in true Valentine Shannon style. Without leaving so much as a trace. Just like those happy times we'd once had in The Manor – all those long summer days when we'd laugh and joke while we watched Betty Boop or Chips – they had simply never happened. Just like he'd never in his life ever eaten a slice of Thornton's – Mrs Thornton's lovely marble cake – apparently, now, it never existed. As, with a single and convenient, quite disdainful flourish, all of those experiences were written out of history. To be spoiled, of course, by expropriating, inelegant remembrances.

Those good times had never happened. Of that he was certain. The Manor had shown him nothing but misery. He was as assured of that now as he was of the love which he felt for his attractive new partner. That is to say, the intrepid and stout-hearted feminist Christine Taylor. Who, somewhat mysteriously, though intermittently, throughout the course of the seventies, had been obsessed with publicising her preference for the sensual attractions of the female gender – almost hysterically lauding the apparent suppleness of their fragrant bodies, their innate understanding of one another's natures. But who, rather contradictorily, six months after they'd met in September '86, had almost cravenly pleaded in his ear:

—Please don't leave us – me and Faisal. I've never met anyone like you, Valentine.

---

Making his approach towards Shaftesbury Avenue, Valentine Shannon reached over and turned up the volume on the radio. The weather report was just concluding and Michael Fish was once again reassuring the public. Beyond all shadow of doubt there would be no storms – certainly no hurricane. He laughed lightly whenever he said this. His words had the same effect on the driver – that is to say, they made him chuckle. He was no longer tense. I made sure of that. Why, he was actually grinning from ear to ear!

# 21

The newspaper vendor by the side of the Regent Palace took an age even to see Valentine Shannon. But eventually his eyebrows elevated in recognition and he approached the car with an attitude of apology – passing the *Evening Standard* through the window. Flicking randomly through its contents, the Renault's now-contented pilot permitted himself the slightest little self-indulgent smile. It was hard to believe but yes, there it was – in broad type printed across the front page – the farcical headline: 'CITY POISED TO FACE UNPRECEDENTED WEATHER'.

Valentine smiled as he drummed on the wheel, thinking to himself just how laughably inaccurate these journalists can be. At least you could always rely on Michael Fish, whose prognosis had turned out one hundred per cent correct. One only had to look out the window to see just how accurate he had, in fact, been. Why, the feeling of calm in Piccadilly at that moment – in one of the world's busiest cities – was nothing short of remarkable.

But what was even more gratifying was how precisely the relative quietude of the surroundings could be said to mirror his own inner state. Something which he now was proud of – and had a right to be, considering what had happened, less than twenty minutes before. When the faintly pleading voice of Faisal Taylor had entered his mind. But not just that – the plaintive cry which had succeeded it. And the awful words – he shuddered as he recalled them:

—*Daddy, please help me. The man says he is going to take out my teeth.*

There was a perfectly rational explanation for all that now, of course – it had been the consequence of an overtaxed imagination.

For the unpalatable facts were that the past few weeks in John Briory had been very stressful – extremely so. There were one or two staff colleagues with whom he could have got along better and Rajesh in 6M had been a source of constant irritation. But, as he folded the paper and edged into the right-hand lane, Valentine Shannon told himself that he was no longer in the least worried. Which seemed to him yet another small triumph – of the kind to which he had become accustomed, ever since meeting Christine Taylor. She had given him such strength, he mused. A thought which he was beginning to enjoy most thoroughly when – as though the radio had inexplicably changed stations – those familiar chords of the overture to *Oliver!* began to sweep out. Yes, *Oliver!* the musical – the show which he had directed, once upon the long ago – in Glassdrummond College. This was followed – already he had grown uncomfortable, he realised – by the song of the Artful Dodger. It was, of course, a tune everyone knew. 'Consider Yourself', it was called.

—It's only a song, he told himself – and bit his lip.

There was a phrase of Christine's – *Feel the fear and do it anyway* – and, as so often now, he found himself returning to it, and indeed to his partner's reliance on such fixed, committed precepts. And, as he gripped the steering wheel, his performance, I must say, was impressive.

—It's only a tune, he continued repeating in a monotone, it's only a tune and it's all in the past.

His lip was bleeding but he dabbed it with a tissue.

—Feel the fear and do it anyway. Fuck 'em! he heard Christine enthuse – as she smiled.

How he loved her. And how she helped him now, as always.

—'Consider Yourself', don't make me laugh! he smiled, gliding past the Cumberland Hotel, turning onto the Edgware Road.

Why, it has to be said that such was the degree of inscrutable restraint that Valentine Shannon was demonstrating now that he might well have been my own twin brother Bailey. How unthinkable would such discipline have been in the past for dear Valentine. When he would have given *anything* to be afforded access to the strength and force of character that his relationship with Chris had bestowed on him. It was she alone who had revivified the man that he once had been. Had given back to him his once legendary facility for quick decision and promptness of execution. It was she who had restored his once much-celebrated authority. A development that had not gone unremarked upon in John Briory. It was why he was made head of department. How warm and worthy it had made him feel! It felt just like the early days in Glassdrummond.

Before the Martin Boan episode had come along to ruin everything. Something which he couldn't understand, to this day. But for which he had shouldered all the blame.

—Prosecuted for something I don't even remember doing, he told himself.

Well, my, my, my, but doesn't that sound familiar!

---

However, all of that was now far back in the past. Like so many aspects of his life, no longer relevant. Belonging to a place he tended to classify as *that other time*. One which, with every single day that passed, receded ever further in his mind.

—*You stupid fucking cunt! Are you trying to kill me?*

The brakes squealed sharply – as a derelict tumbled across the car bonnet, pressing his face grotesquely against the windscreen. He was shaking his fist. Then another similar individual appeared, and within seconds they were screaming at one another, locked in a preposterous, violent embrace.

—I'll fucking murder you, you bastard! Once and for all, I'll finish you off!

The lights changed abruptly and Valentine pressed his foot to the pedal, only succeeding in alerting the warring tramps to the situation. Thin streams of sweat were coursing down Valentine's cheeks. He reached in his pocket for his hankie, without success – just as he heard the side window smashing. A filthy hand was pawing his temple.

—Give me money! Do you hear me, you bastard!

The other derelict had climbed up on the bonnet, leaning down to press a bloodstained hand against the glass.

—For God's sake! pleaded Valentine Shannon.

But there clearly was no point in talking to either of them – the face of the bloodstained one was jaggedly creased with pure mania. He glared in murderously, clawing at the driver:

—*You think he's right – don't you, Michael Fish! Well, that's where you are way wrong, my friend!*

Then he tore off and ran up the street.

---

Valentine Shannon examined his face in the mirror – it was pale and indecisive. If earlier it had evidenced a dignified repose of some considerable measure, scant evidence of it was to be read there now.

# 22

—You'll fucking pay! Make no mistake, but all of you will fucking pay! the tramp had sworn.

He gripped the steering wheel as he drove on towards Hendon. Probably inmates from the local mental hospital, he thought, released under this spurious Care in the Community programme which the Conservative government were so fond of.

—*Don't get me started on that!* he heard Chris wailing.

Realising, to his horror, that the Renault had just now narrowly missed another vehicle. What in God's name was he playing at? he asked himself. His moods seemed to be swinging all over the place. Then – he shivered violently as he felt it glide into his mind – the briefest snatch of an unfamiliar tune, with the singsong jaunt of a childrens's playground rhyme:

—*You'll wonder where the yellow went when you brush your teeth with Pepsodent!*

As, quite startlingly – just like the arrival of the song, he found himself becoming acquainted with an entirely unfamiliar image – that of Bonio, the clown, in fact. Of Mr Pom Pom, with no peer.

—*Consider yourself at home, consider yourself one of the family!* hummed the former Christian Brother repeatedly, in a gallant effort to restore himself – smiling unconvincingly as he urged the vehicle forward – as smoke began pouring out of the bonnet – as, with a heave and a grunt, the Renault finally stuttered to a halt.

As a rule, he eschewed scatology – with discipline and purpose. But on this occasion, Valentine Shannon capitulated hopelessly.

—*Can anything else – can it possibly go fucking wrong!* he snarled, jerkily dabbing his brow as his temples pulsed hotly.

Now where was he – what choice did he have? Jammed chokingly into an unsteady train, its unreliable carriage lighting flickering on and off, hurtling along precariously on the Jubilee Line. As if that wasn't bad enough, being compelled to endure the forced intimacies of the passenger beside him, some clearly mentally unbalanced individual who, with an inappropriateness which ought to have been hilarious, was pressing the works of John Milton on his fellow travellers. Valentine Shannon gripped the carriage pole tight. It was all he could do to hold himself together. It did occur to him, however, that the pest's *modus operandi* could not have differed more from that of the derelicts he had encountered earlier. In fact, his general presentation was in many respects ordinary and quite respectable – he appeared, indeed, possessed of soft and quite refined manners. As he continued, now in full flight:

—By what way are we best to proceed, by open war or covert guile?

Then he grinned inanely into Valentine's face, tilting his trilby to one side. The passenger to his left stiffened and demanded:

—Oh, for heaven's sake! Do we really have to listen to this?

But the poet remained nonplussed.

—This night your city will experience unique havoc.

—Obviously you didn't hear Michael Fish, returned an anonymous voice – pointlessly, with a nervous laugh.

As the lights returned abruptly, blazing back on. And it was at that point that Valentine was permitted a proper look at me, standing directly opposite him in the compartment. As I swayed there, quiet now, swinging back and forth as I stared unflinchingly at him. There was nothing immediately recognisable about my physical aspect but it was clear that he drew something from a slight contraction of the lips and eyebrows that had the effect of instilling the manifest discomfort that comes from faint or ill-defined recognition. Which was what I had intended, as I pressed the piece of paper into his hand. Before doffing my hat – and, with that, I was gone.

---

Emerging from the station, Valentine examined the scrap of paper. It read:

*Be mindful that you have brought this upon yourself.*

---

The sky overhead was metallic, oppressive. Beside him, a willow tree was bending dangerously, tormented by a 90 mph gale. Up ahead a car was lifted right off the ground. Then the heavens opened and he crouched down and tore across the road, just as a clanging dustbin missed him by a whisker. A child's tricycle was bowled along by the wind.

His hands were unsteady as he sat there in the Wimpy, trying his best to lift his cup. But as soon as it touched his lips he lost his grip and it fell to the floor. The woman sitting across from him was so animated that she might well have been mentally disturbed, viewing the scene in the street with wild eyes and parted lips. Then she slammed her small fist down on the table.

—*I don't care what anyone says! Michael Fish is still right!*

The Italian proprietor looked as though he had just been acquainted of some great sadness but was bearing his load with admirable fortitude. He feared, he said, that the enormous chestnut opposite was going to topple at any moment. Repeated calls to the fire department had produced no results, he said. As he turned his back to return to the kitchen – just as the plate glass window came in.

—*You must go home pliss! Pliss all of you, you must go home!* he bayed hoarsely, frantically waving his arms in abject appeal.

It certainly represented a scene of unique havoc – so far from the blissful tranquillity of the west of Ireland where I had sedulously monitored Miss Christine Taylor. In the same committed manner as I now did her companion, stumbling along the road whipped by leaves – avoiding the raining slates and lumbering creaking branches overhead.

*Be mindful that you have brought this upon yourself.* He was far from the logical country now, that restrained, detached place where certitude dwelled. And where existed no promise of imminent catastrophe. Although I really must admit that, given the circumstances, his resoluteness quite impressed me. His show of defiance on the train particularly. Perhaps I ought to have prompted him a little further.

—Very pleased to meet you. I'm Mr Bohan, I ought to have said, I once knew your girlfriend.

---

I have always felt comfortable with the status conferred by the formal honorific of *Mr.* Not to mention appreciative of its efficacy, particularly in the past – when deference to authority, unlike now, was almost immediate. Even back then, in the blistering summer of 1976, Christine Taylor, for all her proselytising, would not have been unduly disrespectful towards *the older gentleman*, shall we say. I mean, she wasn't towards me – or *Mr Bohan*, which was the personification I had elected to assume at that time.

But then, my presentation, although perhaps somewhat remote, in that Bailey Bowen fashion, couldn't possibly have been regarded as threatening. Certainly no appreciation of Mr Bohan as an *instrument of evil* or anything approaching could have been credibly entertained. But then, of course, that had been the way with her old friend Mr Stewart Granger. Indeed the idea of her father's friend ever being of malign intent was entirely laughable. He just seemed so straightforward. Why, even to a child's eyes, for an adult he seemed so innocent – in that dreary suburban land of the mid-1960s, where Gracie Fields still chanted her wartime ditties, and at evening thin curtains closed in preparation for high tea, among other things.

—Take off your sock, smiled her father's friend, and you and me we'll play Sooty and Sweep, Christine.

---

There would indeed have been few in that inexperienced, occluded world who would have identified her visitor as the possessor of a numb and arid soul. Which was why when, sobbing her heart out later, Christine found her claims not only being violently dismissed but was vilified herself for having had the temerity to give them utterance. For whatever else her husband might be, her mother had snapped, Cyril Taylor was not the associate of a degenerate. Why, the man all his life had never so much as said boo to a goose.

—Get up to your room, she said to Christine, reading too many comic book stories!

---

Valentine started when, among the flying tiles, he heard a woman scream:

—I'm ruined! My house! My house! Jesus Christ, I'm ruined!

A car door flapped and banged, as a sideways dustbin filled up with leaves, a rolled-up carpet sailing to rest between two trees.

# 23

I will, of course, readily accept that this narrative contains elements which serve no purpose other than that of my amusement. The Pekinese being bounced on viewless winds some distance above Kew Gardens would evidently belong in this category. What a spectacle it made, what with its hopelessly confused and heart-broken proprietor, a Miss Joan Morrison of Richmond in Surrey, appealing in vain for assistance that would never come. With the animal, poignantly, eventually to break its back against a high-rise tower. Hopelessly oblivious of all such events, Valentine Shannon continued to behave somewhat in the manner of a faulty clockwork toy, crying out in antic semaphore – pleading for any form of transport to take him home. By the time a cab eventually appeared, he had been searching for well over an hour, and was quite worn out with emotion and irresolution.

Paying little heed to the driver as he clambered gratefully into the vehicle. Why, he didn't even notice there was anything in the slightest unusual about the person behind the wheel – much less become perturbed by the knowing, self-satisfied look in his eye. Not even when he heard – which he ought to have done – the already familiar lyric: *You'll wonder where the yellow went when you brush your teeth with Pepsodent!* – unspooling with a detached, controlled restraint.

—Boy, what a night it's turning out to be, remarked the clown, with a leering melon-slice grin suspended between his ears.

When he finally realised – and, in truth, it wasn't all that long afterwards – what discountenanced Shannon more than anything was the strong possibility that the extraordinary events of the evening had, in fact, already not only directed him towards the realms of much-feared incertitude but in fact consummately snared him. That, his immense efforts notwithstanding, he had indeed become captive in the dread country of delusion and irrationality. But his fears were to prove groundless – for it transpired that the clown was just an amateur children's entertainer – from the Harrow area, apparently. And who worked, Valentine was informed, part-time as a minicab driver.

—Bonio is my circus name, he smiled, before continuing:

—I do schools and suchlike, you see, my friend. I work part-time in the morning and in the evening here I am, driving my cab. Isn't that good? Isn't it nice being driven by Mr Pom Pom?

The garishly made-up face turned, eyes goggling as he rubber-necked – with two comical bobbins of orange curls wobbling over each ear. Which, as a matter of fact, Valentine found so disarming that he became susceptible to a growing rush of the most positive feeling. Until a presentiment of sorts – of the kind which sometimes gives its particular horror to a dream – acutely gripped him and he found his eyes riveted to the mirror, in which he discovered a dilated gaze as pale as death. There was something truly awful in the driver's expression. As the vehicle shunted forward and the now mysteriously benign grin hove in with fixed purpose – not without its discernible hint of menace.

—Please call me Bonio, Valentine Shannon.

Valentine stiffened, shrinking in the back seat. His stomach turned over and his fists began to close. But the driver continued talking – quite incessantly, with his grin widening as he became increasingly animated.

—You know, my friend, people tend to misunderstand us entertainers. Not all clowns are alike, in fact not at all. That's what sets them apart from each other. One clown can be shy, another boisterous. One clumsy and another skilled. One can wear bright, colourful clothes and another tattered attire without colour or glitter. Each one should look and act distinctively different. Although it is easy to spot a clown because of the characteristic costume and make-up, each clown should have his or her own character and personality.

The vehicle jerked abruptly as he rubbernecked, grinning ferociously:

—Do you understand what I mean? he enquired, with his shoulders hunched.

But Valentine didn't get a chance to reply as he proceeded, wild-eyed:

—What I'm saying is, sir, too often novice clowns don't pay enough attention to their make-up; they put a dab of eye shadow here, some lipstick there and – presto! – they call themselves clowns.

The brakes squealed fiercely.

—But, I ask you – are they clowns? he demanded.

And again no opportunity was offered for a response. As he continued fulsomely:

—I would suggest not. In fact would go so far as to suggest that what you are dealing with there is – an IMPOSTOR! Do you hear me? An IMPOSTOR!

A current of air, Valentine realised, from the driver's breath had just struck his brow, icily cold.

—You see, make-up and costuming are EXTREMELY important parts of clowning. Often, it is the unique clown attire and make-up that sets clowns apart from other children's entertainers. To be a real clown you must look the part. You see my pompoms? My orange bobbins – do you see them? The way I've painted my mouth at the edges? Which brings me to whiteface.

—Please, pleaded Valentine, almost pitifully.

—I would regard it – genuinely – as perhaps the most elegant and most simplistic of the clown facial designs. The primary colour is white, which covers the entire face. Simple thin features, usually either in red or black, are added to emphasise the mouth and eyes. Few, if any, other markings are present. The facial designs of mimes would be typical examples of this type of make-up. For my own part – as you can see – I tend to apply the greasepaint more boldly. So that the mouth and eyes become a large splash of colour, and the nose – *look!* – puffs into a large bulb. There is also my skullcap, which matches my one-piece jumpsuit well, don't you think? And my pompoms – LOOK!

The brakes screeched and the vehicle came close to striking the edge of the kerb.

—Jesus Christ, man, will you for Christ's sake watch where you're going!

He might as well not have uttered a word – for all the response he received. As, in the front seat – unbelievably, the driver was now jumping up and down, scrunching up his face as he gripped the steering wheel.

—But at the end of the day, what wins out is one's style. And for me it's always music and jokes. Do you like music? Music – do you like it?

—Music? replied Valentine, do I like mu—?

But the driver had already cut across him, wailing in a falsetto trill:

—*Say hello to Bonio*
*Always on his ownio*
*Never will he moanio*
*Because he's your best friend!*
*Collywobbles!*

—What on earth are you doing? Watch the road, I said – will you watch the fucking road!

—Did you ever hear the Michael Fish joke? What did one hurricane say to the other? I've got my eye on you!, he laughed, just as the speedometer needle began to climb sharply, as the vehicle swerved wildly into a side street. A roof directly in front was pared off like cheese.

—Where on earth are we going? demanded Valentine, what in the name of Jesus do you think you're playing at?

Oh yes, he was very concerned indeed, as well he might be, the former dean of Glassdrummond.

Or should I say Judas – erstwhile sovereign of the most odious perfidy. Who would soon be reaping a bountiful harvest indeed.

# 24

It was on the 3rd of July 1969, the day the local sergeant paid a visit to Manor House, that I came to realise my unfortunate demise was now more or less inevitable. What a truly melancholic revelation – compelled to accept that never again would Balthazar Bowen pilot his Trojan convertible through those tawdry, uneventful village streets, picking up Master Valentine before steering once more westward, to crest the waves upon the glorious *Morning Star*.

It was clearly only a matter of time – and, as my brother had predicted, certain conniving voices had begun emerging, slyly adumbrating my guilt.

But what was the exact nature of the crime of which I was suspected? Why, projecting a selection of popular cinema entertainments, most notably *Chips*, *Betty Boop* and, occasionally, The Three Stooges.

As well, of course, as providing what in retrospect were exceedingly generous rations of Mrs Thornton's special confections. Which were greedily consumed by none other than Master Valentine Shannon, one's associate and apprentice and sometime wheelman of *The Morning Star*.

—Did you know that Mr Chipping was inordinately partial to

such confections? I remember observing. He always ordered a walnut cake with pink icing from Reddaway's, in the village!

—Quite scrumptious, I remember him telling me – for he had really enjoyed that particular helping of Mrs Thornton's. But then he always did – and spent his mornings in that tedious old schoolhouse looking forward to high tea at the house. And much as he might have been embarrassed to acknowledge as much, he derived immense amusement from the coquettish antics of Miss Boop, coyly plucking her garter and shrieking with piles of parcels.

But all of that had now, apparently, changed. There would no longer be cartoons and, certainly, no cake, walnut or otherwise. Ever since his visit to the police station, in the company of his mother, the appalling Mrs Dowdy Cabbage, who once more conformed to Bailey's estimation of the indigenous Irish character, displaying a guile quite profound and shockingly nimble, coldly and remorselessly supplanting that ingratiating smile to which I had become accustomed. She and her son had been in the sergeant's company for some hours, it was reported. During the course of which Valentine had, apparently, made certain *accusations*.

We apprehended him simultaneously through the south-facing mullioned window, bearing the familiar gait of the self-effacing but precarious civic guard. Hardly surprisingly, my brother was furious.

—To hell with you, he said, rounding on me formidably, this is the last straw, Balthazar. Henceforth I have no sympathy for you. You have no one to blame, for on your own head you brought it all.

This was more than I should have been expected to tolerate, I thought. As I confronted him in a most uncharacteristic manner.

—But you did it too, for heaven's sake, Bailey! Did you not enjoy Robert Donat's performance? Or Betty Boop? And you certainly consumed your quota of Mrs Thornton's! Please be reasonable. You encouraged me to extend the invitation. You said it was acceptable to bring the boy here.

—I damned well did no such thing!

—You did! You did! It's not fair you telling lies!

—Well, I have never heard such poppycock in my life! It's an outrage you standing there and making such assertions!

But then, as my mother said – I am almost one hundred per cent certain that I heard this, I really am:

—Just what is one to expect from you, Balthazar? Why can't you try and be more like your brother? Instead of hiding under the stairs, playing with that infernal – thing!

—Mr Bones! He isn't a thing! And I expressly remember you giving me your permission! Oh, how I hate you – and everything about you!

—These intemperate outbursts! They are yet another manifestation of your feebleness and mental frailty! And I most certainly gave you no permission – none of any kind! You imagined that! Just like you've always done – dreaming up resentments, contriving absurd conspiracies—

—But why won't anyone help me? I'll never be able to face the shame of prosecution.

—That really doesn't surprise me, nor should it. What in heaven's name do you expect if you play with dolls? You say they provide you with unique solace and consolation? Very well then – go inside and say hello to your friend Mr Bones. Go on!

—Yes go on!, sighed Bailey, shaking his head in sheer exasperation.

Or might have done, perhaps.

If, in fact, I'd ever *had* a twin! Called Bailey Bowen, or anything else.

Tee hee! What larks!

---

The red Trojan convertible was beautiful to look at. And so expensive. It took the village completely by surprise when they heard that I'd driven it into the lake. But what was I to do? My life had effectively ended anyway, what with my having brought shame undreamt of on Manor House and the Bowens' good name. What options did I have? There was nothing left for Mr Bones and me. But I vowed, as I clutched the little black-jacketed skeleton to my chest, whispering into his soft padded ear as we tumbled, plunging down through those weedy, greeny waters, that one day that seditionist Shannon would pay.

—When the time, inevitably, comes.

# 25

—*Pull out his teeth! Then you'll wonder where it went – the yellow! Yes you'll wonder where the yellow went then!*

Bonio was wailing in falsetto as the car shot erratically through the ravaged streets. His passenger, unsurprisingly, was quite at his wits' end. As the driver swung around and leered again – in what was now a familiar hideous fashion. In his mask of whiteface and large-squared chequered suit.

—*Bonio! That's me – Bonio! Observe me as I wrench his teeth!*

The orange bobbins kept bouncing maddeningly.

—Would you like to know what's going to happen, Valentine?

It was more than Valentine Shannon could stand. He hurled himself forward and grabbed the steering wheel – with impressive determination. I have to say.

—You stupid fool! You idiotic bastard! spat the driver as the vehicle slipped right out of his control. Before veering treacherously across the road, almost turning over, and plunging headlong into a lamp-post. A geyser of steaming water shot up from the bonnet. Almost in a parody of some children's story, the clown was still screaming – capering insanely from foot to pompommed foot:

—You're doomed, Valentine Shannon! Doomed – you hear?

Valentine pushed him violently and sprinted down the glass-littered street. Then, out of nowhere, a figure loomed up. Valentine was as close as he had ever been to weeping in public.

—Give me your fucking wallet, you bastard!

The ascetic junkie clutched a hypodermic syringe. He raised it menacingly above his head.

—Give it to me, please – or I swear to God, I'll do it.

The trees on the side of the road were in the process of being wrested from their roots by the tempest. Which qualified as a hurricane now – of that there could be no doubt..

—I have AIDS, don't you see – don't you fucking understand? OK then I'll give you AIDS! You've asked for it!

Such, he now felt, was the absurdity of his situation that Valentine was on the verge of laughing. But then the syringe came plunging down as the point of the needle sent a searing pain shooting through his shoulder. It was quite unbearable already.

—It's your own fucking fault, the junkie rasped hoarsely, but you just wouldn't listen – and now I've got your wallet anyway!

Drops of blood were already staining Valentine's fingers. A cat stood looking at him – as if in an effort to make sense of this latest aberration. Then, quite unexpectedly, it flew into the air. As a branch, like plasticine, twirled downward from a tree. Then he saw that the wound had stopped bleeding – however, just as quickly, it began to ooze again.

I took advantage of this opportunity, entering his mind through the gap in his defences.

—Ah, I whispered, how sweet it can be – the delicious prospect of retribution long delayed.

As I filled him with dread – his heart beginning to beat quite furiously.

—Run, Master Valentine. Run for heaven's sake!

And, dutiful fellow that he is, Valentine Shannon diligently complied. Obsessed as he hastened – not unsurprisingly in the circumstances perhaps – with how long it actually took to die of AIDS.

# 26

But now it was beginning to look doubtful if he would ever make it home. These were the thoughts frantically racing through Valentine Shannon's hot, tormented mind. In the wind-whipped rains that were, if anything, increasing in their ferocity, he feared he might lose his bearings completely. A possibility against which he was straining quite heroically when, through the haze of the flagellating deluge, he descried to his amazement, the familiar frontage of a white Fiat Uno nosing precariously along the hazardous thoroughfare. And beyond the windscreen, to his astonishment, apprehended none other than Ronnie Clegg – ah, yes, my own little sweet caring angel – who, of course, without realising it had been awaiting her signal – in the wings, as it were. And who was a long-standing, deeply trusted friend of Chris's. They had known one another since college, for heaven's sake. But how could this be? But this was no time for futile interrogations – already he could see her beckoning frantically.

—For Christ's sake Valentine, get in the car!

What were the chances of something like that happening? he asked himself as climbed into the passenger seat. Which really – how could it be otherwise? – tickled my funny bone. Not to say flattered me when I considered the precision of my choreography. As Ronnie Clegg pressed her little flat foot to the pedal.

He had been in her company many times with Chris. But now as a new-found comfort overtook him, he realised that the occasion which rose most vividly in his mind was the night they had all enjoyed in the Embassy Club in Soho. He had only known Chris a short while then. He found himself blurting it out.

—It's quite a while ago now, said the middle-aged woman in the loose-fitting tracksuit. It was a poetry reading, if I recall correctly? I think Nest was reading – am I right in that?

—That's absolutely correct, he confirmed, feeling as though against all the odds he had somehow entered some miraculously impermeable world. A safe enclosed place – one where sunken-eyed junkies didn't exist. One where a syringe hadn't been plunged into one's shoulder.

—I'll get you a proper bandage when we get to my place, she assured him.

This is glorious, thought Valentine Shannon. Why, indeed, almost the equal of the Embassy Club that night. Which had seen the beginning of his re-education, effectively – when he had been fortunate to meet people who had not only impressed but quite overwhelmed him with their extraordinarily tolerant, almost indifferent ways. Not to mention the effect of the club itself – with its subterranean subversion and phlegmatic dissension. A *lady* he'd been introduced to had turned out to be a hermaphrodite.

—I'm going to have to go really slow, said Ronnie, craning forward and wiping the windscreen. Did you hear about Kew Gardens? It's completely destroyed.

The very mention of the gardens disturbed him again – immediately returning him to Bonio's hideous expression and flashing teeth.

—I'm Bonio. I'll be murdering your Faisal in Miami. He's fair set to disappear while admiring the beauty of the lovely pink flamingoes.

But that was all in the past, another mad incident on a truly strange night. Just like that unfortunate episode with the junkie. And, as he consoled himself, there was always the possibility that that could have been a bluff – and that the syringe had contained absolutely nothing at all. Most likely the fool didn't have AIDS at all. But of course he hadn't! Valentine felt like laughing at his own stupidity.

—Not every street person in the city has AIDS, you know, he chuckled.

—What's that? asked Ronnie.

—Oh, nothing, replied her passenger, but anyway Ronnie you were saying?

—Yes. I was telling you that these days I mostly teach supply in Harrow. Are you still in John Briory then, Valentine?

He nodded and smiled and confirmed that yes he was. He felt so at ease in the company of Ronnie Clegg. In many ways she was so like Chris.

—I'm only going as far as Kingsbury, Ronnie explained, I'm on my way to see my mother who is sick. As a matter of fact I think she's going to die.

—I'm sorry, said Valentine.

She was talking about her father now. She adored him, she said.

—Unlike Chris, from my earliest days I can honestly say that I was never on the receiving end of so much as a single word of reproach. A caress from my father was as natural as breathing. In this respect—

She hesitated. They exchanged glances and, reassured, she proceeded.

—In this respect, as I'm sure she has told you, Christine was, how shall I put it – *unfortunate*?

The two of them had met on their very first day at Strawberry Hill College.

—We were all of us into politics at that time. That was the way in the seventies, I guess.

She tossed back her head – her tight black curls peeping out from underneath her knotted coloured scarf – and good-naturedly shook her head as she explained:

—Of course, none of us understood the situation in Ireland. We *thought* we did. Do you remember John Lennon? Didn't he buy an island there? Back then it was all *marches*, *marches*, *marches*. We had a little theatre group too in the college.

—I know, smiled Valentine, Chris told me about it. Broken Chains, wasn't that what you called it?

Ronnie's eyes were twinkling now.

—Yes, she continued, it was Chris who came up with that. Any chance she got she made it her business to get us all out on the streets. She used to travel to the Middle East a lot. We put on so many benefits. Do you know that she actually got a commitment from the group Led Zeppelin? They actually agreed to play at one of our concerts. Although maybe being a classical man, they mightn't mean all that much to you, Valentine . . .

—Can't say they do, Ronnie, but I do know that Chris has all of their records. She often speaks of her admiration for Robert Plant – isn't he one of them?

—He sure is. Believe it or not, she actually went to talk to him herself. In the hope of squeezing a commitment out of him. When I think of her abilities. In those days Christine could have mobilised the bloody army.

He could imagine it all clearly as the car staggered along. He could see them squatting there on the floor of the students' union office – swamped by papers and leaflets and fliers. And the woman he loved so impossibly youthful in her black T-shirt. With the logo *Broken Chains* printed there defiantly – with a mailed fist smashing iron links, out of whose sundered remains fell the shattered word *fascist*.

—But it wasn't all work and agitation, Ronnie smiled as she tapped the wheel. Boy, there were times. I mean did we laugh, did we laugh or what.

There were nights at the Hammersmith Apollo, she went on, when they would go along to see Pink Floyd. Or another particular favourite of the time – Jethro Tull.

—I'd have travelled the length and breadth of the country to see the Tull, she told him, for I just loved Ian Anderson. Still do. I used to play the concert flute myself.

—But not any more?

—Not since my mother got sick, not so much. She got Alzheimer's back in March 1980, and since that time I've been looking after her. Up in Stanmore, in the family home.

—I'm sorry to hear that. Is she showing any improvement?

—The opposite, Val, I regret to have to say. And it worries me, her being on her own. But I've still got to work.

—That club we went to. I enjoyed that so much. They were really great times – those early days in London.

—The Embassy? Oh, that was a hangout we used to go to in the old days. It had changed a lot by the time you came around. I remember actually drinking with George Melly there. Met him quite by chance. To be honest, at the time I hadn't a clue what he did – I just liked him. His style was impressive and, let's face it, he could quote the surrealist poets rather well. The two of us stayed there yapping till closing time. I have to tell you, though – Chris was mad jealous when she heard what I'd been up to. We failed our exams through carry-on like that.

—And to think that all this was going on when I was patrolling the night corridors of Glassdrummond College. Boy, when I think of how innocent I was – before I had the good fortune to meet people like yourself. Poor innocent me. I was a late developer, Ronnie, I'm afraid.

—You might have been better off, Valentine, in a way. For we only got through college by the skin of our teeth. Just scraped in after getting our repeats. But of course that doesn't occur to you at the age of eighteen – that this was just the beginning, I mean. It never enters your mind at that age that your mother might end up with something like Alzheimer's. Heaven knows, when I think of it – in the small hours of the morning discussing the French symbolists, unlocking all the secrets of the cosmos – so full of hope. That flat we had too in Shepherd's Bush, it was crazy. At any hour of the day or night it looked like a bomb had hit it. And believe me, Val, Chris Taylor was the worst. Has she mended her ways in that regard now? I hope so – for you couldn't find anything – well, not unless it was a book by Doris Lessing. Or maybe a poster advertising yet another march on the Israeli embassy. We used to have some great parties all the same. I swear to God one night – you'll never guess who arrived?

Val smiled – suppressing a slight twinge of envy as he thought of himself in his black skirts pacing a dormitory.

—*Marc Bolan!* she trilled. And to make matters worse, who do you think it was who brought him along?

—Christine, no doubt, replied Valentine Shannon – and not without some measure of pride.

The driver nodded.

—None other! she laughed. And we soon found out that she had been sneaking off to this hippie bar where he used to play. Which was how of course she knew all his songs. As soon as she was tipsy she'd pick up the guitar and start to strum these tunes –

I'll never forget the lyrics swear to God. *My people were fair they had sky in their hair… But now they're content to wear stars on their brows.* Can you believe the stuff they used to write back then? Then I look up and who's dancing there in front of me with *Marc* in her arms – Christine! Christine Taylor as I live and breathe! Necking with the UK's greatest pop star of the time – the teenybop hero of 1973!

The windscreen was hopelessly blurred as the Uno did its best to negotiate its dangerous path, crawling along through the driving rains. Valentine could make out an indistinct figure of a man, his shoulders elevated to the level of his ears – seeming to cup his hand as he gestured fiercely:

—*Your time is coming! Do you hear me, damn you!*

—*Jesus!* cried Ronnie, jumping backwards.

As a bolt of lightning zipped across the rooftops. And they both braced themselves instinctively, in anticipation of a repeat performance – or something worse.

But which never came. And the man was gone.

---

Ronnie pulled up outside the house in Kingsbury. Valentine's spirits lifted anew when he saw the framed photo of Christine Taylor on the mantelpiece. It was one of a group of girls standing together by a concrete flowerbed, on a beautiful summer's day. Christine was dressed in a blouson jacket and striped tank top. So immersed was Valentine in thought as he examined the slightly faded image that he started dramatically when Ronnie Clegg's hand fell on his shoulder.

—I'd like to introduce you to Mummy's carer. She'll give you a lift the rest of the way, Valentine.

A roly-poly woman in her middle years stepped forward to shake his hand.

—I'm Ann, she told him.

He greeted her warmly, pointing to the photo.

—That's Christine there, he said to Ronnie, and who's this?

—That's Nest and that's me beside them, looking a little bit sheepish there on the left, smiled Ronnie.

His eyes twinkled as she accepted the picture.

—When all this is over, why don't we go out? he suggested. You, me, Christine and Nest – we'll go to the Embassy Club, have ourselves a reunion!

Already Ronnie was looking away.

—I'm sorry, she said, I'm sorry but I thought you knew.

—I don't understand, he began, somewhat hesitantly.

Ronnie abstractedly brushed the photograph with her sleeve.

—Nest was killed in an accident, Valentine. In Tanzania, in '75. She'd gone over to do some relief work, you see. Anyhow, it doesn't matter. I'll go and get that bandage now. You just make sure and get your shoulder tested. Don't take any risks, although I'm sure it'll be OK.

—I'm sure it will be too, he smiled, in fact I'm certain.

Although, in actual fact, he wasn't any such thing.

—Hopefully the storm will soon ease and you can be on your way. Ann will give you a lift the rest of way home to Barnet. OK?

—Thanks to you both. I'm extremely grateful.

Staring out at some flying tiles.

—It can hardly get any worse now, can it? he grinned.

As some guttering came loose across the street, falling to the ground with a deafening impact.

# 27

Arriving into Barnet in the Fiat Uno with Ann, sitting there mutely in the passenger seat, unexpectedly he found himself laughing. It wasn't a normal laugh – not by any means. Of that I made certain. Deriving considerable personal amusement from its improbable enthusiasms. A development which perhaps, in the circumstances, was not all that surprising – considering the quite extraordinary events that were now unfolding. Which saw a ten-foot high fibre-glass replica of a *Masters of The Universe* figure having been torn from its perch on the roof of the Cricklewood branch of Toyland now being brutishly buffeted by unsympathetic gales out across the factory roofs and tower blocks of North London. Before being deposited – with an almost elegant, smoothly practised aplomb – neatly against the brick wall entrance to Colindale station, where it now almost decorously reposed. After the manner of some idler, a stiff-backed, square-jawed, bluish metal-painted malcontent with a purple hood feigning weary insouciance in the face of the world and all its clangorous, militant inclinations.

Faisal, Valentine knew, would have been extremely taken by such a sight – he could just imagine him pasting back the black wing of his hair, animatedly agitating:

—*Grr! Hmmm! The evil Skeletor!*

However, if that episode was diverting and temporarily uplifting in its effects, I regret having to report that what immediately succeeded it proved much less light-hearted.

—*We have got to do something about the evil Skeletor!* Valentine had been imagining Faisal laughing when the brakes screeched again and there followed a deadly, sickening thud.

—*O Jesus!* cried Ann, flinging the door open. To reveal a mangled metal pram. This was the end, he thought. But a reprieve was in the offing – as, queasily, he watched her make her return to the vehicle, with what seemed the headless body of a child limp in her arms.

—Almighty God! he choked – before realising that it was, in fact, nothing more than a plastic doll.

—What in heaven's name can happen next! she wailed, climbing back into the car beside him.

—This is one crazy evening, she croaked, as he stared at the doll's head in the middle of the road – which seemed to respond to his accusations with a comprehending, abject air.

As she started up the engine, in spite of her pale and noticeably apprehensive condition, his driver professed herself *absolutely perfect*. She had taken a couple of tablets earlier, she informed him – which had worked wonders. They were driving for some time before she said, out of the blue:

—I won't tell you a lie, she continued, looking after the elderly, it can be immensely stressful at times. And if you think Ronnie's mum acts badly, you really ought to see what some of my other charges get up to. Only just recently one bit the head off her budgie.

Valentine found himself reflecting ruefully on the events which had just taken place back at Ronnie's house in Kingsbury – somewhat shamefully accepting at last just how credulous and judgemental he had been. At least in the beginning, when both women had warned him just how unpredictable their Alzheimer's patient could be. Displaying amusement in the face of his evident disapproval of the sceptical levity with which they continued to treat the old lady. Who herself could have been said to have been possessed of the physical dimensions of a budgerigar, so tiny and inoffensive did she seem.

But, as Ann had pointed out later, he would not be the first unprofessional person to make such a mistake . . .

—It's the only way you can keep yourself sane, Ronnie had explained, that's why we act the way we do around her. A couple of weeks with them and you'd soon see.

But at the time he had been shocked – there could be no doubt about that. Particularly when Ronnie's mum, having removed her slipper to fling it violently across the room, had moved her chair closer to the television, extending her neck as if preparing to inspect the intrinsic quality of the pixelated image of a folk band playing a tune entitled, apparently, 'Letter From America' – before proceeding enthusiastically to drop a small blob of spit onto the screen and commence tracing a somewhat erratic line up and down the length of the glass – first diagonally then horizontally. Before turning to Ronnie and announcing in indifferent tones:

—I saw the devil in Margate once, you know. He was wearing a raincoat and a little trilby hat. Quite handsome, he was – as a matter of fact, he looked like Stewart Granger.

Valentine had genuinely been affronted by the extraordinarily flippant response of her carers. And had stiffened with outrage when he heard them chuckle:

—Do you hear our mum! Such a silly you are – a real old silly billy!

---

But now he understood. Now that Ann had taken the trouble to outline a more humane and quite logical side to the story. As regards the demands of the elderly, explaining just how lonely even the most resourceful people – such as Ronnie – could actually get.

—People on their own, I mean, she said.

—Are you married, Ann? asked Valentine, somewhat reticently.

His driver shook her head.

—I've never been that fortunate, she told him.

Before adding:

—But it's not that I'm really unhappy or anything. It's just that there are times—

—I feel blessed, he interrupted, surprising himself – you know, having met Chris the way I did and everything. It shouldn't have happened. I mean – who would have ever thought? We're like chalk and cheese when you think about it. She gave me a glimpse into a whole new world.

—It's me you have to thank for that, Master Judas, I felt like saying – but resisted admirably the temptations of vanity.

As Ann continued:

—Perhaps as you yourself did her, she replied, quite affectionately. Changing gear as she added:

—To be straight with you, Valentine, I actually happen to know that for a fact. I know because she told me herself. That you have taught her a lot, I mean. That, in fact, before she met you she was convinced that Ireland was a dark and dangerous place. And that was after only being there once. Back in the summer of 1976, I think. Which of course would have been a difficult time for her, what with the break-up with Salib still very much on her mind. That was the time she stayed in Rosses Point. A lot of odd things happened to her there, you know. I don't know what exactly. Whatever the reason, she said she never wanted to go back.

—It was a bad time generally. The country was practically on the verge of civil war.

—This man she encountered. One of the scariest men she had ever met, she said. But wouldn't say why.

—But then men, laughed Valentine. As we both know, Ann, they wouldn't have been very popular with Chris at the time. Not the way feminist politics were back then.

—This was different. This fellow was different. Mr Bohan was different. If I know Chris, this was a whole different ball game, Mr Shannon.

---

It might reasonably have been expected that after his experiences in Ronnie's house – particularly when Mrs Clegg had begun screaming about the devil – that Val's mental state might have tended precipitously towards a new and more extreme precariousness. Have assumed a character of unbridled turbulence not entirely dissimilar to that so apparent in the world outside the travelling Fiat Uno – as they continued their unsteady journey through the battered, devastated streets.

But such was the common-sense nature and worldly experience of his driver that any such tendency was, happily, nowhere in evidence. The reason perhaps being that, as she had explained, people who care for the elderly, they tend in the main to have little patience with those predisposed to self-pity and indulgent fantasy.

As she had firmly put it, with a section of wrought-iron fencing narrowly missing them as it sailed by, day-to-day living is difficult enough without bringing more trouble on yourself by unnecessary solipsism and quasi-adolescent philosophising.

—As far as I'm concerned, it's asking for trouble, Ann said, positively encouraging delusions, Valentine, a tendency I've seen far too much of in my time. Especially in the world of the arts – and it's an argument I've often had with Christine in the past.

She swerved to avoid a massive lump of chalk that had become disentangled from the roots of an uprooted tree and went on:

—Do you not think it remarkable that it's so often those who are of an ideological bent, vehemently so in many cases, who appear to make a spectacular mess of their own lives? I'm not being disloyal but I can't tell you how mad it used to drive me listening to Ronnie and Christine when Mrs Clegg first got sick. Of course they thought they knew everything – but believe me, it was the sound of their own voices they were paying most attention to.

He found her company so intelligent and reassuring, thought Valentine, that on at least one occasion he found himself compelled to ever so gently touch her on the hand – to thank her for the privilege of having known such women, simply to have had people such as her and Chris as acquaintances – no, as intimates.

For that's what Ronnie and Chris and now Ann were – his *friends*. But of course not just that – after all, Christine *was* his co-habiting lover – something of which he never before would have dreamed. He found himself actually *blushing* when he realised he'd used the word *lover*.

Because for so long, for the greater part of his life indeed, such a term would have had connotations only with the most obscure of girlish romances. Or if not that then the murky world of illicit, and somewhat vague, obscenities.

Once, back in Glassdrummond, he remembered, he

had confiscated a magazine called *Readers' Wives*. Within whose cheerless pages he had discovered the most appalling narratives, detailing the shaming congress of so-called *suburban lovers*.

The humiliation he had experienced on that occasion, he recalled as a burning discomfort declared itself on his cheeks, had provoked within him the same combination of anger and self-loathing as had the unforgivable impertinence of the insubordinate student Martin Boan. The incident he was remembering had taken place that day outside the lavatories, just before study – when the boy had muttered under his breath:

—There he goes, Brother Valentine. He likes me. He likes directing me in the part of the Artful Dodger. Oh, he likes that very much. Such a dark horse!

He could have sworn he had dismissed it forever from the corners of his mind. But now here it was – coming up again.

—Oh, I know a lot of things about Brother Valentine. Look at him go with his big skirts flailing, whispered the boy in question. A student for whom he had once had immense respect.

—And affection!

Don't go forgetting *affection*, Brother Shannon. You've done quite enough of that in your time.

---

He was concerned – no, seriously afraid. But, thanks to the instinctive empathy of his driver, the anxieties stimulated by such unwelcome memories and which shaded into intemperateness and rage eventually subsided – as his palms flexed open and a protracted sigh heaved yearningly from his chest. As the Fiat Uno pulled up directly across the street from his house. And he climbed out, into a post-conflict Berlin of wrecked cars and smashed tiles.

He was proud, he told himself, to have kissed Ann's hand – to have finally plucked up the courage to do so.

—Thank you so much. I really do hope we meet more often – on a regular basis, Ann.

—Me too, she smiled, waving one last time as he began his ascent of the granite steps towards the front entrance of 37 Spenser Grove, Barnet. Reaching in his pocket to search for his keys, just as a bicycle slammed up against the railings – and which undeniably shook him, even after all they'd been through. Not a single leaf remained on the tree beside him. You could hear cupboards banging all along the street.

—*Such a night!* he thought, after much searching eventually locating his keys. But he wasn't in despair – why ought he be, when unlike certain others, he had actually succeeded in making it home? The logic of which induced a mild euphoria which caused him to laugh – and pour scorn on his earlier suggestibility. When he thought of how suggestible he had been earlier on, permitting himself – thanks to a combination of events completely and utterly beyond his control – to be undermined by the machinations of a complete stranger. He even smiled now as he thought once more of the stupid piece of paper. No, in fact he laughed out loud.

Why, he shouldn't have even bothered reading the ridiculous thing, he told himself. Then released a palpable sigh of relief, pushing his key into the lock and thinking just how great it was to be home. And in one piece – thanks, in the main, to Ann and Ronnie.

Architecture was not a subject in which the former Christian Brother would have considered himself particularly knowledgeable – not to any significant degree. But, nonetheless, ever since he had come to London, it was an area towards which he had found himself drawn – deriving immense intellectual nourishment from it.

Which was why, any time he found himself fortunate enough to have a half-day from John Briory school, there was nothing he liked better than to devote so many hours as might be at his disposal to the appreciation of the great municipal buildings such as St Paul's and St Pancras station.

It was for this reason that he perceived himself fortunate to have made the acquaintance of the architect couple who lived in the flat directly above theirs. Ezra the Incorrigible was the name they had given to their pet Yorkshire terrier.

He smiled when he thought of that day when they had first moved in – with Ezra wheezing on the top of a suitcase.

—Look how he laughs, he remembered the young woman saying.

And that little laugh of Ezra's – it had won him over completely.

The gale was now blowing wilder than ever, with bottles crashing up and down the street. Just as a TV aerial looped like liquorice, falling through some trees into the garden. Just as the little dog appeared beside him on the step. It was shivering uncontrollably. Then a glasshouse concertinaed in on itself. Ezra had these mandarin-style whiskers – quivering helplessly, they were covered in saliva.

—Poor little fellow, said Valentine, scooping him up, our poor little frightened little puppy Ezra. How did you get out without your owners seeing you?

The wet bundle under his arm gave a jump and violently sneezed – as Valentine at last turned the key in the lock, confidently striding along the hallway – now climbing the stairs two at a time. Before briskly rapping on the architects' door, calling out reassuringly:

—There's nothing to worry about – I have him here. But I really have to say you were lucky on a night like that. Lucky he didn't get blown away. I wonder what Michael would have to say to that!

He knocked again – then laughed once more.

—Mr Fish, I mean – I mean Michael Fish!

Nothing. He knocked one more time.

—Well, goodbye, Mr Fish! I guess you're not in yet! Not surprising, thanks to the hurricane that never was going to happen! Don't worry, I'll look after him!

He had been overly optimistic, he decided, in expecting them to be home. Everything, any kind of order, all rhythm, had been torn out of sync because of the storm. His expectations were wholly ludicrous. They'd just been delayed, he realised, as he had himself. That was all.

—Probably still stuck in traffic, I shouldn't wonder, he mused.

Downstairs, suddenly, the front door came swinging open, and a student in a helmet struggled helplessly with his bicycle. Tearing at some straps as he growled ill-temperedly:

—Don't talk to me about stupid fucking weathermen. I'll never trust any of those bastards again. Twice knocked over – nearly killed, I was. We don't get hurricanes in England. Oh, no! Well, goodbye, Mr Fish! Goodbye for fucking ever!

Valentine hurried towards their own apartment, tentatively nodding to the student – who clearly was in no mood for any form of colloquy – still carrying the nervous pet as he turned his key in the lock. Striding straight through into the kitchen as he called:

—It's me, Christine honey. I'm home at last, darling – are you in there? Is that you, Faisal?

—Yes, Val dear, she returned, it's me. I'm in here in the bedroom. I'll be out in a moment. Oh, I'm so glad – thank heavens with all this that you managed to make it home safely!

Valentine positively beamed as soon as he heard that.

—Oh, don't worry. I made sure to make it home all right. Couldn't let Christine down now, could I?

A surge of companionship and warmth surged right through him. As he crouched down on one knee and laughed with Ezra, before sighing contentedly and crossing the floor to pull open the refrigerator door.

—It's your lucky day, little doggie my friend! It's a bad day for us but a good day for doggies!

What Valentine found most gratifying was just how extraordinarily calm and composed he felt right now. Most likely, he surmised, the reason being attributable to his being back in what he had always thought of as his sanctuary. He dabbed his forehead with the back of his sleeve. Ah, it was just as he suspected – not so much as a drop of perspiration on his brow. There could be no doubt about it. A new ease had arrived to take up residence in his soul. What a wonderful turn of events, he reflected.

—Wasn't that the most outrageous turn of events? he heard Christine calling from the bedroom. No one has ever seen anything like it – certainly not in this country!

—So much for Michael Fish! Valentine Shannon heard himself laugh aloud.

—So much for who? he heard her reply.

—So much for Michael Fish! he repeated.

Clearly she hadn't heard him.

—So much for *who*? he heard her respond anew.

—Oh, nothing, he said. Listen, Christine – have we any food in here for the dog?

—Hush, dear, she replied, Faisal's asleep. He got a little bit frightened with the storm, I'm afraid. Not surprisingly!

—That's right! Didn't we all? Like I say – didn't we all!

—Why don't you come in? It's so nice that you made it! Come here!

He gasped, becoming aware of what could only be described as a quite blatant husky suggestiveness evident in her voice – which because of its sheer unexpectedness in the circumstances, found him quite excited, to say the least.

Even more so when he detected it again.

—Come in here and show it to me. That twinkly Irish expression that you know I love. That sheer handsomeness!

As a result of which declaration Valentine completely abandoned all thoughts of the dog and his heart began to race feverishly in a combination of love and sheer desire.

—I mean, it might be exciting, what with the storm and everything. And Faisal asleep. What do you think, Valentine?

To his astonishment he now found himself a little embarrassed. Why, it might have been a reprise of Mr 'Top Hat' and his antics. When Martin Boan had made fun of him, scurrilously, muttering out of the side of his mouth.

Then he realised that Ezra was gone – somehow the dog had wrested itself from his grasp.

—Come on, Brother Valentine. Come in and say hello to Christine. Your partner who loves and cares for you. You do want to, don't you? Of course you do.

He was as excited and confused as a gauche adolescent.

—Ha ha, he laughed a little giddily, Ezra for heaven's sake where on earth are you gone?

—Who are you talking to out there, Valentine? Are you talking to Ezra? Never mind the dog. Come in and protect me from the big scary storm.

—Ezra, can you hear me? Ezra – are you there?

Finally he caught a glimpse of its tail behind the sofa. But it turned out to be nothing of the sort – just a piece of turned-up carpet.

—Oh, to hell with this! he cried exasperatedly.

—Valentine darling, I've got something for you.

He couldn't resist it any longer – pushing through the door, consumed by lust and unquenchable desire. To find his partner sitting with her back to him on the bed, ever so coolly drawing a brush through her hair, humming to the rhythm of each languorous stroke. What gave him pause, for a moment, however, was the fact that her shoulders appeared to be shaking – and he could have sworn, for just a moment, for nothing more than the briefest of seconds, that she had, in fact, released a strangely suppressed chuckle.

Not that that mattered great deal – or at all, in fact, with Valentine Shannon in that moment being so consumed that it is likely *nothing* could have dissuaded or distracted him from his intended purpose. As he lunged forward, almost violently bearing down upon his beautiful partner, sweeping her up proprietorially in his arms.

—*Oh Jesus Christ, I just love you so much!*

As his partner turned to greet him with a warm smiling countenance – except that, unfortunately, it wasn't that of Chris Taylor.

—*This is the seal of my hatred on you*, was all I said.

---

And what fun, I must say, we had after that. Why, the things that came into that poor exhausted fellow's mind. I suppose that the storm must have wrought certain effects – for, competent though I am, I'm not that good!

As he sat there, petrified – literally palsied with fear, muttering incoherently about evil and its 'face' and 'mask', I mean, for half the night the poor fellow, he really did look like – well, terror personified. With his hair standing upright as he sat there a-tremble, repeatedly and obsessively wiping the perspiration from his fevered forehead. Irrespective of how meticulously I kept explaining how this was nothing, this represented nothing but a harmless little overture to what was to come, a mere appetiser before the main course.

Really and truly, I have rarely derived such amusement from someone's antics. Such sobs and sighs and earnestly pathetic pleas. As, with starting eyes he again pointed to the wall, where on a grainy, flickering black-and-white screen Betty Boop cavorted as of old – in that impish, impossibly fey way of hers. Only to be followed by something more unpredictable – such as Mrs Beggs, all the way from the old days in John Briory, sporting a *Skeletor* mask but with absolutely no flesh on her frame – Mrs Bones, ha ha! Or an image of little Faisal, so excited as he hummed a familiar tune.

—*You'll wonder where the yellow went when you brush your teeth with Pepsodent!*

Holding his dear lovely mother's hand, standing there in the departure lounge, only moments away from climbing on board that great big airbus and sailing off to glorious Miami – dreaming of hotel rooms and lovely pink flamingoes. As a result of which – really and truly, Valentine's reaction was quite awful! – I had to pacify him with some cake.

—Specially purchased in Thornton's, I informed him, by this gentleman here – an old friend if I'm not mistaken . . . !

And it was then I introduced the facially scarred Martin Boan in his top hat. Striking his familiar 'Artful Dodger' pose but looking the very spit, I exaggerate not in the slightest, of my own dear friend – ah, the ever-reliable Mr Bones.

—Say hello, dearest Valentine! I suggested.

As the poor little fellow looked up, pleadingly all a-quiver. Valentine, I mean – not Mr Bones.

And that, I suppose, was the end of him, really.

As he began to rock back and forth and to sob. Like a baby, in the deathly quiet, the aftermath of the storm. Before I heard the downstairs door close and his partner of some years call out his name. Then climbing the stairs, then two at a time, and flinging the door open to find – well, it's really rather difficult to describe what it was she found, exactly.

But it wasn't the man she knew as Valentine Shannon.

# 28

But all of that, happily, is far behind us now, with the first anniversary of the great October gale actually falling only last evening – a fact of which, of course, Mr Valentine Shannon remains quite blissfully unaware. As he does regarding most of the details of what could be called his former life. Where, once upon a time he had gone and upset poor Mrs Beggs, being much too busy poring over old essays, and longing to be at home with the woman that he loved. Why, I don't even think he remembers what might be described as his rather eventful journey on that night of the wind, tootling away there in his little Renault 5, even stopping over for a prayer in that lovely Spitalfields church. There isn't even a flicker of the tramp who'd assailed him, had threatened to give him AIDS, goodness me! Or of all the lovely things that had happened in the long-ago, when he'd been a happy young fellow growing up in a small Irish town, where daily he would greet Mrs Cabbage in her apron, and who would call out gaily:

—That gallant little boy will one day become one of God's own chosen. He certainly won't be associating with that rascal up in the big house!

Well, is that a fact, Mrs Dowdy Cabbage? So how do you explain the continued attentions he pays to me? As he potters along the empty, echoing corridors, sighing as he opens and closes doors with his heavy keys. Convinced beyond all dispute that he is, in fact, no longer domiciled in the city of London, never mind being incarcerated within the confines of Friern Barnet Hospital (formerly Colney Hatch Lunatic Asylum). For, and with a conviction which is not at all unimpressive, he has succeeded in persuading himself that he is, in fact, President of Glassdrummond College. In the dormitory of which each night he falls to sleep. Before being roused by a soft familiar hand. And looks up to see my orange bobbins bouncing – as I impishly uncoil my little falsetto tune:

—*Say hello to Bonio*
*Always on his ownio*
*Never will he moanio*
*Because he's your best friend!*

—Would you like some cake?

Before treating him, as always, to my *pièce de résistance*!

Which I know may strike you as a tad unnecessary – poking out my tongue with its crimson-stained cargo of little pearly teeth. But at the end of the day you've got to laugh. After all, what else is a clown to do?

—*Collywobbles!*

## ABOUT THE AUTHOR

Patrick McCabe's novels include *The Butcher Boy*, *Breakfast on Pluto* – both of which were shortlisted for the Booker Prize and made into films by Neil Jordan – and *Winterwood*, which was awarded the 2007 Hughes & Hughes/Irish Independent Irish Novel of the Year award. He lives in Dublin.

ABOUT THE AUTHOR

Patrick McCabe's novels include *The Butcher Boy*, *Breakfast on Pluto* – both of which were shortlisted for the Booker Prize and made into films by Neil Jordan – and *Winterwood*, which was awarded the 2007 Hughes & Hughes/Irish Independent Irish Novel of the Year award. He lives in Dublin.

ALSO BY PATRICK McCABE

*Carn*
*The Butcher Boy*
*The Dead School*
*Breakfast on Pluto*
*Mondo Desperado*
*Emerald Germs of Ireland*
*Call Me the Breeze*
*Winterwood*
*The Holy City*
*The Stray Sod Country*

ALSO BY PATRICK McCABE

*Carn*
*The Butcher Boy*
*The Dead School*
*Breakfast on Pluto*
*Mondo Desperado*
*Emerald Germs of Ireland*
*Call Me the Breeze*
*Winterwood*
*The Holy City*
*The Stray Sod Country*

This is *Hello and Goodbye*: two glitzy baubles – generously stuffed with the choicest, rustiest nails, lacquered with dread, and compressed to the point of detonation.

Stay on this side for *Goodbye Mr Rat*, in which a girl from northern Indiana travels to rural Ireland; where, as she bids a friend farewell, she meets malign misfortune.

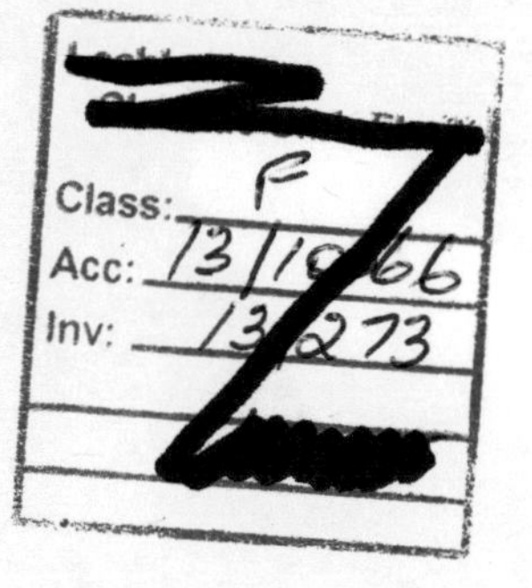


First published in Great Britain in 2013 by

Quercus
55 Baker Street
7th Floor, South Block
London
W1U 8EW



A CIP catalogue record for this book is available from the British Library

ISBN 978 1 78206 013 0 (HB)
ISBN 978 1 78206 014 7 (TPB)
ISBN 978 1 78206 019 2 (EBOOK)

This book is a work of fiction. Names, characters, businesses, organisations, places and events are either the product of the author's imagination or are used fictitiously. Any resemblance to actual persons, living or dead, events or locales is entirely coincidental.

10 9 8 7 6 5 4 3 2 1

Typeset by Ellipsis Digital Limited, Glasgow

Printed and bound in Great Britain by Clays Ltd, St Ives plc

# GOODBYE MR RAT

PATRICK McCABE

For Jon Riley

*The night broke bloody in the quivering, pre-dawn mist, with the cry of the curlew coming eddying through the trees.*

Thus wrote the great Mr Double-You-Bee Yeats of Sligo, when he wasn't fretting over swans or his responsibility for the mayhem of 1916 – or that 'terrible beauty', as he was wont to call it.

I guess it might come as a surprise to certain people when they hear that quite a lot of us had actually read the myopic old josser in prison, figuring it connected us to the high end of art and history or something like that. Way back in the glory days of liberation and romantic insurrection, yeah, those happy-go-lucky Baader-Meinhof Red Brigade seventies and eighties, when I found myself a resident of that bleak grey compound they called The Maze, along with a considerable number of my republican comrades. Or 'terrorists', I guess, if that's what you'd prefer.

We were often persuaded to try our hand at the writing game too. With one reason being that it took our minds off the appalling conditions and another that it fitted in with the way we saw ourselves. As something special, I guess, to be honest – incorruptible defenders in a long noble line of unrepentant stalwarts. Or some similar line of fanciful self-delusion.

Then as soon as the dirty protest got into gear, trying our best to look like Jesus Christ himself, if you don't mind. Our O.C. at the time, an ascetic lanky beanpole by the name of Jimjoe White, had even in recent times begun to sound not unlike him, pacing the wet concrete yard like a Monsignor, dispensing nuggets of would-be revolutionary wisdom.

—Just remember, he said, that we will always have truth on our side. *Semper et in aeternum.*

That was the best advice he could give us, he said.

—Let that be your guide at all times, comrades.

Then, sometime late on in the year 1980, I started to become aware that he was showing a particular interest in me. Which made me a little uncomfortable, to say the least – for there had always been something unsettling about his gaze. Fancied himself as a bit of a scholar, did old Jimjoe. One time when he was walking in front of me, I actually heard him saying this: *A frightful fiend doth close behind him tread*, laughing while he was doing it, whatever it was he found funny about Coleridge. Not that I knew it was Coleridge, not at the time – I had to look it up later, to tell the truth. I could see the *Letters of Seneca* sticking out of his pocket. Oh yes, a very learned fellow was our O.C. Jimjoe White.

—*Ecce veritas*, he said another day, looking over at me with a smile, turning to the others as he gave the side of his nose a little tap.

—Seneca was tutor and later adviser to Emperor Nero, did you know that, Gabriel?

I shook my head. What was he on about?

—But what did he do, didn't the poor fellow go and get himself accused of complicity in the Pisonian conspiracy to assassinate his employer!

⋆

2

I can't remember making any response. Locked inside my own private world, I guess. I've always been a bit like that, introverted. Before I met Beni Banikin, anyway. In that way, I guess, she changed my life. Although I can imagine some people – some of my former colleagues, for sure – having one or two things to say about that.

—It was all he could manage to get, a gay woman. Well if that don't motherfucking beat all!

Or maybe they wouldn't. Maybe I'm just imagining that they'd say it. Prison can make you paranoid that way.

Anyway, all of this happened back in the 1980s – when I, like so many others, had committed myself to the freedom of Ireland and the ultimate overthrow of the British imperialist murder machine, as we called it. Being more than prepared, like so many of my friends, if I had to, to lay down my life, in service of the principles of honour, truth and justice.

That, believe it or not, was the way I felt – and, even after everything that's happened, it still holds true to this very day.

Beni always said that that was what she admired most about me.

—You can be the most exasperating man, she said, but at least I can say this – you know where you stand with Gabriel King.

It was a nice thing to hear, and when she said it – it was in the Trans Am when we were parked in Cincinnati, smoking some draw as we stared at the pines – and it was all I could do not to grab her right there and kiss her.

Beni was a writer too – and a good one. Although maybe not so much in the beginning. She'd had all sorts of problems with her confidence in those days, when I met her first in the early 1990s, when I was working in a bar called Rory's in Queens. She used to

come in there with her friend Mia Chiang, and another guy, a lecturer, a Scottish bloke by the name of Gartland. I gradually got to know the three of them over time. Terry Gartland was knowledgeable, I'll give him that – but he knew fuck all about the Irish struggle. Too much fucking Yeats, I used to tell him. He used to give lectures in the New York Public Library. Mia Chiang was waitressing at the time – before eventually securing a break, off-Broadway. About which more later. For I want to go back to Mr Coleridge 'Seneca' White.

He was standing looking over at me another day when we were walking the circle – before standing right in front of me – sucking his teeth, with his arms folded, smiling. It irritated me deeply.

—What's your fucking problem? I said, like what I'm saying is – what the fuck are you looking at, Jimjoe?

He didn't say anything – just looked at the ground. Then up he comes with this great big smile. What the Americans would call a shit-eating grin.

—The Dog's only foolin', he said with a twinkle.

That was his nickname back in the day. We used to call him 'The Dog'.

I could hear my heart beating as light drops of rain began falling. Now his smile was barely there at all.

—*A frightful fiend doth close behind him tread*, he said softly. You heard me saying that, didn't you?

—The big scholar, I replied as I matched his grin. Coleridge.

—Coleridge. That's right.

He placed a reassuring hand on my shoulder and said he was only having a laugh.

—It's certainly not because I'm trying to tell you something.

He flicked a spit onto the wet concrete.

—I mean why would I do that?

—Search me, I said, fucked if I know, Dog, I'm afraid.

He shook his head vehemently.

—No you don't have to worry about anything, he continued, far from being untrustworthy, anyone who knows him can tell that Gabriel King is the very embodiment of reliability. Unimpeachable, that's what I would say.

He patted me mischievously on the cheek and then began to walk away slowly.

—Truth's sacred keeper – that would be you. Veritas Gabriel. A sweet little angel born without guile.

Looking back on it now, what seems extraordinary is that Gartland and White – they had so much in common, in this sense – that, initially – we had gotten along literally like a house on fire. Until things started to change – don't ask me how. But I guess that's the way.

'81 was a hard year for everyone. None of us knew if we'd even survive gaol – we just kept going from one day to the next. But I could have been doing without White's relentlessly provocative mutterings, whatever the fuck was wrong with him. I was walking the circle when – Jesus Christ! – there he was again. Pressing his lips against my ear, whispering.

—I'm pretending to be your lover, he snorted. I hope I didn't give you a fright!

Then he started to talk about Seneca.

—Among the evils of the time, Gabriel – especially during the reign of Titus – were the prompters. Oh, yes – the whisperers and approvers who had long been given free reign. But do you know, I wonder, what happened to them in the end?

He tapped his foot, remaining motionless throughout. Before continuing in a hesitant, measured tone:

—Some were taken to the Forum and beaten, others exhibited to their shame in the arena.

For some reason – possibly because I really was beginning to loathe his obduracy – I found myself in a state of discomfort even more extreme than usual. Which still had not abated when I looked up and saw that he had gone.

Like I say, he was similar to Beni's friend T.J. Gartland. Who seemed to have been fine until Beni had become successful with her play. In which, of course, he had had a hand. In fact, before meeting him, I don't think she had known very much about Yeats. Certainly not Noh plays. Which he was always banging on about. I remember, in fact, on one occasion him actually saying:

—Are you sure about that? I don't think that's factually accurate, Gabriel.

Referring to something I'd said about Angola. All I can say is I was annoyed at the time – but, on account of Beni, didn't bother making a fuss.

—Screw him, was all I said.

He looked like a second-hand fucking Willie Nelson.

I didn't see much of Jimjoe during the hunger strikes – indeed, like all of us, I didn't see much of anything during the hunger strikes, maddened and completely blinded by grief as I was. Then, out of nowhere, he resumed, I suppose, what you might call his 'campaign'. Addressing Pearse Gavigan, aka 'The Farmer', in a loud voice – clearly for my benefit.

—Pearse, I heard him say, did you ever hear about Seneca and his plot? It wasn't just any ordinary conspiracy, you know – but a

multilayered manouevre that Nero got to hear of. Which was why he ordered the man to kill himself.

As Dog White knew well, Pearse The Farmer didn't care all that much for conspiracies. Nope, doodly-squat as the Texans say. Which is why he just sighed, then shrugged and looked away. Dreaming of one day going home to the valley and smoking some dope listening to his hero Phil Lynott. Yeah, to the great Philip Lynott of the rock band Thin Lizzy knocking more blistering heavy metal tunes out of his axe, miles away from Her Majesty's Prison or anywhere else. You could see it written all over his face – as he imagined himself joining Phil Lynott in a solo. As Jimjoe White just kept on looking.

There can be few sensations to compare with that of being watched and I soon found myself afterwards becoming somewhat preoccupied with shadows and sudden noises – muffled footfalls, distant talking voices. And, to tell the truth, what I began to long for more than anything was the cessation of these persistent, thinly veiled hostilities. But it wasn't over yet. I arrived back in my cell to find a note waiting.

—Being so interested in literature, I thought you might like this little piece. It's from *Paradise Lost*, Milton's masterpiece about His Eminence, Morning Star.

*Beware of the foul and devilish*
*engin'ry of your heart, Mr King.*

—You've thrown your lot in with the ultimate traitor, Gabriel. However, there may still be time to exonerate yourself, he had added.

Whatever the fuck that was supposed to mean.

*

## 7

We'd dream about America as we lay there, tapping out messages – sending our hopes and deepest yearnings in Morse code along the pipes.

—One thing you never try is to put one over on the Iron Valley Boys! you'd hear Donal Givney bawling. And then he'd start into it, narrating this crazy fantastic movie that he'd dreamed – in which the three of us 'motherfuckers' were set to return to our home place as heroes. There was no one to touch him when it came to making up that movie bullshit. And it kept us going – no, it really did. As he described every scene of *Return to The Meadowlands* – along with every single shrub that grew on the slopes of Big Iron Mountain, and along the shore of the lake where we'd spent our childhood.

—Fifteen years and we're out of here – we're gone! you'd hear Gavigan roaring, thumping the wall.

Finally, in the end we had forged a pact – that as soon as we got out we'd buy a heap and travel to America.

—Make it a Trans Am, Givney shouted, scorch the asphalt right across country!

—Coast to coast, all the fucking way!

—Burn rubber, yuh sumbitches! Here we come! The Valley Boys – they are on the road!

And it was in honour of that pledge I eventually made the trip – with Beni Banikin, all the way across America. Just as far as we could go.

The Farmer was always getting things wrong. Singing 'Judas King' to the lyrics of a Thin Lizzy song – instead of 'Eunice King' – which was, of course, the actual name. I had always been on the verge of pointing that out to him, but never had the heart when I'd see him

in full flight – complete, as always, with invisible guitar.

Not that the infelicity appeared to bother our commanding officer a great deal, however. Utilising the malapropism to significant effect, as he saw it – resourceful fellow that he was.

—So, then – how is Judas today? was what he said – and I really do feel, at this point, that I have to acknowledge that in those latter days in the prison my resentment towards Dog White had deepened to such an extent that it was difficult to restrain myself from actually striking him.

—Not many of us lucky enough to have a song composed about us – are we, Gabriel?

I decided it was prudent and wise to attempt to make no response of any kind. As he emitted what I can only describe as a lungless laugh – and again was gone.

Not that he was finished with me or anything, as I was to discover later on that evening, when yet another note was pushed underneath my cell door. A cold dew formed on my forehead as I read it.

—*Goodbye, Mr Rat. Ultinam viscos tuos canes inferni fucking edeant.*

May the dogs of hell devour your fucking entrails.

---

But whatever discord might have existed between myself and Dog White, it made little difference to the men who were dying, as the appalling horror of the hunger strikes continued unabated. Donal Givney made it as far as fifty days and it really was tragic – really and truly awful when he passed. But I don't think I can remember a time when solidarity in the gaol had ever been stronger. With even signs of *our* difficulties subsiding – between White and me, I

mean. With hostilities, or so it seemed, at least temporarily suspended. In fact, now that I think of it, I can actually remember him saying:

—It's gonna be OK, old friend. You don't have anything to worry about now at all.

As, to a man, we all fell to our knees and prayed for the repose of the soul of our revered comrade. Whose devastated body had finally given out. I didn't manage to get a wink of sleep that night, dreaming of touring America in the Trans Am, approaching The Meadowlands, our name for the south, as The Farmer wildly waved a joint – slapping the hood, ecstatic that at last we'd done it.

—Yup, the Iron Valley Boys have made it to the Happy Land!

Except that we never did make it, did we – to The Meadowlands or anywhere else, at least not together. Being as most of my comrades were dead, thanks to Margaret Thatcher and the intransigence of the British government. But one thing wasn't going to happen, and that was the first thing I decided when I got out – that the pact we'd forged would never be forgotten. But how different, I couldn't help thinking, was the actuality of what we had imagined, when we lay there constructing The Meadowlands from our bunks. During those long, bereft, interminable prison nights, at the end of which we discovered that we'd pretty much lost everything that we'd fought for. And, worst of all, that nobody much cared. So that was it then – far from being a hero of Iron Valley, the returning valiant Irish rebel, I was just another burnt-out revolutionary, spending most of the day at the bar. Along, of course – with some of the best and noblest friends anyone was ever likely to know having been taken from me. Bitter? How could you not be?

⋆

And yet somehow, those of us who did survive, we all in our varying ways came through it. Having sustained what by any standards was a monumentally exhausting struggle. And one which ultimately saw some members of the movement – with my old friend Dog White being among them – elected to enter mainstream politics. Which he had never regretted, he told me later on, on an occasion when we'd all met for a reunion in a border roadhouse, name of Mickey's Bar.

—*Slán*, my former commanding officer had finally said, bidding me goodbye on that final occasion, when I told him I'd got my visa for America. With us both acknowledging – we had actually embraced – that whatever might have happened between us, it now belonged entirely and irrevocably to the past.

—Hopefully, I remembering him saying, we will be the very last band of volunteers to have to do it – act out their generation's nightmare of history.

We had all been there that night in Mickey's – Bobby Owens, the Bonners – all of us who'd been in the cages together. They were sad to see me go, they said. And I guess, myself, I too had to wipe a tear away.

—I'll say hello to The Meadowlands for you, I told them, and after that I just turned and walked away.

I even left my old Esther behind – the girl I'd been with on and off over the years. But the truth was I just had to get out of the valley. To honour the pledge and clear my head by just travelling. Wherever the road would take me, I said. To my old buddies the Bonners and a number of others. All of us who had soldiered together, directed magnificently, whatever our differences, by the legendary Jimjoe White, 'The Dog' – commanding officer of the Mid-Ulster Brigade of the Provisional IRA throughout the whole of the 1970s and '80s – right up until the end of the war.

I was all choked up as I got the bus right out of the valley. With the song 'Ashes of Love' still ringing in my ears, to which I had been jiving with Esther McCaul – almost till the dawn broke, if memory serves correctly.

—This is truly the end of the conflict, Dog had said, and whatever they might say, we fought a good fight. And you were among the best of them, Gabriel, *a chara*.

---

That was where I left them, catching the bus at the bottom of Iron Mountain, promising to return one day. And which I'm doing now – unfortunately in a can. Or should I say a polished copper urn.

Which isn't exactly what I had intended. But there's an irony there which I must admit I find amusing. 'Ashes of Love', you know? Although I can't admit to actually *loving* Esther – she could be a right bitch, to actually tell you the truth. Even if I'd probably done so once. And passionately. But we were only kids – things burn out, they die. Is that not what the fucking song's about?

We all die some time. And then we come home in a jar to Iron Mountain.

Now how on earth did that come about? Well, after my diagnosis with prostate cancer, I decided just to be straight with Beni, to tell her the truth. Although it took two naggins of vodka to get me to do it.

—I can't say how long exactly, I told her, it might be a year or it could be eighteen months. Either way I've bought the farm.

Like the Texans say when you get the news that you're fucked.

—I want you to take my ashes home, I told her.

And that was how it started, I guess. Our own personal journey across country to The Meadowlands. She'd been born in Indiana, and we'd been friends now for some years, after meeting around the bars of Queens – long before, of course, she got famous. For which she gave me some kind of credit, even if Gartland wasn't convinced. Or didn't seem to be. She'd been talking about writing for years and had even attempted a kind of verse play about my experiences. But it wasn't until *The Night Visitor* that she really hit the mark. By doing what I'd advised her – drawing directly from her own life – when she'd practically been raped by some Southern bastard in a flat in Queens. The success had come right out of the blue – after her and Mia had put it on in a loft, a tiny place. T.J. Gartland – or should I say, New York City's pre-eminent authority on Irish history and poetry – had taken it upon himself to direct. Then, out of nowhere, it had become a resounding success. Before ending up, for Christ's sake, on Broadway!

—Sure I'll take your ashes home, she'd agreed, but before we do that we're gonna hit The Meadowlands.

And that was how we came to hit the road. With Mia being delighted – taking *The Bones* on tour all over the world. Gartland, of course, was nonplussed as usual – sitting there staring with his little brown beady eyes. Thinking some serious intellectual Yeatsian thoughts. It was him who had given her the title for the play. *Insomnium Ossiae*, he had actually suggested first – before *The Night Visitor*.

—The bereft bones that will never sleep, I remember him saying, staring at the ashes of a dread past in the dawn.

Before delivering another lecture, explaining yet again how Noh plays often focus on ghosts seeking release from passionate sins or errors of judgement committed when living.

—States of unappeasable remorse are what they generally tend to be about, he explained, running his little fat fingers through his whiskers.

He had been involved in the miners' strike, Gartland, in the UK – a place he swore he'd never stand in again.

—Thatcher ruined our country, he insisted, she's a murderer, nothing more, Beni.

Before turning to me with the wine glass in his hand. He was an expert on that too, of course.

—But then you know that more than most, don't you, Gabriel? he said to me – before launching into his analysis of eight hundred years of the Irish troubles. About which he knew everything – including the hunger strikes.

—What was it like inside the prison during the hunger strikes? I remember him asking, raising his eyebrows in that quizzical way of his – like he didn't believe you when you answered his question. He could be a most exasperating man. But very intelligent. Oh yes, very intelligent. Beni was very fond of him – intensely. As I'm sure he was of her.

Not that I care a great deal what he was. But if he was a friend of the girls, then so be it. What Beni and me had together was private anyway, and I got along with her in a way I wouldn't have dreamed remotely possible. After all, my experience with women had been severely limited – not just on account of prison but because of Esther McCaul and her antics over the years. Couldn't go anywhere, not even for a drink, without her appearing wild-eyed, swaying in the doorway – slobbering as she stood there on those skinny foal's legs. So it was good to be fortunate enough to eventually meet someone like Beni. Even if she didn't like men in that way. Or so she said – but sometimes you'd wonder just what you can believe.

Because on one or two occasions she definitely did demonstrate . . . well, affections, I guess – if you could call them that. Although no doubt Mr Gartland would regard that as sexist. Being an authority on the rights of women.

Because Beni – I'll be honest, and right from the start so was she, in fact – yes, Beni Banikin had certain troubles of her own. And I guess that, in a way, made it easy – for the pair of us to get along, I mean. Being as we were, both in a way, suffering from bereavement. Me with my comrades and a struggle that had ultimately gone nowhere, and her with a childhood and adolescence that she had described as a 'vertiginous void'. Which I had actually had to look up after she said it. Unlike TJ, of course, the great Broadway playwright. Who had accused me already of misquoting Yeats.

—*I'm not a fucking university lecturer!* I'd snapped without hesitation.

But do you think did it bother him, little Willie Nelson of the campus, unwavering socialist firebrand?

Oh, why not at all – he simply twirled his whiskers and mused:

—I think, in fact, Gabriel, it actually reads: *I have heard of angry ghosts who wander in a wilful solitude.*

We had been sitting in the mezzanine of their Long Island apartment, I remember, when he said it, on a beautiful balmy summer's day. With the wine flowing and the sun streaming in – just about the last conditions in which you'd expect to find yourself trembling with anxiety and suppressed fury inside, not to mention sitting there like a somnambulist with a dilated gaze as pale as death. But that, I am afraid, was how it was – exactly how I felt at the time. However, thankfully, I didn't say anything. Just remained there quietly, wringing my hands – while Dr Gartland, throughout, appraised me with a number of his customary stealthy glances.

★

That was a week or so before the two of us set off on our journey. Our travels to what I called *Our Home in The Meadowlands*. In memory of The Farmer and all of my prison buddies.

You know, I guess – looking back – in a way our road trip must have kind of acted as therapy, for both of us. As we rode along in the Trans Am (it just had to be that in honour of the pact) just offloading all this stuff, motoring along without a thought as to where it actually was we were going – up and down the length of the country. During the course of which I think I must have told her everything about the struggle. And which really did me a lot of good, just the fact of getting it off my chest. I had even shown her a newspaper report dating back to '79, when I'd already been a couple of years in the field. Detailing an incident which was really and truly horrific – even by the often shocking standards of Northern Ireland. The print of *The Impartial Reporter* was faded and the paper itself was a little yellowed, but the front page photo told its own story – depicting a little humble roofless cabin, with a policeman standing in front of it, with an expression of what can only be described as *agony* on his face. The blunt headline read: BOMB DROPPED IN CRADLE. Those slain by the terrorists 'on this infamous night of horror and barbarism', it continued, included:

1) Nathan Douther, farmer, aged 67.
2) Elizabeth Douther – his wife, aged 62.
3) John Clone – farmer, aged 59.
4) Robert Clone – his son, aged 19.
5) James Cole – aged 23.
6) Joseph Mc Kay – aged 20.
7) Boab Douther (Infant, 6 mths).

The victims, apparently, had asked of their assassins: 'What is it we have done?' Only to receive the following frigid response: 'Youse are Protestants.' I found it even difficult to hold the paper in my hand. As Beni rested her head on my shoulder.

—I'm afraid after that I couldn't take it any more, I explained, driving onward, that's the reason that I finally upped and left. I simply couldn't stand over, condone, operations like that. That's not what the struggle was supposed to have been about. That's just sectarianism – indefensible in anybody's book. You know what I'm saying?

It was kind of beautiful – her kissing my hand.

—I'm glad you did, I remember her replying, for there's enough fucking sorrow in the world without your movement adding to it.

—When I joined the movement, back in late '75, it was supposed to be about freedom. That's what I joined for. And that's what it seemed like, back then – long before the hunger strikes, before the horror of Altnavogue. I couldn't believe in the end what it descended into. So I just had to get away. That's the truth, Beni – I had to shake the dust off my shoes, and just get the hell away from the so-called struggle. Leave it all behind me once and for all.

And how far away all of that now seems as she makes her way back to my homeland in Iron Valley, with what's left of me tucked neat and snug in her holdall, making a special pilgrimage as she gets ready to scatter the last of Gabriel King, fire his grey powder out across the surface of the glimmering Iron Lake. Where Esther and me used to go after the dances, and where The Farmer used to play his invisible guitar. It'll be a humble ceremony – on that we'd agreed. With pretty much nobody in attendance except her. Having given it some thought, that was the way I decided I wanted it.

Quiet, unceremonious. After all, everyone is getting on with their own lives now – and many of them I haven't seen in years. Of course there'll be some who'll be dissatisfied with that – some of my former colleagues, I mean, being as the movement is kind of obsessed with requiem rituals. But I wanted it to be special – between Beni and me. Those were my explicit instructions. Just Beni on the mountain with the copper urn raised way up high – nothing but her and the sound of the breeze. But, even now, I can hear them – what you might call the dissenting voices. With, laughably, His Majesty Dr Gartland the scholar among them. His eyebrows arching as he folds his little plump hands on his chest.

—*Ah, that rascal heart*, I can hear him taunt.

Quoting his idol Double-You-Bee again. Made me sick, the way he went on. Perhaps just as well that he never met Dog. For I can hear him too. Standing in the yard of the prison as I passed, sinking his hands in his pockets as he sighed, before releasing a long, low whistle.

—Yes, there he goes. The man that everyone knows they can trust. I wasn't the only one who had harboured suspicions about you. Beware, my friend, of that vigilant, frightful fiend.

Let them say what they have to – I don't care. All I know is I couldn't possibly have ever lived with what they'd done in Altnavogue. I mean, Jesus Christ – the slaughter of an innocent baby!

—That wasn't how it started out, Beni. It was never meant to descend into something like that, effectively a squalid, bigoted squabble. The reason I got involved was to free my country from what I perceived to be the yoke of oppression – it was supposed to be a fight for national liberation, not the murder of neighbours and blameless children. So when I heard what they had done, what choice did I have, eventually, but to confront them – each and

every one of them, who were effectively my colleagues and comrades-in-arms?

—You call this a fight? I said to Hushabye Bonner and Toby – twin brothers, among the most revered of border volunteers. And I fucking well said it to Dog White too.

How can you possibly tolerate this? I demanded. The whole appalling affair was nothing short of shameful. A shameful episode – a stain on the glorious history of the movement.

—And I just won't be associated with something like that.

It didn't go down well – as I'm sure you can imagine. And – like I told Beni – sowed the seeds of my growing disillusion, until in the aftermath of the hunger strike, it all came apart. When I finally left the IRA for good, deciding it couldn't possibly represent me any longer.

She had always wanted to go to Ireland. Ever since I'd got to know her – from that first night she walked into Rory's back in Queens, she'd never stopped telling me that. And then, when she made her great big discovery – when she fell in love, hopelessly, with the poetry of Yeats, well, sooner or later it had to be inevitable. She had even written some poetry about it – imagining herself same as we used to with The Meadowlands in prison, scaling Big Iron right to its summit, gazing out across country at the soft drifting April rain.

But – *ha ha!* – I can't imagine she expected it to turn out anything like this!

With me standing beside her, watching her stomping along confidently down the main street, with the curtains already twitching as they wondered: who the fuck is this coming along?

Not so much something out of *The Dukes of Hazzard*, maybe, but maybe Ellen DeGeneres come to town – Hey, look out, kids but I've arrived to present my afternoon TV show! – chewing a stick of gum and walking around like she owns the place. Sporting that same tomboy arrogance she'd crafted in her teen years – as a method of camouflaging her sometimes shocking vulnerability.

I'd only become aware of that side of her nature round about '93, after I'd known her a year or two. And which I'd found, I have to say, extremely attractive – that hard carapace splintering to reveal a concealed soft heart. And we really began to get along like a house on fire. Which was great for me – because, apart from Esther McCaul – and, I suppose, a considerable number of ladies of the night in Asia and other places during the course of my travels, I haven't really had all that much experience with women. So I used to get a great kick out of just motoring along in the Trans Am with Banikin, charming the pants off her with my 'old Irish stories' – as she liked to called them.

—You don't mean to tell me you called a band that!?

—Me and Bobby Owens formed it together, way back. Long before the whole thing started. Back, Beni, in the good old early seventies!

How could we have imagined it would end the way it did? I asked her, before wearily adding:

—With Bobby, for Christ's sake, taking his own life!

She didn't bother saying anything – she didn't have to, and she knew it. How great it would have been to be able to love her, in the normal way between a man and a woman. But her heart had already been captured in that way – even if Mia and her had had their troubles. All of which, I am happy to say, is history now – and they're happier than they've ever been in their fabulous Long Island

apartment, paid for by her masterpiece *The Night Visitor* – her 'stunning re-invention of W.B. Yeats', as the *Village Voice* had described it.

—We can never be anything but friends, she'd explained to me very early on.

And I was happy with that. Actually I wasn't happy at all, to tell the truth – I was fucking *raging* when I heard it. But then, after a while, I got used to it. Realising, more than anything, that at the end of the day what Banikin was was a straight fucking dealer – and that's a very rare thing in this world. And is a quality that you ought to value if you're fortunate enough to have it come your way. For, at the end of the day, what else do we have? No one likes a renegade or dissimulator. Jimjoe White was right about that.

—Gabriel and the Fuck-Ups! What a name to call a rock band. Well, all I can say is – I've heard it all now. I've heard it all now, Mr Gabriel 'Looney Tunes' King!, I can remember her laughing – as the Trans Am burnt it, the asphalt all the way across country to the state of Indiana.

---

Yeah, we sure had real good times, me and Banikin – for the most part. Because I'm not going to pretend – not even begin to – that it was plain easy cruising pretty much all the way.

Look, I might as well be honest – all of my problems, with prison and everything like that – they were really, even yet, a long way from being resolved. And I accept that, a lot of the time, I simply fucked up. I really and truly have no problem whatsoever acknowledging those plain, unpalatable facts now. Of course I don't. But when it comes to Banikin I will always tell the truth – and if there were nights when I disappeared without so much as a word, not

bothering even to leave her a note or bother calling her later – then so be it, that was what I did. Vanishing into some roadside dive or other, already shoving down red-eye like it was going out of fashion. Truth is, even yet I don't know how she managed to come around and somehow forgive me – but, believe it or not, she did. And I'm convinced of that, for she told me as much. Not that Banikin was a softie – far from it! With her teeth clenched and that tight little freckly red head glaring at you, seething:

—I don't have to take any more of this fucking bullshit!

A coupla times she had actually struck me – I mean, at times it could get heavy. But then, we'd find ourselves falling asleep – like a pair of babes in the woods, I swear to Christ. In some fucking motel, beneath the vast sky of the American Midwest. Looking back on that trip now, it was kind of half crazy. But she somehow learned to trust me, in spite of it all. Maybe because she'd discovered something – after all, it was after that road trip she'd had her first success – no matter what credit Tubby Gartland might claim. Yes, 'autodidact' felon or not, it was me who had made the suggestion. That maybe she'd been barking up the wrong tree.

—Maybe you ought to forget about writing poetry, I remember suggesting. I mean, after all, there's all kinds of writing.

—You know what? she had said. I think you might be right. It's either that or go on writing this sub-Sylvia Plath shit for ever. *Our skinny breasts, my father's death*. Christ but there's times when I make myself sick.

As a matter of fact, she had written what became the first draft of *The Night Visitor* in a library in Wisconsin after that very conversation.

So screw you, Tubby, and your bullshit 'autodidacticism'!

As she lay there in that motel, I counted the freckles on the upper

part of her nose. Thinking to myself – laughing while I did it – how, more than anything, she looked like Michael J. Pollard! A name, of course, she would never have known – but he was the gas-pump attendant in the movie *Bonnie and Clyde*. It was the way that she puckered her nose when she grinned, and the general little roundy nature of her face. But, man, would she have freaked if she had known I was thinking things like that. C.W. Moss, that was his name in the movie. Then I fell asleep, with my arms around her.

—*Night, CW!* I remember thinking, clamping my hand across my mouth as I did so.

Man, what times we had on that road trip.

She'd been born in a village in Northern Indiana, and been raised there by her Amish parents until tragedy struck in 1983 – when her father had taken his own life in appalling circumstances.

Sometimes, if I'd been drinking, I'd try to press her into making love. Which is something I ought to – *never!* – have done. It was wrong, and I realise that now – have done so for many years. Same as I shoulda stayed away from those roadhouses, and those endless God-awful dive bars that she found me in. Filling total strangers with more bullshit about Northern Ireland. Boy, she could get so mad!

—I ought to have taken the Trans Am and just lit out – for all you are is a selfish asshole! she said one night to me – with her face contorted in a rictus of disdain.

—*Oo-ee!* I couldn't help thinking.

—Sorry, Michael! Ha, ha!

But said nothing. Which was the wisest course of action, in the circumstances – believe me.

★

There's one particular rathole I remember – a juke-joint in Mobile – where, after searching for two hours, she'd finally come upon me – singing the praises of Dog White to a pair of truckers. All I can remember is – shamefully, really – completely ignoring her when I saw her coming in – just standing there in the doorway, staring. I think, perhaps, she may have reminded me of Esther. But I was completely drunk. As off I went, with another elaborate story, concerning the earlier, more glorious days of the struggle. The rednecks I was talking to were farmers who worked on the land nearby. One of them was displaying the regulation beer gut, with his companion, perhaps not a little unlike myself, tending a little more towards what I suppose you might call the feral, with tufted eyebrows and a hard angular face – a set of vulpine eyes darting here and there underneath the bill of a baseball cap. They just couldn't get enough of these yarns I was coming up with – especially, as it turned out, the ones about my time in Angola. As shots of Jack lined up along the counter.

—You might have heard of Mad Mike Hoare. I met him when I was working out there, in Angola. All of which had just come about by accident, in '71. Ran into a couple of guys in London and they set the whole thing up. Not that I saw all that much action as a mercenary – most of the time I was stuck in the bush, looking at seventy miles of impenetrable mangrove swamp. So it wasn't what you'd call difficult, taking the decision to return and fight in Ireland. I reckoned my skills could be put to better use there, freeing my own country for a change – you know?

For days after that she didn't speak a word. We just kept on driving, covering hundreds of miles of highway, with one state blurring into another. When the thaw eventually began to show signs of maybe setting in, I heard her rasp through those clenched teeth:

—Like filling strangers with bullshit about your war, do you,

Gabriel? Well you wanna know something? I'm not sure if I can stand a whole lot more of it.

—Oh, aren't you, Michael? some stupid voice had me almost on the brink of saying. Well, I really am sorry to hear that, that's a pity.

Which would have been just a whole lot of bullshit. But, thankfully, I managed to pull back from the brink. As I reached out, tentatively, to lay my hand on hers. And then she gave me those lovely melting eyes.

—Fuck you! she said – as her face cracked into a smile.

Which led to us attempting intercourse that night – but it was laughable!

—Oh, Mia! she had even moaned at one point.

With my prostate cancer dick bowing his little abject head in shame. As I ran my hands all along her skin, up and down the length of her little squat, plump body.

And everything was fine again next morning – even if we hadn't won 'Lovers of the Year'.

—Tell me about that band of yours again, I remember her saying as we lay there watching TV, hugging as the light of dawn began flickering on the glass – and I pressed my cheek against the tight bristles of her copper hair.

—'Long Black Veil' by The Band, I told her. You ever hear that one in Goshen, Indiana?

—Goshen, Indiana – sure we did, Gabriel – somewhere, maybe, in your Irish dreams. You know anything about the Amish at all? For we weren't allowed to have TV or radio, she explained, but Ta Ta used to sneak off to South Bend. Where we'd listen to Huey Lewis and the News in the mall. We liked them the best.

—Did you always want to get out? Far back as you can remember?

—You think you had troubles? You just have no idea what it was like to grow up there. The dreariness and the endless religious services, not to mention those dour matriarchs with their tedious quilts and insane pattern books – sitting there waiting for yet another excuse to reprimand you. But that wasn't the worst of it, Gabriel. That distinction belonged to the visits into town – in that God-awful buggy, with all the other kids not so much saying anything about you as *thinking* it. Watching as you passed in your stupid dumb lace cap and old maid's shoes. How I loathed them! You know what me and Ta Ta Petersen decided to do once? We had a ritual burning of a pair of button boots! Out at the creek where she pretended to be Huey – hell, if they had ever discovered that! That the two of us had found ourselves a spot in the woods, as she crooned 'The Power of Love' into my hot ear. As I gripped her you-know-what and said, Do you love me, Huey? Please will you pledge your love again?

After which I took her by the hand, and then the two of us just lay there in that motel room – laughing away at the impossible innocence and sweetness of it all.

And it was right at that moment that I found myself thinking of Esther McCaul. Standing in the doorway in that infuriating red leather coat, snivelling into a scrap of a tissue.

—All this time I thought you loved me, I heard her say.

As a crystal tear came strolling down her cheek.

And then I was gone. Off to the States – never to return. Except perhaps, I remember thinking, in a box. Or a jar, as it happened. An urn. Although, of course – I didn't know that then.

That idiot Esther had followed me to the bus station.

—You're a piece of shit! I heard her calling after me – just as

the coach was idling there in the forecourt. It was deeply embarrassing.

—Everyone hates you! You're nothing in this valley, King! Nothing! And you'll never be anything other than what you are – fucking vermin! Goodbye, Mr Rat!

Charming, I must say. You can imagine how glad I was to get shot of her. Even if I loved her. Which I absolutely did, and with all my heart.

Ha, ha!

But not in the same way I loved Beni Banikin – or should I say, Miss Daisy 'Dumpy' Duke, barrelling along now in those hefty rigger boots – acting like she's in a movie about to be shot in Iron Valley. One that might be called, I suggest, *The Last of Gabriel Gervase King* – and in which she shall be seen to scatter my ashes all across the surface of my favourite lake – in a final act of glorious valediction – representing my final farewell to my home in the valley, and the wonderful community into which I had been born. And for which I was prepared to lay down my life. A people, I like to think, for whom I – hopefully – had done my best. And among whom I'd been happy – in a way inconceivable in any other part of the world – even America, in which I'd been so happy. And where I'd met so many really terrific people – Yeats scholars, lesbians – all of them waiting out there to be found.

What a magnificent place, I really have to say, this wondrous world in which we all wander.

---

But enough – of all that rumination and philosophy – *already*, like Mia Chiang is fond of saying. Yeah, let's leave that to the likes of

Dr Gartland the lecturer, plucking his whiskers as he asks you what university you attended. And who then, when you tell him *Her Majesty's Prison, The Maze*, starts to fawn over you until . . .

Well, until he changes his mind about you again. The people you meet – how strange they can be.

However, as I say – no more about that, for we have much more to do, what with accompanying Her Highness Beni Banikin Ellen DeGeneres Daisy Duke, thinking to herself as she arrives at her hotel: I mean what the fuck, is this place America, for it sure don't look like Ireland!

With country and western hits blaring up and down the length of the main street, just like it had always done, with pride of place being accorded to Esther McCaul's old favourite – yes, the one and only Big Tom and the Mainliners, whose wailing harmonica and quavering pedal-steel bleated songs of faith and family, love and redemption from the speakers above the station located right slap-bang in the middle of the town.

—*Broadcasting all day, every day on RV109!* chirped BJ the DJ, as I thought of Esther's sobs that day. Because, I swear to God, she had been playing Big Tom's 'Ashes of Love' before I left.

—You've left me with nothing! All those years I visited you in prison! We were supposed to get married, have kids! Just what is it with you, King? I used to look into your eyes and thought I saw something – now I don't know what I saw! But I have a suspicion that it wasn't something good! Something maybe that wasn't good at all!

BJ was grinning absurdly through the plate-glass window facing onto the main street as the smalltown pedestrians went flowing by.

—*Yeehaw!* he roared, *Goddammit, yeehaw!*

It was hardly surprising that Beni might be bewildered.

*

You know, looking back on it now, I'm glad that I kissed Esther. Just gave her a little tender peck on the cheek, before getting my backpack and turning to make one last farewell. Because I know, let's face it, there are people who would have hit her. But that wasn't something I was prepared to do.

—Goodbye, I said, and went off to catch the bus.

All could see was her shaking in the doorway.

The very same doorway, as a matter of fact, in which Banikin was now standing. As this young fellow rolled up and handed her a shiny brochure.

—*The Best Little Film Festival in the Midlands!* read the programme cover.

As off went the youth, haring boisterously down the road.

—As well as our kids' programme, we proudly introduce a season of Irish political films this year – screenings which include *Angel*, *In the Name of the Father* and *Some Mother's Son*, Beni read.

The latter was upsetting her – as a matter of fact, she was close to tears. Especially when she saw the Jesus Christ figure – for her, a truly startling image of an emaciated, near-skeleton breathing his last on a rough plank of wood. It wasn't hard to see that she was hearing my words as she clutched the brochure.

—After the failure of the hunger strikes, the war was more or less over for me, Beni. Fifty-five days fasting – it's more than enough to break any man. And I gave it my best shot. But, in common with a lot of my comrades, after that I found I just didn't have the stomach for it any more. I guess you could say that I had nothing left in me to give.

I was moved, I have to say, by the sight of her lips miming my name as she stood there, shivering – opening up her wallet. Before removing a picture I had given her in the States. The one

which she said had made me look like Levon Helm, the drummer with The Band. Especially when I wore that cutaway denim jacket, with my skinny arms completely covered in tattoos, and my angular face, quiffed sandy hair and tufted eyebrows completing the picture she had of me – she was always going on about what she described as my enigmatic 'Lean Wolf' smile – complete with missing incisor, which I'd lost somewhere in a fight in Asia.

I almost wept as I watched her place a small kiss on the programme page, as she stood there in the main street. Like I'd told her, Bobby Sands had actually been out-of-shot in that picture. Bobby Sands, aged twenty-seven, had been on hunger strike for sixty-six days before he died. Eleven more, I realised she was reflecting ruefully, than her friend and admirer Gabriel King. Who, perhaps, all his life, had dreamed of dying for Ireland. Of distinguishing himself by literally offering himself up as a sacrifice. Just like Jesus. Just like Jesus – Our Lord, ha ha! Who is always claiming to have done so much. Like Tubby Gartland – ooh, such a saint!

But then, of course, things are not always as they seem.

For what are his so-called efforts on our behalf? Only a thinly veiled exercise in narcissism – selfishness, in fact, if you want to get down to it. With things, just as Jimjoe 'The Dog' used to whisper in the shower:

—Not always being as they seem, I'm afraid!

For so-called 'hunger strikers' just as much as anyone else.

*Because he knows, a frightful fiend*
*Doth close behind him tread.*

It can still send shivers rippling down my spine.

And which it might have done for Beni too, had she been aware of it – for Jimjoe White had literally appeared out of nowhere – just as she was on the point of returning to her hotel.

—*Céad mile fáilte romhat!* she heard him exclaim, I am happy to welcome you to the valley! Yes, a hundred thousand welcomes, as they say, Miss Banikin!

Dog had recently been elected mayor – and was looking the very picture of officialdom in his neatly cut three-piece herringbone suit. With his shining platinum hair reaching halfway down his back – looking, for all the world like Tubby Gartland's Irish twin. Another veritable biblical, Willie Nelson-style pontiff. Rocking on his heels as he snorted with laughter.

—With them shorts on you, ma'am, he told Beni, I might have taken you for something out of *The Dukes of Hazzard*!

Beni was impressed. You could tell that straight away. But then, for her, the accent would have been enough. Oh, those sweet and gullible Amish! He wasn't a bit like a smalltown mayor, she was thinking – not stern and pompous like an official you might encounter in Bloomington or Mishawaka. Why, on the contrary, Mayor White was impressively tall and most distinguished-looking.

—A regular silver fox! she kept thinking.

Before The Dog began checking his watch, good-humouredly announcing:

—Well, unfortunately, I'm afraid I have to dash. But hopefully I'll be seeing you soon again – will I, Miss Banikin?

How had he known her name? she wondered – as off he trooped with a familiar knot of sycophants – including my old friends the Bonner twins, Toby and Hushabye, trotting along in his wake with their folders.

—You're on the third floor, Miss Banikin, said the desk clerk again when she reached the hotel. I really hope you'll enjoy your stay with us. Even if I'm sure you're accustomed to much better than this in America, ha ha!

What on earth could she have meant by that? wondered Beni, but just as quickly dismissing the thought, riding the elevator to the third floor. Wondering, should it give her reason to be paranoid?

A question to which the answer was:

—Yes.

Because, of course, in the valley, paranoia is a way of life. S.T. Coleridge would have enjoyed a stay there.

---

She found herself flopping giddily onto the bed. There indeed can be few sensations to compare with that of being watched. And, being more than aware of Beni Banikin's inherited medical condition, I wanted to do nothing that might induce that endemic 'hunted' tendency, I suppose you might call it, which had dogged her pretty much all her life. And which had been the first thing I had noticed about her – constantly half glancing behind her, seeming as one haunted by a fixed delusion or one perhaps oppressed by a guilty conscience.

Already she was in the throes of hyper-analysing the desk clerk's comments, investigating them for possible significance. Realising how, in times gone by, such observations might have made her deeply resentful.

But thankfully now, it wasn't former times!

No, absolutely not, it wasn't the old days, she told herself – as I sighed with relief.

It not being something I intended to enjoy – not with Beni.

With Beni Banikin, no. Whatever others in a comparable psychological imbroglio may have thought, such as certain New York Library blatherers.

Already she was considering ingesting a capsule of Cymbalta, for the routine purpose of calming her down. But, of course – as was her wont – convincing herself that there wasn't any need.

So she wasn't – *not in the least!* – worried about that. But her entire body was now beginning to tingle. Something which, of course, began to seriously worry me – I mean, I knew so well that that was the way it always started. And already the faces she had encountered in the valley were beginning to seem strange – as though morphing into *commedia dell'arte* masks, floating about a stage in the tiny crowded theatre of her mind – including not only that of The Dog but also the genial, smiling receptionist. Who already – it seemed to Beni – knew way too much about her.

Realising, only now, just how clammy her skin had become. Before climbing off the bed and stretching herself up to her full height – commencing, as so often before, that familiar variety of breathing exercises. A process in which she had been so expertly tutored by Mia.

But this time the feeling failed to abate. In fact, if anything, it grew even more acute.

—This is getting ridiculous, she laughed impatiently, as her heart continued to resonate furiously.

—I shouldn't have to do this stuff at all – not at this stage. Didn't the doctor tell me I was more or less cured? Why on earth should this be happening now?

Then she noticed a strange disquiet appeared to have overtaken the room.

Me, I knew only too well the likely consequences of that growing bloodless pallor – and the lurching dramatic mood switches, those

startling episodes of grandiloquence which were already threatening.

—*Breathe in, breathe out*, she heard Mia urge. Before beginning to pace the floor frenetically, thinking of her very first day as an orphan. In a home called Maria Coeli – which was located in New Orleans – in Storyville, Louisiana.

But why should I want to dwell on *that*? she asked herself. She'd been over it all, why a million times!

Stupid old school! she told herself.

*Wa-a-a-y* better to think about her lover.

Yes, to dwell over and over on the sweet Mia Chiang, her dancer-partner who had only just recently stormed New York with her performance as Olympia, the automaton doll in Offenbach's opera *The Tales of Hoffmann*. In an interpretation, incidentally – she laughed, tossing her head back in an attitude of mock hauteur – which had been variously described by a number of critics as 'sulphurous' and 'incandescent'.

With her voice on opening night soaring, attaining an almost unearthly pitch as she leaped and glided across the stage, the notes spiralling in that magnificent coloratura style:

*—The birds in the arbour*
*The sky's daytime star*
*Everything speaks to a young girl of love!*
*Ah! This is the gentle song,*
*The song of Olympia! Ah!*

How had it happened?, Beni asked herself, wringing her hands, before returning to the bed and wriggling excitedly, exulting in the very passion and good fortune of being alive. Never in her life had she felt so good.

But that was before the memory of Pastor Braam edged itself

slyly into her mind. How I wanted to reach out to her when I sensed it coming! You have to believe me – it really is true!

—At all times be vigilant in order to protect your holy purity! she heard her mother cry. And beware of rogue angels!

Ta Ta Petersen had heard about them too. But her attitude had been different. As a matter of fact she said that she didn't care about angels, rogue or otherwise, and that whenever her chance came she intended to run away from Goshen – and that then those stupid angels could do what they damned well liked.

And I have to say that that amused me. 'Rascal hearts', Beni had called them in her play. Which made me smile as I watched her lying there, dreaming of Ta Ta touching her 'downtheres'.

—You like that, don't you? she had said, when the two of them had crawled underneath a bridge.

—Yes, Beni had replied, but I hope he doesn't see us.

—Who? asked Ta Ta.

—The Rogue Angel, the one they call treacherous Morning Star!

—Ha ha! chuckled Ta Ta. If he does, we'll pull off his feathers and stuff them into Pastor Braam's mouth!

But laugh though they might, there had been times when, in the shadows, Beni had seen something. Shifting furtively, then not moving a muscle. Other times she would hear just the softest whisper, followed by a steady padding tread behind her. And would turn on her heel – only, to her horror, to discover – nothing.

Absolutely nothing at all.

---

By the time she had reached the age of ten, it had become the custom of her mind to make daring incursions into the realm of the unreal without renouncing residence in what might be described as the region of certitude. So vivid in character did these excursions come to be that she could entertain no other possibility than that they represented presentiments of some kind. A conviction which could not but become firm in the aftermath she had experienced, and in which she had apprehended the shadow of a human being dangling from a rope.

And the following day they found her father in a barn. Pastor Braam had called to the house to give them the news.

---

I too have known one – a pastor, I mean. A man of elaborate and stiff civility who might have belonged in one of Tubby Gartland's adored Victorian novels. And who favoured elaborate language in that vein – speaking effusively of evil angels and death. And, in particular, as they pertained to what had happened one certain night in Altnavogue. Of course, I know now what he means. Watching over all with my basilisk stare – my impotent gaze, I suppose you might say.

Just as someone similar might have been in attendance that particular night. When a certain disciplined party of men began hovering into view, approaching that very same town-land. With their storm lamps swinging as they emerged from a line of firs, with their bombs primed and ready. Elizabeth Douther had been the first to expire, reproaching the intruders with her dying breath, and in particular the man who had just murdered her husband:

—I never expected the like of this of you, Dog White.

*

Yes, the pastor in question had delivered the oration, in fact, at those funerals. And in the blinding rain, had said to his numbed congregation:

—Nathan Douther and his wife appealed for mercy from the killers but with oaths and obscenity it was refused.

A second unit of terrorists, he continued, had meanwhile attacked the home of John Clone, who resided there with his wife and two sons – Robert, aged nineteen, and William, aged sixteen. Who had taken refuge in a barn where they were subsequently discovered by the assassins. Who then killed them and proceeded to burn the Clone home to the ground.

That was what had happened in the small hours that Altnavogue morning, on the twentieth day of March, in the year of Our Lord 1979. When the men left the cabin and were swallowed up by the woods, disappearing like ghosts along a line of dripping firs.

---

Long ago – during the war.

—I didn't even know that they had called it that, I remember Beni shrugging at the time – as we shared a toke, in a car lot in Cincinnati.

—Whether it was or not, that was how it seemed to us. There was no choice, really, after Donal Givney was arrested. We were all drawn into it, more or less. He was sentenced to seventeen years, you see. I was given the news when I was over in Angola.

—So then you went straight home?

—What else could I do? Right back home to the valley, I went. Just as soon as I heard.

—And after that you started bearing arms?

—I went on active service after that. And this time I knew we were going all the way. All the way with my loyal, noble comrades.

As a matter of fact, about the actual conflict we never talked a great deal – and with good reason, for she had never left me under any illusion about what her feelings were towards violence. Anyway, in those days, really, I was so fond of her that I had no desire whatsoever to cause any unnecessary difficulties between us. Particularly during those first few months when I had still been so naive as to actually think that maybe – somehow – we could sexually 'get it on', like the Yanks say. Before, of course, I contracted prostate cancer. Which was going to make it a whole lot more difficult. Even if she had wanted – which she didn't, and you know the reason why. One night I had said to her:

—I mean you can't be *all* lesbian!

And she had looked at me like she was shocked. Which she was, of course. But it's still true, isn't it? But after that, I never alluded to it again. Just got used to 'One-Eyed Charlie'. And how I'd never get to ever 'getting it on' with anyone, ever again. Then one night we had a blow-up in Ohio – I suppose I was still smarting over her response. I'm not saying it was logical. Or retrospectively trying to justify my actions.

—This is bullshit, Beni, you know that? This whole road trip, it's a waste of time. We're fooling ourselves – for men and women can never be friends! Not really – not in the true sense!

Regrettably, at that time, I'd had no knowledge whatsoever about her experiences at the hands of Karsten Bloch – not to mention the assault which had taken place in Queens. During the time she'd split up from Mia. And I have no doubt that, had I become acquainted with them, then those facts would have made a considerable

difference. But up until then she'd kept all of that secret – something which, even yet, and in spite of myself and my best efforts to overcome it, I can find still annoys me. Which is embarrassing, really – considering how close we'd become, you know?

And we really had.

You see, Bloch had been her housemistress in the Maria Coeli orphanage during her teenage years in Storyville, Louisiana. And their strange relationship had continued to haunt her all her life.

—Your breasts are temples, the tall gaunt housemistress would routinely announce, pale globes of innocence – inviolate holy sculptures. At least they ought to be. But not for you, my dearest Bethany. Because for you they are something else entirely. Tell us what you dream of having done to them, Banikin. Tell the truth to all the other girls.

—I want Ta Ta to bite and to kiss them, Miss.

—Flagrant sinner, she would hear her hiss contemptuously, the heavy oaken door closing behind her with the remorseless finality to which she had become accustomed.

Initially, I have to admit, she had fed me some few meagre details regarding this period of confinement – how unpleasant and damaging it had been. And, of course, having been unjustly incarcerated myself I knew what such circumstances might lead to – for anyone, really. Had more than an idea of the sheer *complexity* of human relations. Now when I say she was sparing with these morsels of information, in all truth I don't think she had ever told anyone else – not even Mia. And certainly not Tubby. No, the eminent Dr Gartland was to remain relatively uninformed about that period of her life – in a way that he wasn't about British social and political history, the collected works of Shaw and W.B. Yeats and – if you

were to believe him – the various intricacies of thermonuclear fucking dynamics.

Bloch would just appear at the bottom of Beni's bed – and just stand there motionless with her keys hanging from her belt.

—I remember literally stiffening with fear when I'd see her there, I remember Beni saying. Not so much as uttering a word, Gabriel – sighing away in that baggy old fisherman's sweater of hers. In the moonlight she might have been seventy years old, I guess – although she couldn't, realistically, have been very much more than forty. I could see her taking the keys from her belt – her chest rising and falling. I braced myself as they bulged in her fist. *Flagrant sinner, this time you'll get it!* I remember her saying, through those thin and loveless lips. Thin cruel lips.

She paused then and said:

—At least that's what you think.

I didn't know quite what she meant by that.

—That's what you *think*? I quizzed as I lit a rollie. What did she mean? I had to know.

And then, what does she do? Clams up altogether. I guess there must have been something in my tone.

But a couple of nights later, she came very close to telling me everything.

—I got this nose bleed, and it was as if, somehow she knew, she began, because when I looked, she was standing there, as always. Then the next thing I knew she was undoing the back of my nightdress.

She shivered violently before continuing.

—This will cure you, Banikin, she went on, before stroking my head, just the kindliest, gentlest mother in all the world as she pressed the heavy cold key against my back.

—I hate to see you suffering, my love.

At that point, then, I remember her looking fearful.

—Maybe you don't like me talking like this? she said – tremulously.

As I shook my head and told her I loved her, as we lay there listening to the 'symphony of the cicadas', as she sometimes called it – clicking away far beyond in the desert.

---

It wasn't long after that before I divulged my own unfortunate little secret – that I'd already been diagnosed with advanced prostate cancer, and that it had already travelled as far as my bones. A disclosure which saw her looking frail and shivering, like what I'd just said somehow fed into the play that she'd been writing – her 're-imagining', as she called it, of Yeats. But it was good that it happened – and I think that night we were as close as we'd ever been.

—Yeah, I told her, when I was seventeen I decided to go to Africa, head off to Angola where there was plenty of work in the mercenary line. I had an address of a guy I knew in Cape Town, Beni, and it was him who pretty much organised everything. You wouldn't believe how simple it all was, guys. And before I knew it I was right out there in the thick of it, in the jungle. You ever hear of Mad Mike Hoare? I got to know him pretty well in the end. Can't say that I cared for him much, though. Too much of a psycho if you ask me. In the end, in any case, all I wanted to do was get out of the place. I'd already seen too much, and the truth was I was getting older. Not to mention the fact that things were hotting up in the conflict back home. After Kingsmills, it looked like civil war might very well now be on the cards.

—Kingsmills? What was that? she asked – half, as so often in the past, not wanting to know at all.

—It was one of the cruellest episodes of the struggle. Even worse than what my hardened and deluded former comrades were responsible for at Altnavogue.

—What did they do, your comrades – at Altnavogue?

—What did they do? Murdered an entire family – dropped a bomb into the cradle of a fucking infant. That's what they did. That's the legacy of that night in Altnavogue. Even, long after, when I was wasting away in that prison on hunger strike, what had been done in the movement's name would return to haunt me. And I began to realise that no amount of atonement could remove that stain. No hunger strike nothing. So was it any wonder that, in the end – after the strikes had more or less come to nothing – I'd want to renounce my membership – and to get the hell away, once and for all, from what our so-called struggle had become? That's the reason that I had to leave the country. Just get on a plane and run – and keep running. To Malaysia, Thailand, wherever it would take me. Because I had almost gone and sacrificed my life for nothing, Beni. In the end, we failed. No matter what anyone says, Thatcher and the British government defeated us in '81. Leaving us with nothing, only the memory of Altnavogue. And horrors like it.

—Jesus, she said, shrinking back in revulsion.

And I didn't blame her. But, like I say, for the remainder of that night I never felt closer to her.

---

Almost as close as I am to her now, watching her standing on the shores of Iron Lake, with the mountain behind her, that great

majestic peak, in this very same spot where all of us spent the great part of our youth. Yes, all of us old pals – me, the Bonner twins, Donal Givney and The Farmer. With the future stretching before us like some fucking diamond highway, as Bob Dylan might say. And it's hard not to be moved whenever I think of her agreeing that day – to ferry my ashes back to this very place.

—You speak so fondly of it, how could I not? she had smiled as she looked at me. To tell you the truth, I can only regard it as a privilege, Gabriel.

—It's so good, swear to God, that you feel like that. And I'll tell you this – I don't know if peace, real peace, can be found in this world. But if it's anywhere you'll find it on that mountain. You'll find it on the shores of the beautiful Iron Lake.

Then I saw that there was a tear in her eye – it had just appeared.

—How can I conceive of a world with you not in it? she had said, before hugging me tightly.

It really had been such a lovely moment.

Michael J.Pollard? C.W. Moss? How could I ever have called her that?

She really was gorgeous.

---

Before even thinking of going anywhere near the Iron Valley or our country, Beni had buried herself in various libraries in order to learn about it. Its social history as well as the conflict in which I'd taken part.

—You don't think you were appreciated, do you, what you and your comrades did for Ireland?

I had to admit it.

—It was hard. Lying there – wasting away, your body giving out. I mean, for Christ's sake – fifty-five days! But then to come out – and nobody cares?

—And then, of course – *Altnavogue*!

I nodded bitterly.

—I never wanted to see Ireland again. I just longed to travel and never stop travelling. Half of Asia I covered in a month.

That's where I got my tattooed arms. One every night.

She studied the place until she knew it inside out. Knew all the place names – Tempo, Blacklion, Swanlinbar – until she could recite them like a mantra in her sleep. With 'Swan' as we'd always called it being the very place where I'd initially been sworn into 'the movement' myself. By none other than my old friend Dog White himself.

That would have been around the time of the very first hunger strike, when Frank Stagg had lasted sixty days. It had been a deeply unstable period. With central government remaining terrified that some form of political coup, sooner or later, was going to be attempted. Slowly but surely – to paraphrase old Double-You-Bee – things could no longer hold at the centre. And 'mere anarchy' would soon be loosed upon the world. Not that it appeared to bother The Dog. No, the subsequent mayor of the valley had remained at all times cool as a breeze. Because of the fact that his people had been associated for generations with the struggle for national liberation, The Dog was spoken of in terms close to awe.

—You'll be good for us, Gabriel, I remember him saying, most particularly because of your recent experience in the African conflict – you'll be seen to bring a bit of mettle into the ranks. Because, to tell you the truth, what with the quality of some of the

volunteers we've been getting lately – Jesus Christ, I can't begin to tell you!

That he meant The Farmer and Bobby Owens, I knew only too well – with the pair of them barely out of short trousers at the time.

To tell you the truth, looking back on it now, Pearse Gavigan should probably have never been admitted to the organisation at all. I mean, sweet Jesus, when I think of it now, that very first night of our so-called 'inaugural operation' – raiding the Dundalk train, when he was laughing and cheering like the whole fucking thing was some kind of a game. For all we knew we might have had to stiff the driver – I mean who knew what the fuck was going to happen? – and there he is, entirely off his head, chortling away and waving the shooter like a lunatic. But I'm happy to say that somehow we made it through all right, managed in the end to get away unscathed.

Set the movement up for years financially that one did – and the cops never so much as suspected we were responsible, in spite of interrogating the lot of us one by one.

Those were the good days – before such cruel debasements as Altnavogue appeared on the horizon.

Because it just wasn't like that, way back in the early seventies. In many ways those days now seem so breathtakingly innocent. There wasn't even one of us who broke during interrogation – not a single one of us who sang. No weak links, we gave them absolutely nothing.

And I look back on it almost fondly. For we really felt like warriors – connected, as I say, to that noble line of unrepentant stalwarts of whom the great Double-You-Bee had written. It was a good time, you know? The possibility of defeat never entered

our heads. For in your late teens and early twenties you ain't just inclined to think about the future. Or the possibility that one day – and a lot sooner than you think – very soon you're going to find yourself lying stinking on a bare plank starving half to death – in the cold grey hell of a British concentration camp.

Where I was incarcerated for eleven years with some of the finest men it has ever been my privilege to know.

Among them Hushabye – or 'Send-'Em-Home' Bonner, as he was affectionately known by the other members of our unit. I used to sit with him while we watched poor Donal Givney die, preparing bit by bit to perish from the earth. Hushabye had a reputation for being fearsome, with some saying that he got a kick out of 'sending people home', his own unique private term for the final act of execution. But I would say that someone like that wasn't the guy I knew at all. With any evidence you might need being provided by his response on the night that Donal's wracked body finally gave out. When I watched him sobbing helplessly as, I swear, he shivered and cried like a baby. Clutching the hand of the dead man. That's if you could call it a hand, of course – a white bony claw about the size of a bird's talon, more like – as he lay there, a skeleton, stretched out on bare boards.

He'd been hallucinating vividly for days before the end.

—I'm finally going to The Meadowlands, boys, he kept saying, to that land where the heat-haze quivers as in a dream.

And then, couple of days later – he was gone.

But to tell the truth, nobody but me and The Farmer understood him. Well, we would, wouldn't we – haven't been through it with him so many times, over and over? *Riding to The Meadowlands*, like he used to call it – which had all been started by Robbie Robertson

and The Band, a song that had never been off his cassette. *Way back then, in the winter of '65*, he used to say, where the broken defeated soldier dreams of going back to the heartland. Where, once upon a time it had all made sense.

—Here where I belong, in The Meadowlands of Winter, he sang.

Giving us another instalment as we lay there every night, his muffled voice coming through the walls.

—We's harbouring a hurt them city slickers will never understand, he'd attempt in a Southern accent that was hopelessly unconvincing, and that's why we pledged our loyalty to The Meadowlands, and to what its glorious freedom represents. To this humble country boy whose only crime was to follow the dictates of his heart.

That was one of her favourites.

—Tell it to me again, Beni would smile – just like she did that day in Cincinnati. When we were parked in the car lot, with the engine ticking over as the two of us watched the light coming needling through the pines. I kept on talking about The Farmer, poor old Pearse.

—Gavigan was probably the most authentic country boy of us all, I went on, with all that simple, disarming sincerity of his. He'd have been happy all his life just driving a tractor. Would have fitted in perfectly right here in Ohio, just squatting there on a John Deere machine. For when the rest of us were bragging and blowing, Beni, about literature or history or whatever the fuck we were on about – Marx and shit, Frantz Fanon, I don't know – all he wanted to do was talk about fucking tractors. Dog used to laugh his head off at the poor bastard – How in Christ's name he ever became a volunteer is beyond me, he'd say.

I shook my head, passing her the toke as I turned away.

—Not that it matters a whole pile now – for it's all history, ain't it. But boy, did it end badly. Things just seemed to get heavier and heavier as time went on. Do you know what happened to Pearse? After we got out of prison, he turned informer. Yes, became perhaps the most loathed and despised figure in Irish history: *a rat*, in other words. What a dreadful development. Sold God knows how many of his comrades down the river. I really never thought it would happen to someone like Pearse – simple country boy or not.

—What way did they do it – turn him, as you call it?

—Oh, they have their ways, believe me. But even so, when I heard it, I couldn't believe it. It was the last operation I was on before I left. The straw that broke the camel's back, I guess. Even yet, I find it incredibly hard to talk about. But we were left with no choice. To become a tout – working, literally, as their agent under our noses. Christ almighty knows what he had told them. So we were left with no choice – we had to shoot him.

I remember her turning pale and pulling away roughly.

—Am I fucking hearing things or what? Did I just hear you saying you shot your comrade?

I explained the situation as best I could – placing the regrettable episode in context.

—It was Dog White pulled the trigger, Beni. But the army council had already decided – that we'd simply got no other option. I mean, those were the rules. You sing, you die. Because the organisation was already in complete disarray after the hunger strikes and Gavigan's behaviour had cost us God knows how many lives. Anyway, that's the way it is whenever you join the movement. You abide by its rules. But he was interrogated fairly. It was White himself who conducted it, actually. He always did jobs like that.

But the Bonners were there, too – the twins, and a couple of the others. But it didn't end good. He was guilty on all counts.

—To be murdered by your friends, in the loneliness of the mountains just before dawn, she murmured absently, the joint quivering, what a fucking way for someone to end up.

—War. It's so ugly. It took me years to get over it, really. All over Asia, I tried to erase the memory of that night.

In spite of what Gartland or anyone else might think.

—I don't believe you, I remember him remarking, one night we were eating in their Long Island apartment.

—I'm sorry, I replied, but I didn't quite get that.

Really, what a guy! Looking at you there with a forkful of spaghetti, arching his eyebrows and then, for ages, saying nothing.

—I used to have this nightmare down in Storyville, Beni said – this voodoo doll used to appear at the bottom of my bed, Mr Bones, he was called. You'll find his name in a work of the poet John Berryman. *Dream Songs*, I think it's called. Jesus, he was hideous – appearing there, clicking – with this awful knowing grin and a rattle in his hand. I still get sick whenever I think of it. It had happened many times, but it wasn't until TJ insisted I go to Belle Vue that I actually remembered it happening at all.

—Why did you go to Belle Vue? I asked her.

—Because the senior consultant psychiatrist there was a long-standing friend of TJ's. It was there I discovered what was causing me all these problems. Above all, I was warned against alcoholic drink. That, more than anything, is fatal for someone with a bio-chemistry like yours, he told me. Not unless you want to find yourself sliding off a roof! Which was how I'd described the

symptoms to him – that feeling of the moorings somehow slipping and being loosed off into who knows where, you know?

Then she had begun to give me details of the assault – which, as I say, had taken place when she and Mia had been parted temporarily. And when she had encountered this particular individual in a bar in Queens.

—His name was Johnny Roxbury, she told me, and the motherfucker, he looked like the young Elvis. I'd been drinking all day, drowning my sorrows in that God-awful dive.

Which was only around the corner from Rory's, in fact.

—Hi, I'm Johnny Roxbury, he had said, I'm a software engineer from Starkville, Mississippi.

—The hell with Mia, she had found herself saying, and you know what? The hell with fucking writing! And Anne Sexton and fucking Sylvia Plath!

It had all been going kinda swimmingly up to that. He had seemed so cool – with a knowledge of music and Southern literature she'd found compelling. But once inside her apartment, there could be no mistaking the change that had come over this new acquaintance. The shark-faced menace, that malign intent.

—Just my fucking luck to pick me a psycho, she found herself muttering, in despair, to herself.

As he slowly began to approach her across the floor, in his hand-tooled leather boots which he had pointed to impishly as he stood above her with legs akimbo.

—'Wantcher bones and you're gonna give 'em to me, ain'tcha? Yup, being a good gal, you're gonna let me have 'em!

When Roxbury was finally sated, he tossed his butch-waxed hair with a snort and tugged up his jeans.

—Ah's laaks 'em bones, she heard him say.

And then he was gone – vanished into the maw of history, and after that she never saw him again. Consoling herself – especially when the 'turns' would come upon her – that at least she got her play *The Night Visitor* out of the fucking bastard! In which he'd featured, obliquely, as a minor character.

But all of that might have taken place a hundred years previously – as, excitedly, she prepared herself for her trip to Iron Lake. For a *recce*, you might say. As she placed me tenderly on top of the mantelpiece, smiling as she kissed the urn tenderly – almost unthinkingly, in the most beautiful way. Hoisting her shoulder bag as she called across the room:

—Soon, old friend, you'll be going home. Back to the shores of your favourite lake!

Which had the effect of making me think about Esther again – saddening me, right to my core, I swear. Because, you see, we used to go there regularly when things were good between us. More than anything, I have to say, I hadn't wanted those two women to meet. Because I had never mentioned my common-law wife. Which, in the end, was what Esther McCaul became and who now was standing directly across from Beni's hotel – in that same cheap leather raincoat as usual, trembling as she dragged on a cigarette. As if somehow organised, Big Tom's 'Ashes of Love' was crackling away on the speakers down the street, something which, no doubt, added to her state of anxiety and bitterness – as she looked about her, furtively – in the same way, so familiar, she used to do when she'd come out looking for me – hauling me out of various bars. Making a show of us, really, to tell the truth. Bawling country and western songs in public – claiming, for Christ's sake, that they told *our* story!

She knew every one of Big Tom's songs – 'The Old Rustic Bridge', 'The Cold Hard Facts of Life'. You name it, Esther knew it.

But more than any of them – 'Ashes of Love'.

And now there it was, blaring away. How more appropriate, in the circumstances, could you get?

But, in all of the years that the pair of us had been together, and through all the various troubles we'd experienced during that time, I had never seen her look anything quite like the way she did now. There was really something fierce about her stare from across the street. It seemed so sickeningly vindictive – even for her – and I didn't fucking like it. Moreover, it was clear she'd been standing there for some considerable time. Not taking her eyes off Beni now – who had just emerged through the doorway onto the main street. Making her way past the monument – when, as if out of nowhere, who appears, only Jimjoe White – sporting a spotless Panama hat, which he doffed in a most decorous manner.

—Ah, Miss Banikin. I was hoping I might run into you again. You see, when we met earlier on, you neglected to inform me that I was enjoying the pleasure of speaking to a dramatist of some distinction.

You could see Beni wondering:

—How could he possibly have known that?

Out of the corner of her eye, she could see the woman in the red leather coat attempting to conceal herself behind the monument, a limestone obelisk erected to the memory of Ireland's dead. The mayor shaded his eyes and smiled.

—Ah, poor Esther McCaul, he sighed, turning back towards Beni, she's not the worst, no matter what they might say.

He placed his hand tenderly on Beni's shoulder, brightening as he continued:

—But tell me, Miss Banikin, things are going well for you in New York? I spent a lot of time out there, you know. I had all sorts of ideas when I came back from the States. Do you happen to know Gary, Indiana at all?

Beni shook her head. And in fact what she said was absolutely true – she didn't know the city, even though she'd grown up in the state.

Jimjoe White turned his hat in his hands.

—After my wife took sick, he murmured, I'm afraid I had no choice but to come home. The irony is that after all this time she's still with us. It's a wasting disease. Some folks thinks that maybe it's already gotten as far as her brain. Well, anyway, right now I've got to go home and look after her. I mean – I'm not like some people. I mean, what I'm saying is – I'm not like one of these self-serving rats! Who care about nothing only themselves!

—Rats? she replied – understandably flummoxed.

He laughed uproariously.

—Goodbye, Mrs Rat! I'll be seeing you! he said.

And then was gone.

As a matter of fact, and to Beni's utter astonishment, he was actually already halfway down the street. A development which she was on the verge of analysing when she found herself once more taken aback by the sudden sound of an elderly voice. The stooped, grey-haired lady was crossing herself gravely as she made her approach.

—You're from America, aren't you? she said, I *know*!

Continuing to stare at her intently.

In spite of her seeming frailty, Beni found her presence quite overwhelming. As she spurted through thin lips:

—They've been trying to turn this place into a pit! Into a Godless, whoremongering pit! Like the place you come from. Is that

what you're here for – to give them assistance? Along with that fellow you were smiling and joking along with just there – the one they used to call 'The Dog'. Do you know that he once cut a man's finger off – and made him eat it in front of his children? That's a great soldier – a right fellow to be electing mayor! Perhaps you think I'm wrong for saying that? Maybe you have fellows like him in America. Well – do you? Do you have them in New York, which is where you come from – or so I'm told, Miss Beni Banikin!

Did they know absolutely everything about a person in this place? you could hear Beni thinking.

With a wisp of smoke coiling against the steely backdrop of a lowering sky. As I knew only too well, it wasn't a good thing to have happened, for it brought her back to the words of her Belle Vue psychiatrist.

—Are you familiar with the work of Sylvia Plath? he had enquired. After which, as a matter of fact, she had become acquainted with her fellow American's famous novel *The Bell Jar*. Which, as she turned the pages, had really quite astonished her, for she might have been reading a description of her own emotional life. Detailing minutely – as it did, and quite breathtakingly – those shockingly debilitating sensations of vertiginous panic that had assailed her sporadically – for as far back as she could remember. And for which the imaginary figure of Mr Bones from her time in Storyville might have been some horrid physical manifestation. But the unfortunate thing now – again she felt queasy – was that she could sense it beginning to happen all over again. She trembled coldly and went back inside the hotel. Behind her Esther peeped out from behind the obelisk.

Hunted, white-faced and biting her lip so hard it almost bled.

*

It was like the world was proceeding beyond glass. So she knew what was coming. But she had strategies now – and had no intention of letting it overpower her. One thing for sure – and her psychiatrist had been of immense assistance in helping her to realise the importance, nay the sheer *necessity* – of this decision – she certainly wasn't going to seek refuge in alcohol.

—That's just about the last thing, in any circumstance whenever these feelings begin to threaten, that you want to do, the doctor in Belle Vue had warned her numerous times. It didn't matter, for anyway, she felt much better now. Why, it was really quite extraordinary this time! she thought – all of that without even the aid of a single tablet!

Unzipping her iPad, she tumbled luxuriously onto the bed. As I sat here, fretful, watching her from the mantelpiece – where she had temporarily set me down again. Grinning delightedly as the machine began to power up and a trio of glistening bodies filled the screen, writhing underneath the masthead *Sapphic City*. She emitted a cry of physical desire, unbuttoning her shorts as she forcefully gripped her loins.

When had she ever felt so good? she asked herself.

—*Bell Jar!* she grunted, imagining herself in bed with Sylvia Plath.

By the time she was finished, she was really quite exhausted, and a woman in leather lingerie was staring at her from the floor.

---

After that she fell asleep. And it was then that she saw it – the narrow-looking face of the black-clad Johnny Roxbury, like some lopsided Elvis in a white-stitched black denim, standing by the mantelpiece with his crooked grin and butch-waxed hair.

—I fucked you before and I'll fuck you again, he taunted.

There really can be no describing the degree of quite appalling anxiety she was now beginning to experience. My heart went out to her, but I mean what in Christ's name could I do from the mantelpiece?

Then he was gone – just as unexpectedly. And in his place – a familiar chilling voice – that of a certain housemistress from the long ago.

—She commits herself to bodily pleasures. That is what she does. Many times I have looked in her mind and read there appalling desires of which I shall not speak, for I would not dare to.

Her tone was as firm and stiff as ever, standing there in her fisherman's sweater.

—Did you know I wanted to be an actress when I was young, Bethany? she was saying now. But I never got the opportunity, I'm afraid. Not that it matters – for Karsten Bloch, she isn't bitter, Bethany. But to make up for it now I have come to request a little assistance. You see, I want you and I to put on our own little play. One in which you shall play the part of my own litttle mousey. In the play my new name shall be Mr Carson Block, and what fun we shall have as I stroke my little mousey. With my great belly puffed out as I woo my pet and tug her by her little tail. That will be our own special play. The beginning of which shall see me arriving up to the door of the orphanage, to request my Bethany, who I shall then take with me to my sweet home in the heartland.

—Ah, The Meadowlands!

It was hard not to think that as I stood there watching Bethany dream. Powerless, condemned to be utterly ineffectual.

—As together we return to my home in the good place, to that hazy land of the blood-red setting sun – where as one we'll abide

in my mansion with its garden of solfaterre roses. So come here to me now, my perfect little mousey, and give your Karsten the sweetest little kiss!

—*I'm not a mouse!* Beni screeched as she shot awake – with her face entirely covered in perspiration. *I'm not a fucking mouse, you freak!*

Once in a Goshen garden Beni had come upon a thick black mass of what she had taken to be an old tennis ball secreted beneath a hedge that, to her astonishment, had transpired to be a thick black mass of cobwebs, which, when stirred gingerly with her stick, had sent several large spiders running out of it along the grass. It seemed to her as though her thoughts were those very spiders now. Returning to scamper across her cold moist skin, with thread-thin legs traversing her entire body, fanning out in military platoons.

In times of trouble, when her body stiffened – just as it was beginning to do again now in the silent gloom of her hotel room – those spiders would march in regiments across the surface of her cold skin. She could feel their wiry crooked legs so intensely as she lay here.

One of the spiders had a face like Johnny Roxbury.

—*Yuk! Yuk!* he snorted, they is yo' bones and ah'm goan jump 'em!

And throughout it all, I had no option but to watch. Devastatingly, humiliatingly impotent.

That's been the legacy of Gabriel King – erotic failure, superannuated soldier.

---

I had known for a long time she had attempted various poems on this theme of sexual confusion – but had never been happy with any of them.

—Sometimes I make myself sick, she had confided in me. As she quoted John Berryman's poem about Mr Bones, in which he refers to his marvellous good fortune.

By which he meant he died.

—Jesus, babe – I could be doing without that, I said.

But she just stared straight ahead, and didn't speak for the rest of the afternoon – the whole day as a matter of fact, if I recall.

That was the fall of 2003 and we had already been travelling for three weeks or so. It was after that 'confession', if you could call it that – more of a hapless attempt at self-analysis – she'd made the suggestion that maybe it might be an idea to head down south. Which was why we'd ended up in Storyville. Where, I guess, she just wanted to confront her demons, insisting that we head down to Baton Rouge, where Karsten used to take her and her little friend Li for a drive every Sunday. That was the day I gave her what she called her *eureka moment*. We'd been just sitting there, chilling, toking there in the Trans Am.

—I can't pretend to know a whole lot about literature, Beni, but I've done a bit of reading here and there, and it seems to me that whatever the source of your troubles might be, part of it has got to do with the fact that you don't have the guts to bite the bullet. If you don't confront things and keep on making excuses all that will happen is – these insecurities of yours – they'll just go on growing inside of you like a cancer.

—I know that, Gabriel. But the truth is I just can't seem to write any more. Everything I do, it all seems so fucking derivative. Like bad Anne Sexton, third-rate Sylvia Plath. Jesus Christ, there are

times when I literally cringe with embarrassment at some of my efforts. And if I can't write I'm nothing, believe me.

I tried to comfort her as best as I could – using my own experiences, for what they were worth.

—You know, there are ways out of all these things, just so long as you don't panic. Try not to get so agitated, Beni. And I only say that because I know exactly what it's like myself. Over in Africa if I hadn't ultimately faced my problems – look, I came to the conclusion that if I didn't address them I was ruined. And it'll be the same for you, Beni – you've just got to work this problem through. As well as that, you've got to get back to the place where you and Mia once were.

About that particular relationship she had pretty much told me everything, revealing details I wouldn't have expected her to share. But she couldn't have helped herself even if she'd tried – she so admired and truly loved Mia. Who became what they call her 'muse', effectively. You could see that onstage. Especially in *The Night Visitor*.

—The truth is, Beni, out in Africa we didn't actually do very much at all. I mean there were swimming pools, naked parties, but generally very little action. Fact of the matter is, there were guys out there who were so coked up most of the time that they didn't know where they were. I figured pretty soon I was going to go the same way myself. Then out of the blue I received the letter from Jimjoe. That was really the beginning of it all. Dog had already done a stretch and was a hero, even at that stage. He'd been arrested and charged with crimes against the state, but from the moment he'd been lifted had defiantly declared that he would never wear 'any convict's uniform'. I thought about it long and hard, Beni.

I remember a long, contemplative silence – but a close one, and a warm one.

—It wasn't a decision that was easy to make, though, I told her, coming back from Angola to fight in the North of Ireland. But sometimes you've just got to face things – stand up for what you believe. Comes a time when you've just got to look things square in the teeth. Like you, in your own way, have got to do now. It's clear you got a gift and you know that. But you have to have the courage to honour it.

After their break-up Mia had been given custody of William, their adopted son. Principally because of Beni's drugtaking and recently diagnosed mental instability, for which the doctor in Belle Vue had prescribed Cymbalta. And which had been the most significant intervention – acting as a stabilising agent that had, effectively, changed Beni's life. And helped her and Mia at last to get back on track.

—Did it ever occur to you that you mightn't be destined to be a poet at all? I suggested – it was a possibility that had been on my mind for a long time. Initially she had seemed deeply shocked. Really quite affronted. But I had gone so far now it didn't matter a great deal. So I just continued:

—That some other form might be more suited to your talents – the theatre, for example?

I had taken the liberty of buying her the book – the collected Noh plays of W.B. Yeats – just on an impulse in Barnes and Noble. And I have to say that the effect they had on her really was quite extraordinary. For almost as soon as she read them, she became obsessed – that's the only word I can use – and wouldn't leave them out of her hands for a second. Her *eureka moment*, she started calling it then. I was pleased with that.

—I wouldn't have had the confidence to tackle it before, odd as it might seem had never even considered the stage. Your faith gave me confidence, she told me, along with the sheer electricity of the

Noh play form. Not to mention the creative possibilities!

And a month or so later had shown me what became the very first page of *The Night Visitor*, a 're-imagined version', as she called it, of the celebrated Yeats ghost-drama *Dreaming of the Bones*. In which, with distressing familiarity in the light of subsequent events, a shade seeks release from passionate sins committed when living.

—You're halfway there. Now all you got to do is go all the way, I suggested.

Which she did. To, as it proved, triumphant effect.

She had finished the first few pages in the Wisconsin library.

—You know what it was like, Gabriel? she said to me afterwards. Like I was coming home, that's all I can say about the effect it had on me. Writing all those pages without so much as pausing for breath, all twenty of them, in an unbroken succession of images. You know what it did? That play – it saved me, Gabriel, I swear to Jesus that's what it did. And it would never have happened without your advice.

But neither of us had been remotely prepared for what transpired – its extraordinary success off-Broadway, initially. Before it transferred onto a major stage.

It was just about the last thing we had expected, to be honest. Not to mention the rave in the *New York Times*:

A *W.B. Yeats dance-drama on poppers:* The Night Visitor *defies all expectations – readers, please welcome a literary sensation!*

---

*Thank Christ it's morning at last!* Beni Banikin was thinking – lifting my own spirits as much as her own in the process, making her way out of the hotel onto the main street.

Before, to her dismay – and, of course, hardly surprisingly, mine also – catching a glimpse of Esther McCaul, standing across the street as before, crouched in the doorway of a dilapidated pub. McHugh's, as it happens – a place in which we had spent our share of time over the years. Frantically smoking again as before – with her head like a small bird's shooting up and down the length of the street. But now there was something different about her – a new sense of purpose. The source of which wasn't hard to figure out – I had seen it a hundred times, as I did again now, watching her shove the empty naggin bottle back into her handbag. As she bore down on Beni – looking utterly drained from her night of broken sleep and erratic dreams. Snapping bitterly, wringing her hands as she did so, attempting as best she could to suppress her violence:

—*I've got something to say to you! Are you listening to me? I lived with Gabriel King and knew him far better than the likes of you ever will. So get out of this town while you can! Do you hear me, Yank? If you know what's good for you!*

And that was it – she turned and disappeared into another bar.

One thing about Beni – long as I've known her, I knew how in extremity she could be capable of a fierce, cold, calculated defiance. And which was now yet again in evidence even as she did her best to steady her cold, shaking hands. Thinking to herself, well, if that little episode was supposed to intimidate her then that little lady had better go and have another motherfucking think to herself.

As all the spiders scurried away. And she imagined herself confronting her adversary inside the bar.

—You're going to be allowed to bother me, girl? You think that that's gonna be the way it is, that that's gonna be allowed to happen? Well, somehow I don't think so! Look at me!

Repeating it when she'd been sufficiently cowed:

—*Look at me!*

And in her mind's eye seeing all of the other smalltown barflies turning away.

As once more off she strode, with a renewed determined purpose making her way in the direction of Iron Mountain for her *recce*. Eventually arriving at the quarry where she found the landscape littered with torn-up machinery and old rusted wrecks. In the middle of enjoying Yeats's peace coming 'dropping slow' as she stood amidst the debris before becoming arrested by a flurry of rocks which suddenly came rolling towards her down the slope. Clearly caused by the arrival of the hulking overweight figure standing staring at her from the summit. Where he remained for some considerable time – before arriving up beside her with the sweat cascading onto his shirt. He must have been in his seventies, she thought – hopelessly out of breath, and with such a high colour she feared he might have a heart attack on the spot. A couple of sad wet strands of grey hair limped apologetically across his shiny crimson dome. As he mopped his moist forehead with a massive white handkerchief.

—What do you think you're playing at? she demanded edgily. Have you been watching me? How long have you been up there? Did you follow me out from the town – well, did you? *Answer me!*

—I hope I didn't startle you, Miss, he said. If you like, I'll go off – I'll go away about my business. It wasn't my intention to upset you in any way.

Then, to her astonishment, he burst into tears.

—It's just the time of year, he began explaining, every time it comes around I tell myself I won't do it – no, I won't go out to the lake, I say. Ulick, for Christ's sake, stay home, I say. But it's

like something inside of me compels me, you know? And then there I am – going through the whole dreadful nightmare again. When, that day in '79, when I received the news that was to change my life. Not that you should be expected to know about it, daughter. It was just a bad time in this country, that's all. Nobody seemed, really, to understand what was going on. This much I do know, however, and you've got to believe me. And that is – that my son Bobby would never do anything bad. He was a good boy, Miss. A great boy, really, to tell you the truth. His mother died, you see, when all of them were young. I have three other children. They're all away now.

Drawing his clenched fist towards his chest, he closed his eyes tightly, almost lapsing into a trance.

—He was hardly gone nineteen. There was all this talk about impending civil war. Any time now – that was what they were always saying, *any time*. But Bobby didn't care. The only thing he cared about was having a laugh. You know what he did? He played with his pals in this little band that they had. Forget what it was called – some daft stupid name.

—*Gabriel and the Fuck-Ups*, I cried out – but I might as well have been the wind.

There were tears in his eyes and he gripped her firmly by the wrist – abstractedly.

He didn't even know that he was doing it.

—They were always hanging around the house, you know? And I knew something was wrong with Bobby but I couldn't say what. He became sullen, withdrawn. But I had never expected anything like what happened. Absolutely not, Miss – you've got to believe me. I got the call at around 3 a.m. When I arrived out here – at the lake, I mean – the place was already swarming with police. Police and ambulances. They had found him slumped in the cab

of the truck, they told me. Then it didn't take long for the rumours to start. About his having committed suicide and all that. People can be cruel, Miss. So cruel, Miss, insensitive and cruel. That's all of thirty-five years ago now, believe it or not. Then they started saying that he'd been planting bombs around the area for some time – and had been responsible for shooting an off-duty policeman. They had even suggested he might have been at Altnavogue. My boy! At Altnavogue! Jesus Christ, did you ever hear the like! Even the very possibility of such a thing would make me want to die! Killing a little baby infant like that – throwing him into the fire! But my conscience is clear regarding that – because I know it isn't true. Ah, well. I suppose I'll be meeting my own end soon. You have to know that I loved our Bobby so much. I'll be glad, in a way, to get to the graveyard. Then the two of us might be together. You never know. Well – I guess I'd best be off. It was really nice to meet you, Miss.

---

I would have done anything to stop it happening – shield her eyes so she wouldn't make the discovery. But that isn't possible – after all, it's been ordained. Well – hasn't it? What choice do I fucking have? Anyway, it was the first thing she saw as soon as Beni opened the door of her room.

*Get out of town, interfering Yankee bitch!*

The message was scrawled on the mirror in lipstick.

---

Which, obviously, was the main reason that the spiders made their return. That night, and in droves. With their feet stiffening

like bristles as they marched in formation – just like they used to when the Amish women would beat her. Whenever she had reported, in her innocence, what she thought of now as 'the pictures' – portents, essentially, presentiments – often chilling. And which, she could feel it, were coming again now. She saw herself standing at the edge of a wood. Where a party of men was approaching through the trees – a symmetrical line of stirless Scotch firs. It had been raining earlier but now the air was steaming, refreshed. One of the men was wearing a Panama hat. And she recognised his face immediately – how could she not? It was the mayor, Mr White.

—We do what we came to do, then we go. That's all he said.

With not a trace of emotion in his voice.

Then they emerged into a clearing, before approaching the small stone cottage. There was a rain barrel to the side of the little cabin and pecking around the back, a few scattered fowl.

—I never thought my neighbours would do the like of this to me, said the woman, pleading on her knees, to the masked man with the rifle.

—I'm sorry but we have to. The reason being that youse are Protestants, you see.

As a shadowy figure stepped out from a recess, standing staring above the baby's cradle.

And it was at that point she woke up, drenched in sweat, with the spiders running amok all along the length of her body. Without thinking, clambering over to the closet to check that the urn was still there where she'd secreted it after the 'mirror' episode. To her immense relief, finding that it was.

Exactly where she'd left it.

—Hi, my name is Johnny Roxbury, I'm a software engineer

from Mississippi and ain't nothin' ah laaks better'n makin' out with dykes. So if you'll do me the honour, Miss . . . !

A spider with a head like Elvis. A tiny little Elvis head and little wriggly furry legs. She felt like crying – almost dropping the urn. But she couldn't – she *wouldn't* – let this happen!

But that was easier said than done, and when another regiment of the insects returned, with – it seemed – considerable reinforcements, it was hardly all that surprising that her already hot mind, troublingly fevered as it was, might begin to make daring incursions into the realm of the unreal. Only on this occasion – principally because she had omitted to ingest her Cymbalta – already showing familiar – at least to me – signs of renouncing residence in the charted regions of what is commonly called certitude. She couldn't stop walking around the room – fearful if she slept that the spiders would devour her. Outside, the world proceeded as if behind glass – thick glass, like that of a bell jar. Thinly, but frenetically – that was how it seemed to her. As the *commedia dell'arte* pictures began to form.

It was a quiet night in the serene little Amish village. All the children had been put to bed and the mamas and papas were weaving and quilt-making or else quietly reading the Good Book by the fire. All except Cooper Kemble, who was trembling in the silence of the barn where he had been waiting for some considerable time in the quiet. Trying his best once more to resist the temptations which had been plaguing him relentlessly all that day. But try as he might, he could not reject the overwhelming allure of Fannie Banikin. The neighbour with whom he'd enjoyed illicit congress the previous Sabbath. And was now on the verge of doing it again.

—Her body is the rock upon which I shall perish. And there seems to be nothing in this earthly world I can do about it, for Fannie Banikin, the temptress, has me in thrall.

---

For those trapped in the bell jar the world itself was the bad dream – for they themselves were blank and stopped as a dead baby. But at least, she thought, at least Sylvia Plath – she hadn't had to contend with spiders, tunnelling mercilessly underneath her skin. At least she hadn't had to endure that.

—Like I do! she moaned.

Before emitting a long and almost convulsive sobbing wail. When the handle of the door began to vibrate and, with a gaze as dilated as that of a somnambulist, she cried aloud as the door came bursting open, splintering soundlessly before her very eyes. As a Kawasaki motorbike came gliding through the astonishing light-filled aperture – soundless, without ceremony. It seemed the most natural thing in the world, just like a scene she might have dreamed up for her play. Elated, she realised – because of the fact that the rider actually knew her name!

—I've brought someone with me!, she heard him declare.

He removed his helmet. It was W.B. Yeats. With his great leonine, aristocratic head held back in hauteur.

—I believe you know one another, said the poet.

The pillion passenger was courteous and elegant.

—I'm the Countess Cathleen, Miss Banikin, she said. Perhaps you might recognise me from one of the maestro's most celebrated works, the eponymous CC – a verse-drama in which I'm to be found scouring the famine-ravaged countryside in a search for the souls of the ragged and starving – extending her hand as Beni Banikin fainted.

★

Lying there still asleep on the bed, it seemed like she was miles and miles from her home in Long Island but somehow the poet was observing the Manhattan skyline.

As the Countess Cathleen, attired in tweed skirts, paced the floor wringing her hands in deep contemplation.

—It's been a long and arduous journey for you, Miss Banikin, she was saying, and don't think for a moment we aren't aware of that. But be assured that Mr Yeats here and I – we are convinced that you have the makings of a world-class dramatist.

The Countess was grinning quite impishly as she stood over her. And Beni was not entirely surprised when she felt her cup her vulva in her small firm hand.

—Can you feel that? she whispered.

—Yes, Beni nodded – a little fearful, as the aristocrat's tweeds billowed around her buttocks.

—Easy, *alanna*, no need to be afraid, all I want is your body and your soul.

And it was at that point Beni felt the thrust of the leather phallus – thick and hard as it pressed against her.

—*Hush now!* urged the Countess, and through pleasure I will release you from the torment of your anxieties. Through pleasure and excess we will bid goodbye to the spiders. And when you wake in the morning you'll be spent. Yes – and happy, my dear.

W.B. Yeats was still standing quite motionless by the window.

—You know, these charlatan physicians such as those in Belle Vue know nothing of artists such as us. So let me say this – whether it be the pleasures of Cathleen or those afforded by the imbibement of alcohol, what I have to say to you, Miss Banikin, is – *play on!*

—Fuck me, Countess! She groaned, as she repeated, Yes, *fuck me*!

With their bodies writhing far into the night. All through the dream where the spiders remained in pacific slumber, leaving the

field clear to an aristocrat with a basket, ever so patiently trawling a scorched and devastated land.

However unexpectedly, I in my own way knew about similar, quite unearthly hallucinations – and the mood of exhaustion which inevitably succeeds such states of heightened awareness – that strange emptiness that so often follows hard upon them. Principally, I guess, because on the fortieth day of my hunger strike, I had become been visited by a similar figure who might well have been conjured up by Mr Double-You-Bee Yeats. Standing, sepulchrally, staring right at me – from the bottom of the rough plank that served as a bed. Smiling as he approached me, attired in his waiter's livery, complete with dicky bow and crisp white gloves, ferrying a silver catering dome. Underneath which, as I was to discover, when he removed the gleaming hood with a flourish, lay a single snow-white orchid on a plate. Accompanied by a note printed in italicised gold leaf, which read: *A single flower for the unmourned dead.*

—Don't you ever feel guilty? smiled the waiter as he made his departure.

A question which he needn't have bothered his fucking ass posing – because of course I did – absolutely, I felt guilty. Was it not, for Christ's sake, the reason I had straight up disobeyed a direct order from Dog White?

—You've been selected to take part in the raid on Altnavogue, he told me.

Well, I don't for a moment regret standing up to him, even though I knew what the consequences might be. But it meant the beginning of the end for me in the IRA, and wasn't without its effect on my close comrades either. But, like I said to the Bonner twins:

—I'm sorry, Toby – I regret it, Hushabye, but this has all the hallmarks of a sectarian operation and I simply cannot condone or be a part of it.

It was unfortunate, all of it – but sooner or later it was bound to happen. I didn't like the way the movement was going – it had been dishonoured far too many times already, as far as I was concerned.

—That's just the way things are, I said to White – as he gave me that look, not saying a word.

—I see, he said, staring at me resolutely, unflinching.

—I see, Gabriel. Well, if nothing else, you've made yourself clear.

When she awoke the following morning Beni felt quite delirious, purged in the most magnificent way. It was unlike anything she had ever experienced before, and both her cheeks were touched with a roseate shade of post-coital bloom. It was as if the bell jar had been inexplicably hauled away – as though it had never existed, in fact. And as for spiders – especially those with a face like Elvis Presley's – well, what were they?

—This is the first day of the rest of your life, she laughed.

Ta Ta had used to say that in the mall, whenever they rode on the bus to South Bend.

---

Down in the lobby the festival festivities were already in full swing. There was a Cadillac streamered in pink on a rotating stand. Locals got up as various screen characters were milling around everywhere – among them Clint Eastwood and Mr Potato Head, the character from *Toy Story* so adored by their son William. And who, as a

matter of fact, made Beni laugh aloud, cartwheeling hilariously the way that he did, after thrusting a flyer into her hand.

—I love Vangelis! she heard Mia murmur, as she passed by a huge billboard advertising *Blade Runner.* Their music just takes me to some kind of arcadia, a place where everything just seems to make sense. That beautiful unicorn – ice-cream white, cantering out across the heavens.

—Do you know why he appears?

—No, replied Beni.

—He comes to give form to the love that we feel.

It was through art that everything had happened for her and Mia. That was what the Countess had been trying to tell her.

—If you hadn't had the strength to find yourself through art it might never have happened for us, Mia had insisted, but somehow, eventually, and indomitably, you did. And now little William is our endless source of pride and joy.

She felt so proud. Because it was nothing short of a miracle, what had happened. But there was one person who'd helped her whose name had not been mentioned. And that was Gabriel King, she thought. As a single tear moistened her eye.

She nearly fell over as Buzz Lightyear gave her a push.

—*Toy Story* is the theme of the festival this year! *Toy Story*, *Toy Story*, *Toy Story*, hooray! he squealed.

As Mr Potato Head performed a series of cartwheels.

---

She sat at the bar but wasn't going to have a drink. What on earth would she do that for? She didn't need one. How would you need

one when you actually felt exultant, elevated – delirious, indeed, having succeeded in banishing all those motherfucking spiders and smashed the glass of a bell jar – on your own! Then she thought of the great W.B. Yeats, her hero. And how he'd described the peace that 'came dropping slow'.

As it did like a floating silken parachute, billowing softly out over her soul as she sat there, trying not to indulge in thoughts of her recent extraordinary success – which had changed her life, validated her in a way that heretofore she would not have imagined possible. And for which she owed an enormous debt of gratitude – to two people.

—Go off and find yourself, Mia had advised – in fact demanded. Look at yourself every day in the mirror and decide whether or not you like what you see. Do what you have to do, I implore you. But make no mistake about this, Beni – I won't go on paying the price for your neuroses. Find yourself, you hear me? And then – just maybe – you and I can start over.

—Did you ever think, maybe, that poetry isn't your thing at all – that your talents might lie in some other form?

—Such as drama, she heard herself whisper – as a radiant smile broke out across her face. And she felt like crying to the entire hotel lobby:

—Thank you, Gabriel! Thank you, Mia! How, oh my God, I love you both!

---

I knew it was hard for her to reveal the details. A lot of things she hadn't admitted to herself. We'd been heading for Graceland when I heard her say in a cracked, tense voice:

—I want to tell you something.

We had come pretty close to the truth, again, that evening. When we'd gone to Suzie Mae's to hear some music. She was lashing the brandies down, as I remember – something which she had been mortally warned against – by, among others, Dr Gartland, the world-famous psychiatrist and physician. She was white while she was telling me. But after that night a new kind of closeness began growing between us.

—Sexual confusion, she had whispered, all the while shivering – and after which she had clung to me almost hysterically.

Back at the motel, a lot of the time she was incoherent – and couldn't manage to sit still, pacing the room – I guess, like she says, in flight from the spiders. Who, if she lay down, would go to work on her comprehensively.

—I even have dreams about her being jealous – of *you*, for Christ's sake! she wept.

I dampened a cloth and insisted she lay down. Then I placed it on her hot forehead and gripped her hand, telling her:

—Breathe in and out.

Which she did, like Mia showed her. Gradually her heart began slowing down.

—I had always suspected she was mentally unstable, she began, trembling, the things she used to say. In the dream she was standing there just like she used to. In that stained old sweater, white with fury as she fumbled with her keys. So you think you've trumped me, do you, Madam? she kept saying. Think you've got it made now with your gallant Irish soldier by your side to protect and look out for you? Feels good, does it, lying there guarded by your handsome IRA warrior? But when are you going to tell him the *real* truth? About how it was *you* who loved *me* and not, as you say, the other way round? When are you going to tell him

. . . *that!* You enjoyed Baton Rouge and don't you ever dare say that you didn't!

And she remembered it well. How could she not, when it was the best show ever in the state of Louisiana. Beni and her little fellow orphan friend Li had been allowed to dress up especially for it. Li had been given a majorette's uniform, with Bethany permitted to hold her hand in public. She was wearing white gloves the housemistress had bought for her. And now here they all were, lined up in front of the stand, holding their breath with luxurious apprehension. Already a constellation of coloured balloons had been released. With the trumpets and trombones playing gaily and the cadets looking splendid in their military tunics.

—Isn't this just the best? It's an amber day, my sweet girls! Karsten Bloch had trilled, triumphantly handing her 'special pupil' a tray of sweet potato.

—With cinnamon, Bethany! she cried gaily, which I know that you love!

As the cymbals crashed gaily high upon the stage. And Bethany Banikin found herself quivering with desire – even to the extent of being jealous of Li. Fearful that their housemistress might demonstrate more affection for her – burning Bethany up in a fire of total shame.

---

Like had happened on so many previous occasions, I knew I oughtn't to have left her in the motel, but that's what I did that particular night in Cleveland. Which was more unforgivable than usual because I suspected that she'd been drinking again – brandy,

too, which inevitably proved fatal. She and Mia had had a row on the phone.

—Fuck you, then! I'd bawled and stormed out, through the blinding rain towards the bar – any bar. Far behind me I could hear her pleading:

—Gabriel, where are you? Don't leave me, Gabriel! Gabriel, I don't feel so good! Come back! Will you – please?

The bar I ended up in was another juke-joint of sorts, and wasn't all that far away as it happened. But by the time she discovered it, I was already far gone. Soon as she came in, a couple of barflies eyed her keenly, pool cues in hand. She looked wretched – wan and bloodless – just like she always did whenever she'd been drinking. If the doctor in Belle Vue was a quack, like W.B. Yeats had suggested in her dream, then I'm afraid it didn't look like that to me. He was right about everything he had told her. Strange thing was, she reminded me of Esther. Frangible – is that the word? – and on the verge of slipping off this roof she was always talking about, into the yawning maw of a vertiginous pit.

—What's he been telling you? What's he been saying? she had screeched at them, zigzagging palely towards the bar counter.

—This guy? one of them had shrugged. Half the time I couldn't honestly say for sure. Couldn't make out all that much of what he was trying to say. Just kept going on about Africa and shit. Guess they fried his head or something over there – huh, lady?

Can't say really how she forgave me for that one. Maybe on account of being impressed with my resilience or courage or something – I don't know. Because it was the first time, I suppose, that I'd actually described my experiences on my hunger strike in any detail.

—Fifty-five days, I kept repeating, it does things to your mind.

And maybe she felt a certain sympathy. Perhaps thinking of me lying on those rough bare boards, with my ribs sticking out and with only a matter of mere days to live.

—I love you, you bastard, she had said, against the odds.

And after that I had made her a promise – resolved not to repeat that behaviour again – all that bullshit – getting drunk, disappearing – whatever.

—You promise?, she had said.

—My word is my bond, I replied – nodding vehemently.

And it is.

Just as it always has been.

For if you don't have that – then what do you have?

I loved Beni Banikin – she meant everything to me.

And I loved the movement, same way as I love my country.

Which is the reason I would willingly lay down my life. Even yet. Even after all that's happened.

*Sandy & Ginger* was a movie we had made up one night we were stoned, the pair of us just lying there listening to Elvis crooning. 'In the Ghetto', as I recall. I elected to be 'Sandy the drifter'.

—Levon Helm, that's who we'll get to star as you, with your sandy hair and all those tattoos.

—Yes, I laughed, and although she didn't get quite what I meant, it had amused me when I said:

—And Michael J. Pollard to do your part. Ha ha!

I had almost collapsed with laughter when I thought of it. Looking back, it's just as well she didn't understand what I was saying. For I can't imagine her taking it too well.

—C.W. Moss! I kept on laughing – in falsetto!

It really was just as well she didn't know what I was on about – I mean, I *know* she would have freaked!

I guess, who wouldn't?

As we kept on cruising our way across the country – Sandy and Ginger in their busted-up 'Chevvy'.

—Freebie and the Bean, Smokey and the Bandit.

—Tango and fucking Cash, she laughed, skinning up another jay.

—You're a real Southern boy at heart, ain't you? she said. Looking like you do with that missing incisor and that hard angular redneck jaw of yours.

—Maybe, I agreed, but you ain't no Amish – leastways not any kind that I been used to.

—You're the man from The Meadowlands, Gabriel, she said, the lone warrior that got out just in time. And I'm glad you did. I'm grateful, more than anything, that you somehow managed to survive that awful conflict.

—If we ever had a kid, that's what I'd call him, Beni, I grinned. The Prince of The Meadowlands – I've decided that that would be his name.

—The Prince of The Meadowlands. What a lovely idea. Maybe we could make a little movie with William.

—William could be The Prince of The Meadowlands, I agreed. You know, I think you're on to something there!

Then we fell asleep like a pair of kids in one another's arms.

It was the first time we came close to actually making love, or anything like it.

—I've never trusted anyone like this before, she said.

—My word is my bond – for if you've not got that you've got nothing at all.

I liked the way she admired me for saying that.

---

And now as she stands there in her sawn-off Wranglers, with that tight, copper buzz-cut slap-bang in the middle of Iron Valley, she might as well be back in the old home place of Indiana – or anywhere at all in that big-sky country. With everything in the valley looking exactly like it does over there, from its long lines of hoardings and brand name American franchises, to the incessant blinking green neon 24/7: STEAKS ALL DAY. BUD ON TAP.

As now, finally, she vacates the Valley Lodge Hotel – and in the height of her excitement and anticipation of what wonderful discoveries might yet be awaiting her in this most exciting, intriguing place – actually omitting to bring me with her. Which was why she had come in the first place, for heaven's sake! So I had to follow her, and willingly, from my squat place of incarceration, a little brown urn in a dark closet in a hotel.

And leaves it far behind, stomping off with the soft breeze in her face – lost in her memories of Mia and myself. Until, emanating from just beyond the hill, it begins to gradually reach her ears: the most beautiful ethereal gospel choral singing.

—Why, it's just like home!

And, boy, was she a long way from the bell jar now! Not to mention Johnny Roxbury, the spider with the stupid face.

As, exultant, she added:

—I just can't wait to see Mia's expression! What will she say when she hears that, at last – I've cracked it at last!

BJ the DJ had parked his caravan outside the churchyard gates – sitting inside in his Stetson, grinning. As what appeared to be the entire population of the valley came sweeping in waves through

the doors of the small wooden chapel. A child in calipers had been installed in a chair directly in front of the altar, flanked on either side by a number of sombre clergymen. The lachrymose hymns being relayed through the speakers and the sound of her mother's sobs were exerting a heart-rending effect on all present. As, to tremendous applause, the guest of honour was now introduced.

—I thank you for that, said US Congressman O.C. Brewster, for I know you all well enough to know that it comes from the bottom of your hearts.

OC had been coming to Iron Valley for over twenty years, he explained, and now – by this stage – felt it to be his second home.

—When I was first asked to come here, he continued, to be honest with you people, I could not find it in my heart to accept. And do you know why that was? Not because I didn't want to, or had no desire to do so, but because I did not feel worthy enough to perform the tasks that might be required of me.

Mayor White, seated in the front row with his Panama hat placed on his lap, nodded to Beni as he watched her take her seat.

—It wasn't that I wasn't qualified for the task, he elaborated, no, it wasn't that at all, believe me. For indeed, as had been suggested to me at the time, with my background, raised as I was in a divided society – how could Virginia not be, with its unfortunate history, with its many sad episodes? No, that wasn't it, for ever since I was knee-high to a rooster's hind leg—

This last remark, perhaps predictably, elicited a peal of warm recognition.

—Ever since I was so high I'd been used to tensions and difficulties of all kinds – even in that small and frankly nondescript village. Why, perhaps it was even more pronounced for that reason, so close did we live together, black and white side by side, used from the day we were born to fear and suspicion and religious intolerance.

Except that, as you all know, in great part – not entirely, perhaps, but almost – those anxieties which for so long were a part of growing up in that part of the world have been seen off. And not just by the passing of time, either, not entirely by accident. No, for people have laboured assiduously over the years in order to ensure that exactly that might happen. Just as these good people here have done.

He coughed and turned to call on Canon Bly to speak. The pastor was somewhat stooped as he crossed the floor and made his way to the lectern. From the moment he began speaking there could be no doubting the authority of his presence.

—It was the year 1976, he said softly, and I hadn't been ministering very long in Iron Valley. I was only just coming to know you all individually – and the true nature of the horror that had grown up in your midst. Of which I admit at the time I had little experience, having exercised most of my ministry abroad. Well, I was here that morning, my brethren. I happened to be here at the service, on a calm and unremarkable Sabbath morning. I was indeed present when the bad men came. Men who had nothing but hate in their hearts. Even to think of it now fills me, not with resentment, but a heartfelt pity. Pity for people who could find such brutality in their souls. I recall being made to kneel on these very steps, to fall before these masked men as they raised their weaponry. They destroyed many sacred objects in this church that day, as well as ending the lives of many innocents. Three people were left to die that morning, brethren. And do you know what those men said as they departed, having completed their work? 'That'll give you something to think about.' That's what they said. But that wasn't the end. No, horror was heaped upon horror that year. After that we had the very first hunger strikes. And tensions were as high as they could possibly get. There were a thousand troops drafted

into the valley the day the very first striker was buried. The following week there was a car bomb in Breen. On the sixtieth anniversary of the Easter uprising, it was genuinely felt that the centre could no longer hold.

At those words, Beni found herself excitedly shifting in her seat – immediately recognising the quote from her hero, Yeats.

—Mere anarchy is loosed upon the world, continued the canon, and not long after that the most closely guarded diplomat in the history of the state was blown to pieces. Not an hour's drive from here.

He turned to the congressman who now joined him at the lectern. O.C. Brewster cleared his throat.

—But like every conflict at some point, at some time, surely – it all has to end. I mean, who would ever have thought that one of the bitterest struggles in all of human history, that between the north and the south of my own country, would ever have been resolved the manner that it was? And it was, my friends, with the result that if you come and visit me in Virginia I can take you out and show you one of the most beautiful and peaceful villages that God in His mercy has ever seen fit to place upon this earth. On a sunny Sunday morning such as this, you and I can take a stroll amongst those very same people – the descendants of those who once upon a time would gladly have taken the lives of their nearest neighbours, in a manner almost unthinkable to any God-fearing human beings, and now what will you find? You will find the same economically modest but proud and religious individuals going about their business in a manner that any decent human being would approve of.

---

Outside in the hard sunshine, OC was conversing animatedly with BJ. They looked, for Christ's sake, like two extras from *Bonanza*!

But maybe that's unkind – for OC was sincere. At least he sounded like he was as he continued:

—You see, my friend, history must always reach its inevitable conclusion, for people cannot simply go on killing one another forever. Sooner or later they come to realise that.

—Sure, nodded BJ, absolutely one hundred times yes!

Then I went cold, for who came waltzing up? Only my two old friends, the fucking Bonner twins, of all people. Smiling in the company of Jimjoe White.

—Did you ever hear tell of a Roman called Seneca? he asked the congressman – who stroked his chin a little contemplatively before shaking his head.

—Not that it matters, laughed the mayor lightly, he was just an old philosopher I used to read in the old days. In prison, like.

—Aye, said Hushabye Bonner, Dog was always a great man for the reading. In the H-Blocks.

—Reading, aye, agreed his brother, nothing like a bit of hard reading.

—Seneca, laughed Dog.

—Aye, *Sennikka*, chortled Toby, he'd be the quare boy now all right!

As Hushabye leaned over, cupping his hand over the mayor's ear as he whispered:

—Aye. But just make sure the plebs don't do too much of it. For at the end of the day, people are like mushrooms. All you have to do is keep them in the dark but make sure to feed them plenty of shit.

—Ha ha, laughed Toby Bonner.

—Desperate men, all the same, the Romans – did you ever read about the Pisonian conspiracy?

—Naw, said Toby.

As his brother Hushabye shook his head. Before Dog White smirked and hooked his thumb into his waistband.

—They didn't fuck around, he said, do you know what they did when they unearthed such a thing as treason?

—I've a fair idea, replied Toby Bonner.

—Cudgelled them to death like rats in the arena.

The mayor sighed, and stared off down into the valley. But, as he turned, we might have been back in The Maze in the early eighties. The way he was looking – it seemed, right at me: although all he could have been seeing was the breeze.

I felt sick.

But everyone was smiling and laughing now, for all in all it had been a glorious afternoon. Then what did she do, Beni Banikin? Suddenly remembered! Why she had come to the valley in the first place!

It was time to get ready for the funeral, she decided.

Yes, to cast the ashes of her close friend, say goodbye to lovely Gabriel, right here in his beloved home place.

—Come on, Gabriel, it's time to go home, she sighed – with such a degree of genuine affection that it just about tore me up.

And that's the truth. You know you can believe it. No matter what White or his ilk might like to say. Whose motivation proceeds only from my reluctance to permit myself to become complicit in unnecessary murder. That night in Altnavogue, and a number of other occasions I won't go into.

He never forgave me for that – that's the truth.

Screw him – for if you don't have principles, what do you have?

Irrespective of national liberation or anything else.
And if they can't see that – well then, too bad.

---

The only reason, as Beni well knew, that the shrink in Belle Vue had advised her not to drink alcohol was not, as Yeats had suggested in her dream, because he was a quack or a charlatan or anything else, but because at the time he had given the advice she'd been *sick*. Which, magnificently, and for whatever reason, she certainly wasn't now. As she lay on the bed without so much as a spider near her skin – in it or under or anywhere near it. How lovely it was to be able to say that!

—One thing Yeats was right about, though, she found herself accepting – with a detachment and clarity she truly found remarkable – is that artists are different. And, yes, for them excess so often can prove to be the portal of discovery. And as well as that, I'm burying my old friend Gabriel! So I'll just have a single miniature from the minibar – and that's it! One and only one – no more, no less!

How wonderful it was to be in a place where not only Johnny Roxbury but the dread of the bell jar was little more than a distant memory. After another brandy, she still could not believe, though, how lucid she was proving to be. And, even after four, seemed perfectly capable of quoting favoured swathes of Willie Yeats as she lay there, flushed. Before jumping up suddenly when the knock came to the door. Opening it, expecting to be confronted, perhaps, by the turndown service. Which would normally have been the case, except not on this occasion.

His face was distorted in the sputtering wall-lamp but there could be no mistaking the face of Johnny Roxbury. With his butch-waxed black hair gleaming in the light.

—Please, she pleaded.

But already her visitor had closed the door behind him.

—*Ah's goan rape yuh!* he said as she woke up.

Realising she had just dozed off – and that she had, in fact, been lying right there on the bed all along. But with the problem being – whether she admitted it or not, and with the assistance of five miniature brandies, she had made the mistake of admitting the spiders back in.

—Nice, she heard him say, yup, jauntin' yuh bones is finger-lickin' good!

---

Staring dumbstruck at the mirror, Beni read:

CEAD MILE FAILTE ROMHAT. 100,000 WELCOMES. ROT IN HELL, BITCH!

She must have struck the desk bell six times. Finally, exasperatingly, the female clerk decided to put in an appearance, bustling up to the desk with a great big disarming smile.

—Miss Banikin! she cried. How nice to see you again. How may I be of assistance today?

—Someone has been in my room! said Beni. And I want something done about it immediately!

—What's going on? demanded the manager, arriving gravely at her side.

But the desk clerk assured him that already she had the matter

under control. Pledging to do whatever was in her power. Appearing genuinely horrified when she heard about the mirror graffiti.

—Oh, my goodness! Whatever must you think of us? Miss Banikin – that's disgraceful!

Continuing to proclaim herself 'quite mortified' by these truly dreadful developments. Which she did her level best to explain.

—You see, perhaps regrettably we have a lot of younger visitors in town for the film festival. What happened might somehow be connected with that. Miss Banikin, I simply can't tell you how sorry I really—!

But Beni was more than happy with that – quite exhilarated, in fact, if the truth is to be told. And was on the point of making her feelings clear – of protesting 'No! No! No!', in fact, reassuring the desk clerk that everything was fine – when, out of nowhere, she was knocked backwards on her heels, with her head beginning to spin – actually blacking out for a period of time, however brief.

—Jesus fucking Christ! the desk clerk screamed. At the out-of-breath youth in the Mr Potato Head outfit.

—I'm sorry, Mary! I'm sorry I'm sorry! he cried, pulling the fibreglass head off his shoulders.

—Why in Christ's name can't you watch where you're going? For the love of Jesus, watch where you're fucking going! snapped the manager, giving the youth a vicious shove. Before calling to the desk clerk:

—Call the doctor, Mary – do you hear me?

But by this stage Beni had already begun to come round.

Hearing the desk clerk shriek in the distance:

—Jesus! What in Christ's name do you think you're doing, Nuttsy? Do you want to disgrace the hotel and ruin our business?

*

With the assistance of a bellman, the desk clerk assisted Beni onto a chair.

—I have a good mind to have you all thrown out! she snapped anew at Mr Potato Head and his friends – eventually returning sympathetically to her guest.

—Are you all right, Miss Banikin, do you think that maybe I *should* call a doctor?

—No, replied Beni, I'm going to be fine. I've got something important to do. Right now, I think that I'll just go back to my room.

---

Which she did, for just one final miniature brandy. At which point – as I watched her rocking back and forth on the bed – I felt it was my turn to cry out from the pit. To call to my old friend right across time into the cosmic vastness of the town and Iron Valley. Reaching out to catch Beni, who was like a doll blown by a tornado – plucked from a Storyville orphanage long ago, borne now aloft by a raging, relentless twister. But one which, inexplicably, abated quite suddenly, and ever so gently set her down. Before out of the murk emerged Karsten Bloch.

—You're just like your mother, then, an irresponsible alcoholic?

—No, Ma'am.

—You're just like your mother then, an irresponsible alcoholic?

—Please, Ma'am.

—Your mother, in fact, who was even worse than that. Being as she was, in actual fact, a practising prostitute.

—Please, Ma'am don't say that.

—That's why she left you in the orphanage, isn't it?

—Yes, Ma'am.

—And maybe ensured that in time you yourself would become a deviant. A full-time resident of that place they call *Sapphic City*.

Beni's cheeks burned and she did her best to look away. But already the large hand was cupping her vulva.

—Please, croaked Beni.

—Hush, said Dr Karsten.

As the Countess Cathleen stepped out from the shadows.

—I'm afraid it's true, she heard her say.

Her eyes shot open as her body tightened and she felt the spiders.

—*Finger-lickin' good!* said Johnny Roxbury, running a tiny steel comb through his hair that was like furred and wavering little black legs.

As a result of which she found herself longing more than anything for the snap that gives release to strain. As she saw, to her horror – this could not be, not after the lobby incident! – that there was, in fact, someone moving about in her room! She had lost track of time. The clock dial read ten minutes after three. The scream issued from the very core of her being.

—No! Please! Don't scream! It's all right! she heard a pitiful male voice plead.

As the lights went on and she realised that it was the same swarthy idiot, the drunken moron who had knocked her over earlier, in the lobby.

—Please don't report me, will you? Don't report me! I'll do anything! – as a furious pounding came to the door.

—Are you in there, Corrigan! Corrigan – are you in there? Is Nuttsy Corrigan in there, Miss Banikin? Can you hear me? Nuttsy! Answer me, will you, you deaf and dumb fucker!

Within minutes, the contrite miscreant was being shamefully led away. This time, she was informed, they fully intended to deliver him into the custody of the police.

—This type of behaviour just cannot be tolerated, the night-manager continued to insist, with the visibly shaken desk clerk nodding vigorously in agreement.

There was only one thing Beni could think of doing now – she had, above all else, to call Mia in Long Island. In spite of the fact that she feared that Mia would know – instinctively intuit – what she had done, with the miniatures. Something which could see – she almost fainted at the thought of it – their relationship being sundered all over again. But in spite of her repeated efforts, the phone rang out. And, eventually, she decided to give up in despair. Lying there with her eyes alert and open. But this time Johnny Roxbury failed to materialise. And even the bell jar – it didn't come down. But nonetheless, her heart kept pounding. As an ice dew of perspiration, all night, seamed her forehead.

The next thing she knew was – two small taps were sounding on the door. Which she opened to find the receptionist outside, handsomely attired in a fresh new candy-striped blouse and satin cravat.

—I really am so sorry about last night, she began, thrusting a huge bouquet of red roses into her arms.

As, once again, the manager appeared, in a similar state of abject remorse.

—It really was so unfortunate, what happened, he added, offering her a box of chocolates.

—I didn't want to say, the desk clerk explained, but Nuttsy Corrigan is my brother, I'm afraid!

—Oh, that Nuttsy! Man, he's an awful character! moaned the

manager. Some of the lads around here – they really can be incorrigible!

—It's the film festival, you see, it's gone and turned the whole place upside down!

Beni saw the night manager nodding again – even more vehemently, if that were possible – wringing his hands helplessly.

—If there's anything we can – absolutely anything, Miss Banikin—!

At which point the telephone began ringing inside in her room.

—*I've got to take this!* cried Beni suddenly.

—Thanks for all your understanding!

Her heart was pounding as she gripped the receiver. William was talking non-stop about movies.

—Mr Potato – he's my favourite!

In the aftermath of that conversation, Beni decided that at last she was in a position to reassure herself – she was finally, happily, back to herself.

—*Absolutely one hundred per cent!*

—Hello, repeated Mia, hello, Beni – are you there?

As the receiver just hung there, dangling from its cord.

—Hello? Hello? Hey, Beni – are you there?

She might have been striding on stilts along the main street. Ambling into McHugh's for a shot.

—Set 'em up, Joe, she said to the barman – just joshing, that's all.

—Whee-hoo! she heard herself laughing, shaking her head and brushing the tears from her eyes.

—Are you all right, Miss? the barman asked anxiously. I mean, strictly speaking, it's way too early. I could get into trouble for serving you like this . . . !

But she couldn't seem to settle in the chair.

—*Come to picturesque Altnavogue in South Armagh!* urged the old-fashioned watercolour railway poster in front of her. As an orange sunset lit up a line of firs.

—Get out of there, Beni, I heard myself plead, please will you do that for me – get out of McHugh's? Esther McCaul might arrive in any time. Please leave that bar – get out of there now!

I didn't want her to look at the poster. I didn't even want her to see the townland's name.

Then her nose began to bleed. As she choked, *Please! No spiders!* – rocking back and forth on the chair.

—Like I say – are you all right, Miss? repeated the barman.

Then, slowly, grandly, they began to appear – in spite of my best efforts to prevent it happening. But it was out of my control, as I soon began realising – as one by one they emerged from the trees, stealthily appearing out of the woods, all along the line of dripping Scotch firs, pushing back branches heavy with rain. As they made their way determinedly in the direction of the isolated stone cottage, the little humble cabin where Nathan Douther lived with his wife Elizabeth, along with their infant son Wee Boab, and some other relatives. The gravel crunched beneath the sound of heavy boots.

—I never thought on you to do the like of this, moaned Elizabeth Douther as she died, and us 'n's neighbours this long time past.

All of the intruders were masked, but Nathan Douther found that he immediately recognised them all. Which was the reason why he got shot in the face – by Toby Bonner.

—No stir out of this one anyway, observed his twin brother,

turning over a corpse with his toe. As Jimjoe White handed over the bomb.

—Here you are, Gabriel. It's all primed and ready.

As I removed my balaclava to get a better look at what I was doing.

That night in Altnavogue, as the wind swept through the trees.

—Drop it in the cradle, Gabriel. And that'll put an end to it, once and for all.

---

As I have indicated earlier, it was T.J. Gartland – or, should I say, *Dr* T.J. Gartland, the eminent lecturer and authority on Irish history – who had insisted on bringing Beni to visit the consultant psychiatrist in Belle Vue Hospital, in the hope of ending her persistent sleepless nights, among other things. Gartland, admittedly, was an intellectual of some considerable abilities, and a long-standing friend of Mia's. Whom he had met after his arrival in New York, subsequent to the failure of the miners' strike in the UK.

—I will never again stand in my abased native country, he told me.

Initially, I really do have to say, I liked him – and a lot. Especially when he called Margaret Thatcher 'The Iron Bitch'!

—She fucked your people over, too, Gabriel – the very same as she did ours! I remember him saying.

Yes – I liked him. I have to say that I genuinely did. And admired his scholarship immensely as well.

It's just that I don't like people looking down on me, you know?

—I think you're actually misquoting that, Gabriel, was, in fact, what he had said.

When I'd casually dropped Mr 'Double-You' into the conversation – maybe, in retrospect, to impress Beni and Mia.

—*The night broke bloody in the quivering pre-dawn mist, with the cry of the curlew coming eddying through the trees: the damning screech of the cat-headed bird.*

—*The cat-headed bird* is certainly correct, he explained, but I think what you've actually done is conflated a number of Yeatsian quotes. Hang on till I check – I'll get my copy of the plays.

And of course he was right. But so what? Not that it seemed to bother him. Once he had corrected the 'autodidact' – which was how I'd overheard him describing me, one other day when I wasn't in the room. Because now he was blathering away about his mother.

—She was bipolar, you see, and you didn't know just what to expect. From one day to the next, well I guess anything could happen. Maybe that's why I understand Beni.

Yes, it could be that, I remember thinking. In the days when I still remained reasonably favourably disposed towards him. After all, Beni had learned a great deal from him. But of course it was Gartland who had kick-started her career. After all, what would I know? All I am is just a hill-valley, redneck country boy *autodidact*, ha ha!

And so on it went: the Long Island series of nightly lectures, with T.J. Gartland at the podium. With his little stubby hands folded over his waistcoat, teasing his whiskers as on and on he droned:

—Gaelic lore, as Willie Yeats knew so well, is much preoccupied with liminal states of being caught at a precise point of temporal change – much of classical Noh drama focuses on ghosts seeking release from passionate sins or errors of judgement committed while living—

I suppose I *was* a little envious – not just of the breadth of his

knowledge, but of the effect – certainly after her time in Belle Vue – which he appeared to, commendably, exert on Beni.

—I think that TJ's advice may have cured me, she told me, for without him I would never have consented to go to Belle Vue. He really is a most wonderful man.

Then, one night, entirely out of nowhere, what did I hear him say? Only:

—How many days, exactly, Gabriel, *were* you on hunger strike?

And, with the way that his fuzzy little eyebrows rode up, I might have been back in The Maze with Jimjoe White. Leafing through his copy of *The Ancient Mariner* as he sighed:

—Ah yes. *A frightful fiend doth close behind him tread.*

Then – and it quite alerted me, I have to say – just the sheer impertinence of his attitude, I suppose – when I became aware that he was still awaiting my answer.

—Well? he said, with the fat fingers still drumming on the armchair.

I didn't respond – just sat there staring over at him. For the way I reckoned it, if TJ felt, or for some reason was under the impression, that I would hop whenever *he* decided – well then, I'm afraid, he had another think coming.

So I didn't say anything, just gazed out of the window.

—I tend to feel very calm with him, she had confided to me once, and so does Mia. He really is a most extraordinary man – like a shaman who brings knowledge – and yes, a certain *calm*, wherever he goes.

---

A calm, however, which would seem to be very much under threat now, as the person in question continues to incessantly mop his

brow, making his way with a wheelchair towards the airport terminal exit. Looking resplendent in his paisley waistcoat all right, but with his little heart pounding as he tries to find the words with which to greet Mia. Advancing towards the arrivals hall of JFK Airport in New York City, where a beautiful Chinese dancer is awaiting him. Yes, for T.J. Gartland, of course – but also her partner, to whom she is devoted – who else but the lovely Beni Banikin, lately the toast of Broadway and beyond? However, it won't be the girl she has known and loved who will be returning. No, because the girl she loved is now irreversibly brain-damaged, I'm afraid. Yes, destroyed physically, I'm sorry to have to say.

And it's all my fault – for suggesting she ever make the fucking journey in the first place.

'Ashes of Love': maybe I ought to have called my story that.

Or, perhaps, just 'Love's Ashes'. The conclusion of which sees Beni Banikin appearing at last in the door of the arrivals hall – rather shabbily attired in a brown velour tracksuit, sporting a pair of great big puffy gloves, not unlike the paws of a bear, which have been generously provided by the hospital medical staff in order to ensure she does herself no serious harm. What a to-do. In the course of human affairs, it really was just about as bad as it could get. Well, it must have been – to discommode the celebrated Yeatsian authority in such a distressing fashion. As a matter of fact, Dr Gartland was actually on the verge of crying. Who ever heard of such a thing? Dr Gartland! Well, honestly! But that is the truth – that's the way it really was. Which maybe is understandable – for, after all, it was TJ who had been compelled to make all the arrangements, being as Mia was 'down under', on tour with *The Tales of Hoffmann*. And from which she had returned as soon as it was humanly possible.

★

So, I guess let's be realistic, it was hardly going to be surprising, faced with this entirely new and quite horrifying set of circumstances (Beni could now only consume food through a straw), that Mia might find herself disturbed at a level she could not even begin to comprehend. How was she ever going to cope? she asked herself. Would she be capable of living with a lover who was a cripple? And, perhaps, even more ignobly (and which, I must admit, had the effect of providing me with considerable amusement, however regrettably), – how it might possibly affect her *career*?

A variety of similar, comparably unedifying thoughts continued to career inside her mind as she scanned the faces of the approaching passengers.

—Easy, Mia! she told herself. Get yourself together – it's gonna be OK!

Succeeding in calming herself a little – before setting to biting her nails once more, and applying added pressure to the mystified William's hand.

—*Ow!* he exclaimed, releasing a short and embarrassed little laugh.

Enquiring again:

—Are you all right, Mommy?

Before tugging at Mia's sleeve and asking her once again:

—Please, Mommy! Why will you not say anything to me?

—Damn it, William, will you let go my shirt! she snapped.

There could be no mistaking the boy's crestfallen expression – or the renewed remorse which now overtook his mother.

How could it be, she asked herself, that the Beni she loved could possibly now be gone forever? What was she talking about – how *could* it be? Was it not already a *fait accompli*, for Christ's sake!

The Beni with whom she had stood on a balcony in Tokyo, telling her all about her childhood in the small Chinese village of

Matisi in the province of Gansu Sheng, where she had spent her adolescence dreaming about meeting someone like her.

—In Maria Coeli, I was the very same, Beni had responded affectionately, yearning for the day when I'd eventually be released and maybe, somehow, meet someone like you. In fact you remind me of my little friend Li – she might have been a version of you, the lovely Mia Chiang in miniature – preparing the way for this beautiful, longed-for dream.

---

—Mia, Mia, please don't cry, pleaded William, will you, Mom!

As the glass doors parted and T.J. Gartland, portly but dignified with his Willie Nelson hair tied back in a ponytail, appeared behind the wheelchair in the company of a flight attendant. It was all Mia could do not to evacuate the contents of her stomach right there on the concourse where she stood. Especially when she saw Beni's bear-paws in her lap.

---

Gartland thanked the attendant, placing his hands on the wheelchair's rubber grips, as Beni's head rolled from side to side on her shoulders. Her eyes were glazed and lifeless, and her tongue was protruding from the side of her mouth. How could this have happened, after all that they'd been through? Throughout all those days when, together, they had visited Belle Vue and triumphed. Bitterly crushed as he clearly was – perhaps characteristically – T.J. Gartland succeeded in rallying admirably.

—You sure are some dude, William son, I gotta tell you that! How about you and me go to the park later, huh?

They often went to the park. Almost every day, as a matter of fact.

—Sure thing, Teej! pealed William heartily.

He often called the doctor *Teej*.

It was kind of a private game with them.

But you could tell that the boy's heart really wasn't in it. How could it be, for it was slowly beginning to dawn on William just how serious this new set of circumstances actually was. As Beni writhed uncomfortably in her chair.

—*Mnnngh!* she groaned as they made their way towards the car lot, a dribble of saliva trickling down her chin.

---

I might have been sitting in the back with them as we drove, feeling myself also, in a special kind of way, coming home – as the taxi cruised in the direction of Long Island. With Mia still agonising over what exact story she was going to tell William. Knowing in her heart she was going to have to tell him something. Most likely *everything*, she eventually acknowledged, certainly at some point. But how much of the story did she herself know? That was the question I was posing as I sat there, examining my fingernails as I emitted a weary sigh.

Well, not a great deal, if the actual truth be told. And certainly very little of what had actually transpired on that sunny Sunday morning, back in Iron Valley, when Beni had found herself sitting on the back of a horse – and a white one, no less! – already making her way to the regatta on the lake at the insistence of her new-found friend Walter Reilly, a horse dealer who might have been a hundred years of age, for he seemed to have been in the valley for – well,

certainly as far back as I could remember. She had happened to meet him by chance on the road, making her way out at the invitation of the redoubtable Jimjoe. He said he'd have to accompany her all the way.

—Hop up there, Missus! he said, and flourished his stick. Turned out he wouldn't take no for an answer.

—A dealing man about these parts for fifty years, he told her.

Beni was in a state of radiant transcendence. Even America seemed far away. Walter had lovely dimples and eyes, she was thinking. Why, she could have listened to this fellow talking for hours, she felt so good. So far did she find herself from America – and the Amish.

Where she had found her father dangling motionless in a barn – as a consequence of her mother's relationship with the tormented Cooper Kemble. Her mother Fannie Banikin would have to quit the village at once, the elders decided. In the merry month of May in the year 1986 – as an eleven-year-old girl in Goshen, Indiana. Where her mother had commenced a thriving career in a brothel – but which Bethany didn't learn about until later – being left to the mercies of Dr Karsten and Maria Coeli.

The horse gave a whinny and they looked up to see a fellow approaching along the road, all decked out in his glorious Sabbath finery.

—Well, Walter, he exclaimed, I suppose youse are headed out to the regatta?

—Indeed and we are! Me and this lovely young girl from America!

And, before they knew it, they had arrived at the lake shore, with the frolics already in full swing in the marquee. As Tom Cruise

and Green Lantern drank beer with Marty Robbins, who ascended the stage in his white sports coat and pink carnation, calling insistently for hush.

—This fucking festival is now open! he roared, most surprisingly inducing in the process a great bout of hilarity

—I said I solemnly declare this party is now starting! he bawled again.

As, to my dismay, the band started up with 'Ashes of Love'. Sometimes my mood, you know, changes just like that. Maybe I should book an appointment in Belle Vue.

The following couple of hours proved to be among some of the most enjoyable Beni had ever experienced in her life.

As she found herself, only a few short hours later, certainly having fallen off a roof, as she often described it, but vertiginously ecstatic, and with not so much as a hint of anxiety anywhere. And certainly no hint of spiders coming travelling! Now that she was in the company of all her new-found friends – right back there in that hotel room, trying on dresses from an assortment of vintage gowns.

—This can't be happening! she kept telling herself, flushed with all the excitement.

But it was indeed. Indeed it was.

Yes, happening right there in the Valley Lodge Hotel, with Beni's bosom heaving like that of an overgrown debutante. She couldn't even remember whose idea it had been.

—I have nothing with me except jeans and T-shirts! Beni had complained.

But she didn't have to worry, Esther had told her.

Yes, you heard me right – Esther McCaul. My old common-law beauty.

I could see everything coming – but what was I in a position to do? Except wring my hands and lament the existence, sadly, in this world, of 'rascal hearts'.

Maybe Dr Gartland might have made a better night-wanderer? Do you think?

—I'm not quite convinced, I remember him saying another night, are you absolutely sure that that's the case, Gabriel?

But anyway, as I was saying – yes, Esther McCaul had come up with the solution.

—I know what we'll do! she cried, clapping her hands. If you want to go to the regatta dance, then here's what we'll do – are you listening to me, Beni? Beni Banikin, do you hear me?

Having apologised profusely for their 'bad start' as she'd termed it.

—Now you don't have to worry about a thing! she reassured her.

They would soon find her a dress, all right.

—It'll be just like home! What with you being an Amish and all!

Most of the gowns had been used in their production of *Oklahoma!*. There were aprons and prairie bonnets and voluminous gowns of pink calico, along with button boots and wide sweeping frocks with crocheted edging.

—If only Mia could see me now! laughed Beni – performing a bit of a girlish twirl.

—You look absolutely wonderful! chuckled Esther McCaul. You really do, Beni – honestly, I'm not kidding!

---

—*Oh, the farmer and the cowman should be friends!* laughed Maudie Breen, Esther's closest friend – or interfering bitch, if you'd care for my forthright opinion, spreading rumours about me when I'd been living with Esther. And who, according to herself – as she elbowed Beni in the ribs repeatedly – had received great praise for her part in the musical.

—And she's going to do it all over again tonight! enthused Esther. We've been planning this dance for over a year now!

—You can represent America in it, Esther laughed gaily, opening the packet and offering her a cigarette.

—What a great idea! they all agreed – especially Maudie Breen, who gripped her by the wrists. Gazing intently into her eyes.

—It will give the valley a great lift, Miss Banikin, it really will!

—What with you being our special visitor!

—Beni Banikin, our wonderful new friend! I can't tell you just how welcome you are to our little community here in Iron Valley!

I knew that tone of Esther's so well.

—*Whee!* she squealed again, spinning around the room excitedly, before concluding her dance with a great big huggy embrace for Beni.

—You know what I'll do? I'll fucking destroy you. That's what I'll do, Mr Gabriel King! I can remember her saying one night she was drunk.

—If you think you can turn around and just leave me like this then you had better have another think to yourself. I'll fix you, you snaky bastard.

---

Now if I happened to be a person of learning – like a certain rotund hirsute 'natural' scholar that I know – as opposed to an 'autodidact',

that is to say – I would advance the opinion that, in mythopoetic terms, the stage was already being set in the valley – keeping my nerves at a pitch of attention and sustaining a sense of the deepest foreboding.

A situation for which I have no one to blame but myself. And I accept that. Condemned to seek release from a serious error of judgement, or as Gartland might put it, licking his thumb as he leafs through his erudite volume:

—*An angry ghost who wanders in wilful solitude* – like the protagonist in *The Dreaming of the Bones*.

Fuck him.

---

Beni had already mislaid her mobile phone – ensuring that Mia, in spite of repeated efforts, wouldn't be able to reach her. What need did she have of a mobile phone? she asked herself. Striding on stilts across the Iron Valley.

—It's happening again, Mia agreed, I can sense it. She's omitted to take her medication.

—Jesus, said TJ – mopping his zealous, concerned, earnest brow.

---

The hotel room now was buzzing like a hive of bees. They were throwing down wine now like nobody's business, with Maudie Breen bleating that her best friend Esther was indeed a 'terrific character'.

—You can always be sure of a great time with Esther, just as soon as you see that girl coming! she cried.

Spiders? What spiders?

—Here! Give me another glass of wine! demanded Beni, for I fully intend to be the belle of the ball!

—It's great with the American accent, isn't it? Maudie snorted.

—Ha ha! Yes, chuckled Esther, it really is some crack! She's just the spit of a Yankee movie star!

More bottles were opened and further glasses went sailing around.

Subsequent to which, what might be described as an alarming 'incident' was seen to take place. Not that the occurrence itself could be said to have been particularly remarkable. Certainly not as far as I was concerned. Having travelled with Beni I knew she was capable of a great deal more outrageous acts than that – *kissing* someone!

But then I realised, true to form, it had all been part of Esther's plan – connivance – call it what you will. Not that Beni, of course, had ever suspected. Having thought nothing, in fact – or almost nothing – of the famous 'kiss' that had caused all the trouble. For her it had represented nothing more than a mere gesture of affection.

Even if she had, in fact, gripped Esther forcefully – a great deal more than she had intended to do – or perhaps ought to have done – kissing her, passionately, in fact, on the lips. As she pressed her body up against the wall. And in the process cried out:

—Darling, I love you! Esther!

Not having the faintest idea, then, what was happening. As she looked up to see them exiting – and the door of the hotel room closing gently behind them.

Although she had accused me of the very same thing, Esther had always been a very fine actor. The traduced, wronged and

misunderstood party. Why, that was a role she could play like a dream. Even if it was exactly what – many times – she had insisted *I* was doing.

—Jimjoe was right about you from the start, she said, you were never to be trusted. Look into his eyes, he used to say, he's made of stone – with the natural cunning of a serpent. Next thing she'd be quoting White in Latin.

*Ultinam viscos tuos canes inferni fucking edeant.*

May the dogs of hell devour your fucking entrails.

Charming. What wonderful people I've known down the years.

---

But at least there was Beni – who made it all worth it. And to her my heart goes out as I watch her delighting in the sweep of her calico gown, arriving on those cold familiar shores of Iron Lake. Just as the jaunty lilt of an accordion concluded, succeeded by a joyous, spontaneous burst of applause. And just in that instant she might been back in Goshen, Indiana. For everywhere you looked there were broughams and gigs – buckboards and landaus and old-fashioned wooden carts, with farm girls moving around and in their knitted shawls, ferrying woven baskets filled to the brim with fruit. As she stood there waiting by the side of the enormous striped marquee, with its coloured pennants and GOOD OLD DAYS slogans, thinking of those childhood days – and, in particular that winter morning. When, on account of the burst pipes, they had found themselves informed that the old wooden schoolhouse had been flooded. And that they had no option but to take their books into Pa Larsson's barn where they could resume their schoolwork and lessons, just as normal.

Which meant – even now she could feel the goose pimples once

more on her neck – she would be sitting close to Ta Ta Petersen. Her own special friend about whom nobody was ever to know. Because that was the promise she had made to her 'girlfriend'. That was what Ta Ta had made her swear that day they had both crawled in under the bridge.

—What's my name? her new girlfriend had asked her.

—Your name is Amy Petersen, Bethany had replied, shivering shakily – but quite deliciously.

Before Amy Petersen shook her head, taking one of Bethany's hands and placing it first on one small breast and immediately afterwards on its delectable twin.

—This is Ta, and this is Ta. So then, may I ask you, what is my name, sweet plum Beni Banikin?

—Ta Ta Petersen. That is your name, Amy, you are Ta Ta.

—Yes, that is my name, Ta Ta, my dear. And so from now on you must realise that you and I have been secretly married, but that it always and forever has to be kept hidden. Do you understand that, nice Bethany Banikin?

—Yes, she had nodded, for she would have done anything that Ta Ta had demanded.

Then they lay down together in the snow.

—You are my wife and you must make me snitz pie to have with some ice cream. Whenever I come home from chopping all my wood. I will eat it then and say that it is *gut*. I will come and live with you because I don't like my *Daed*. Would you like that?

—Yes I would, Bethany had replied, especially if you wore a leather jacket like Huey Lewis and the News.

—Oh, but I will, and I will sing you 'The Power of Love'.

—I can't tell you how happy that would make me.

⋆

Sometimes I wonder – and I know it's not right – but how could she not have loved me like that. Even for one night. I mean, one night, for fuck's sake!

That wouldn't have hurt her.

Why not even just for a single night?

Not that I don't still love her. Of course I do!

I love her with all my heart. It's just that—

It's not easy having prostate cancer, you know.

Why, I often wonder, did it have to be?

I'm not a bad person. Of course I'm not.

Sometimes, too, I wonder: did she do it with Gartland?

But I never found out. So I couldn't say if she ever did.

Not one hundred per cent, for certain.

Not, most likely, that he would have had the time.

Being so busy emancipating miners.

---

Beneath the swinging coloured banner, on the gig rig erected beside the marquee, the festival band had already started into their set. As the drummer tossed his sticks and treated Beni to a great big wave. The massive oaken table to the side of the tent groaned helplessly beneath the weight of its mouth-watering fare. As Beni was introduced to everyone – before being led over to take her seat. Everyone in the valley appeared to be there. At the far end of the table she could see Esther and Maudie – waving away as if nothing at all had happened. Which, as far as Beni Banikin was concerned, was in fact the case.

A regrettable appraisal of affairs, as I knew only too well – and which she would find herself discovering, and not so very long afterwards, either.

Maudie was smiling as she raised another glass of red. As if she was genuinely delighted to see Beni. Or 'that fucking swank queer', as Esther had called her earlier – just as they left the hotel after 'The Kiss'.

O.C. Brewster was fulsomely singing the praises of the food.

—Wouldja look at this, friends! gasped the congressman, tucking his napkin into his shirt. I swear to God I'm getting as drunk as Billy be damned!

—Drink up! laughed Hushabye Bonner, reaching across for the carafe of wine. And always remember there's plenty more where that came from, Mr Brewster!

As Big Ulick Owens raised his glass and called for a toast. To 'all of the good people from the valley here present'.

Before arriving over, to heartily slap the politician on the back.

—I hope youse are all having a good time, are youse? How are you doing there, Congressman Brewster? Working your way through them grits then, are you?

—*Haw haw!* laughed the politician.

—Eat up, ladies! chuckled Hushabye Bonner, as he lifted his cutlery, for in Ireland, as youse are aware, the next famine's always just around the next corner! But Iron Valley will live to fight another day!

—Damn right! cheered Congressman Brewster. We'll rise again, and anyone as says that ain't the case, well they's ain't of no more use than tits on a boar!

—I hope you like your barbecued ribs, Miss Banikin! bawled Toby Bonner suddenly – gesturing good-humouredly from the bottom of the table. Well, do you?

—Sure do! replied Beni. But I didn't expect this kind of lavish treatment!

—Och, sure, aren't we glad to have you! called out Maudie Breen, much to Beni's delight.

—That's right! agreed Esther. It's a pleasure and an honour to have someone like yourself. Someone who writes all them great big New York plays! *The Screaming of the Bones* – boy, but that's a great name for a play! No wonder that you're the toast of New York!

—New York? Ha ha – don't make me laugh! scoffed O.C. Brewster, I used to be ashamed when I was growing up, but then I realised we were as good as those uptown nobs – yeah, and better! Smart alecs!

—Yeah, Mr Brewster! Them sumbitch fuckers! laughed Hushabye loudly in a mock Southern twang, spearing some chicken. We's'uns belongs to The Meadowlands, ain't it?

I didn't want to hear him say that. The Meadowlands had nothing to do with him. For if it belonged to anyone, that story was the property of three other people. Who had soldiered together and starved themselves for their country. And Hushabye Bonner had had nothing to do with it. He wasn't even there in the prison when we created it.

—All we have got to remember, boomed OC, is that all of us, we're in it together – right, folks?

—All for one, and one for all! agreed Toby Bonner.

—And if one goes down, then all of us go down! Whaddya say, men? That we'll all hang together!

—Right you are there, Congressman friend! cried Jimjoe White, genially tipping the brim of his Panama.

As, completely out of nowhere, what can only be described as an anguished howl interrupted the proceedings – resulting in all of the exchanges literally dying right there on their lips. And, to their

amazement, they found themselves looking up to see Big Ulick Owens – with floods of tears coming coursing down his cheeks. With his glass of Merlot falling out of his grasp, splintering in shards between his feet underneath the table. As he trembled violently, like a wounded animal.

—Fuck youse all, do youse hear me, youse bastards? After what youse did to my son! What have you done with my Bobby – where is my boy?

A close friend rose from his seat, going immediately to his aid, and doing his best to placate him – with some small degree of success. But not much. For Ulick continued to present a pathetic sight.

—A big fellow like that, blubbing away like a girl, muttered Hushabye Bonner resentfully behind his hand.

With the unease persisting until more wine was opened, being consumed with an avidity bordering on the frenetic – until at last everything appeared to be on the verge of returning to relatively normal. Then a glass broke loudly and the voice of Maudie Breen rose above the chastened hubbub of conversation:

—She's not the only one we've ever had, you know. There was another lesbian here one time!

She glared quite fiercely along the length of the wooden table.

Subsequent to which there wasn't so much as a sound, and for some considerable time indeed. There wasn't even so much as even a sob from Big Ulick. Until, finally, clearly incapable of tolerating the tension any longer, Hushabye Bonner rose to his feet, calling loudly for everyone's attention. Before proceeding to congratulate all who had been associated with the theatre guild's recent production of *The Good Old Days*, the successor to last year's extraordinarily successful *Oklahoma!*. Singling out Big Ulick Owens, he said, on account of his magnificent versatility during the run of the show:

—Congratulations, Ulick, you really did yourself proud this year! As always!, he beamed.

With everyone clapping as they turned to face the big man.

—Don't talk to me, you terrorist bastard! hissed Ulick fiercely, knocking over a pile of dishes with his elbow. The crash was deafening.

Many, including Mayor White, clearly were not at all pleased by this renewed outburst, tensing up and determinedly looking away.

As Beni, hopelessly inebriated now, lifted her head to become aware of a familiar set of eyes, a pair of unflinching orbs which were deliberately, icily fixed upon her – and her alone. Esther McCaul had changed places and was sitting directly across from her now – strained and pale and ramrod stiff. Coiled.

—Ah, there you are, Esther! chimed Hushabye Bonner, grabbing a bottle and offering her a glass.

But Esther didn't make any reply – clearly extremely intoxicated herself – lighting a cigarette, which she managed to succeed in dropping twice. Before knocking over a cafetière, which fortunately didn't break, its contents dripping languidly onto the grass. Looking at her there, I have to say she looked even more malnourished than usual.

—You think you're special, don't you, bitch? she growled at Beni, with her small hand trembling as she tapped the cigarette. Huh – well, don't you? Don't think you can ignore me! Look at me!

Where the strength came from within her, Beni couldn't say – all she could think was: What a pity it hadn't been there the night that Johnny Roxbury decided to come calling. And there wasn't so much as a spider in sight. Just like the poet said, peace had come dropping slow – a zen-like calm had descended upon her being.

—Once upon a time I would probably have reacted adversely to this inexplicable development, she told herself, but not now. Not when such a feeling of belonging and homeliness has somehow, almost miraculously, been gifted to me. Here by the shores of the beautiful lake, beneath the peak of this majestic mountain, where my old friend Gabriel has lived all his life. It's just not going to happen.

She felt like a bluebird perched upon a glass – upon the dome of a bell jar, chirping. Gazing in cheekily as if to say: *I'm free!*

Resolving now, privately, to accommodate Esther in whatever way she could. Because she knew a hurt soul whenever she saw one. As Mia might say, why would she not – when she in her time had been one herself? Bruised and vulnerable and hopelessly misunderstood. She reached out to take her hand. At which point Esther McCaul turned the colour of parchment.

—Fucking American tramp! she grunted, jabbing the cigarette viciously as she hissed:

—You've made another big mistake, my friend.

As Hushabye Bonner again intervened.

—Ha! he laughed mischievously. Do you hear that old Esther! Giving out about the Americans now, are you? Go easy on the vino, love – just in case Mr Brewster might hear ya!

—I don't see anyone talking to you, Bonner! she snapped. I don't remember anyone talking to you, Mr fucking Know-It-All! How about you, maybe, piss off, Bonner! Huh? How about maybe you try doing that!

This time, however, his reaction was far less conciliatory. To put it mildly.

—Don't be unwise, Esther, he advised menacingly. That mightn't be such a good idea, if you know what I'm saying.

Then, again unexpectedly, he grinned from ear to ear. Before turning to Beni.

—You don't have to worry, Miss – believe me. It's just that Esther's had a wee bit too much to drink.

Beni smiled. Of course she didn't mind, she assured him. Before becoming aware that Maudie Breen had now joined the company.

—Think you can ignore my friend, do you? Is that what you think?

She placed her hand on Beni's shoulder, stiffening her fingers as she gripped it harshly.

—Listen to me, you!

—Don't look away from her when she's talking to you! roared Esther, suddenly screeching – and swiping the wine glass right off the table.

Now it was Beni's turn to grow pale. And for those first few tremulous seconds she was on the verge of, actually, simply rising from her chair – and getting the hell away from there. Without a word of explanation to anyone. Maybe flee into the sanctuary of the woods, she thought, just like she used to when she was with Ta Ta, repeating the name of her lover over and over, discarding her clothes one by one as they fell, peeling away like the softest petals.

—Mia! My Mia! You are my beautiful doll, my Olympia! – as she imagined herself leaping and extending her wings.

But she didn't do that. Because, of course, now she knew better – having learned the value, as she told herself, of simple willpower! The sheer power of a strong nature mastering a strong will.

—There's no need for anger, she smiled beatifically, looking directly into Esther's eyes After all, we're both hurt souls, are we not?

Before finding herself roughly grabbed by the wrist.

—I know what you're here for. I know you brought that

miserable bastard back. But make no mistake, I won't let you get away with it. For there's only one place that that bastard belongs – in the trash with all the other rats!

Hushabye leaned over, covering his mouth.

—Keep your voice down, Esther, do you hear me?

—You've no right to give me orders! Do you hear me, Bonner? You've no right to go ordering me about! You or any of your Altnavogue cronies. I'm not afraid of the tough guy Bonners!

She tried her best to light another cigarette but dropped it again. As she rose to her feet with the blood draining from her face.

—I'll be seeing you later, bitch – this isn't over!

After which Beni drifted off into sleep. Before sensing a meaty hand gripping her firmly by the shoulder.

—It's time we were heading to the movies, compadres! declared Hushabye Bonner.

As Maudie Breen gently took Beni by the arm, leading her towards a waiting pickup, laughing as she told her they were all sorry.

—You don't want to mind Esther, Beni – like all of us here her bark is worse than her bite! So come on ahead and we'll all have a ball! Will you? Come on now with us, Miss Banikin – please say you will!

—Of course I will! replied Beni – with her spirits immeasurably lifting once more.

Yes, this was the way it ought to be, she told herself – before climbing into the truck behind Maudie and seating herself squarely in the seat beside Esther.

Sadly – I swallowed in anticipation – there was no chance of things being turned back now. Although Beni couldn't possibly have

known that. Tragically, in fact, now thinking the opposite. Finding herself, in fact, immensely grateful when she heard Esther agree she didn't have 'any problem at all' sharing a ride with either the 'American visitor' or the Bonners. So what if she'd been a bit drunk and lost her temper earlier, she laughed contemptuously – who in the valley didn't do that from time to time? And at the end of the day were the Bonners not her 'oldest pals'?

—Sure are, laughed Hushabye, pressing his foot to the pedal and hurtling forward.

As the pickup continued rattling along the road. Lulling Beni into a state of soporific calm, taking her back to that day in Cincinnati, where she is mesmerised looking at the shoals, those needles of light – coming at intervals through the trees.

As a closed fist rises up and strikes her on the jaw – and she turns to see the *commedia dell'arte* face of Esther McCaul glaring:

—Maybe that will put manners on you, bitch – do you hear?!

The sound of the blow had been surprisingly dull. As Esther hesitantly drew back her arm.

—*Whore!* she snapped.

—Esther, have manners, demanded Hushabye, turning around in the driver's seat.

—Why – you going to shoot me if I don't? she cackled.

—I'd send you home in a heartbeat, babe. And don't think I wouldn't.

—Like you and your brother did to plenty in your time, she answered defiantly. Watch out, girls – here's the murdering Bonners.

—You hurt me, Esther! Beni wept helplessly. I hope you know that fucking hurt! I hope you know that hurt me, God damn you!

Esther pulled out a cigarette and stiffened.

—That's what you get. We don't take kindly to them dyke types in the valley!

—For Christ's sake, Esther! bawled Hushabye.

—Screw you, Bonner!, Esther rejoined.

The twenty-foot screen attempted to rival the height of Iron Mountain, or so it seemed. As an enormous Buzz Lightyear clambered out of his toy box, with the blue beams of his eyes trawling the great big inky-coloured cut-outs of the countryside.

As Esther appeared to lose control. Reaching over, doing her best to grab Beni's hair.

—Don't you fucking touch me! squealed Beni, striking out wildly – to no discernible purpose.

—For Christ's sake, Esther, will you leave the girl alone! shouted Hushabye. I always knew that you were trouble, you know that? I even warned him – that motherfucker, King!

—Don't even mention his name, do you hear me! growled Toby. You listening to me, Hushabye? Don't even mention the turncoat bastard!

—You hear what he's calling your lover, dyke? You hear what they're saying – they're calling your lover a fucking Judas tout!

—Don't you dare say a word against him! Beni screamed. You have no right to say anything about my Gabriel – he was a hero!

—She doesn't know the first thing about it, does she? Esther chuckled. She really does not have the slightest fucking clue!

—A hero, eh?

—Eleven years in prison. Fifty-five days on hunger strike – and this is what he gets! So this is how the Irish treat their heroes!

—There were plenty of men prepared to lay down their lives, but rest assured he wasn't one of them. Did a couple of months in

The Maze, before they turned him into a rat. Brought nothing but dishonour and shame to the movement. Took part in Altnavogue and one or two other operations – then went and pissed himself with fright. Gave them every name he knew. Told them everything, going right back as far as the early seventies.

—He returned from Africa to fight for his country!

—The bastard was never in Africa in his life!

—He was a mercenary in Angola, what in hell's name are you talking about?

—You ever read *The Dogs of War*? You ever read that more or less forgotten piece of pulp trash by Frederick Forsyth? That's where he got it, his fairy-tale history, the compulsive fucking liar – for that's all he was! And fed you a pack of bullshit into the bargain – fool that you are, believing it all!

—You couldn't believe a word out of his mouth. Even took part in the killing of Pearse Gavigan to try and save his own skin. Why do you think he went to America? Sure, he was there the night we stiffed The Farmer, you idiot, irrespective of what bullshit he may have fed you! So what do you think of your Irish hero now? Still sweet on the infamous Gabriel King now, are you?

High above them on the screen, Woody and Bo Peep, *Toy Story*'s pastel-coloured twenty-foot dolls, were bathed in light, grinning inanely as they came strolling through the park. Esther stabbed her heel into Beni's ankle.

—Like screwing my husband, did you then, bitch?

Grinding it viciously into her calf.

—Should have pulled a black bag over his head and popped him. Ought to have given him the Farmer treatment, stiffed the fucking rat and shoved him down a hole.

Beni decided she could bear it no longer. God, I was proud of her. Yes, I have to say that I really was proud.

—I don't believe a word of your bullshit, she shot back defiantly, he came home from Africa and was prepared to give his life for what he believed in – and this is what he gets in return, you bunch of ungrateful, heel-flinging rednecks!

An icy silence, with no peace at all, began to descend. Dropping very, very slow indeed.

—You've gone and made a bad mistake now, lady, said Esther.

As Hushabye Bonner laughed that she was only joking:

—We're all just getting a little bit carried away. Whaddya say we go for a drink?

And the truck went roaring in the direction of Mickey's Bar, like a toy rattling past the flickering screen mounted high on wooden stilts, on through the valley towards the back of the mountain where the late-night soirée had been prearranged. But not before making a pit-stop at the hotel. For the purposes of collecting a certain item. Which, as they discovered, had been secreted in a closet, and once more heading off – cheering! – to Mickey's. Where the doors were flung wide open to admit 'the funeral party', led by Hushabye with his squat copper receptacle. Containing the star of *Ashes of Love*. Or, if you prefer, yours truly, insubstantial night-rambler, solitary protagonist of a Noh play yet-to-be.

---

So whether or not you believe me – and I really can't say that I'd blame you if you didn't – that's exactly what happened on that warm midsummer's night during the Iron Valley movie festival. But it would be a long time afterwards before it would ever be referred to in any detail again. Before anyone in the valley would find themselves comfortable enough to even begin to broach what

had transpired. Not that that wasn't understandable, for who could have been proud of what had eventually taken place behind the locked doors of Mickey's Bar? Even if, strictly speaking, as many would argue later, it had been no one single individual's fault? It was just a pity that things had 'got a little out of control' in the end. That was all you could really say about it. 'That dreadful night in Mickey's Bar' – a subject which was set to remain undiscussed for quite some considerable time to come.

Although in terms of sheer gravity, at least, it could hardly have been compared to another, I guess, out-of-control happening – which, of course, had taken place in a certain town-land called Altnavogue many years before. And regarding which, similarly, one was expected to turn a blind eye. Unless you wanted to be 'sent home' – either by Hushabye or one of his lieutenants.

Like poor old Pearse Gavigan, obsessive fan of Philip Lynott and Thin Lizzy. How Hushabye and Toby had begun to suspect him of revealing seriously compromising information to the authorities nobody had ever really established for sure. But those in the movement were now adamant that he was 'a rat'.

The most loathed figure in all of Irish history. An informer, a tout.

—The lowest form of human life imaginable, said Jimjoe, *vile*.

Which was why they went to see him that day – drove up to his farm, after which he was never seen alive again.

---

When the news got out, no one could believe it. Because Pearse Gavigan had always been extremely popular locally – quiet, sure, but extremely generous and good-natured, puttering about the

district in his John Deere tractor, playing his Thin Lizzy tapes on an eight-track. It all proved to be too much to bear, the thought of it.

Which perhaps provides the reason why anyone present in Mickey's Bar that night might resort to the tried and trusted comfort provided by the kind of irreverent humour that was so common in the valley over the years. With everyone straining to be that little bit more outrageous than their neighbour, taking pains to emphasise the fact that their particular conscience was clear and, after what had happened, that as far as that 'bloody festival' was concerned, there were times when you thought maybe it was time to 'wind the whole thing up'.

But always tending towards the conclusion that, after all, when you weighed up the evidence in a fair and reasonable and objective fashion, what had happened that night to Miss Banikin the American amounted in the end to just 'one of those unfortunate things' – a deeply tragic and regrettable episode. For whom nobody, really, ultimately, had been to blame.

Because, as they all knew, there were very few citizens residing in Iron Valley who did not, at the end of the day, have the welfare of their community at heart. Yes, of course, certain people had gone and made complete fools of themselves during the festival, with well over a dozen people being arrested, not to mention the business with Nuttsy Corrigan getting drunk and breaking into poor Miss Banikin's hotel room. But surely, it had to be agreed, in all honesty, that it was hardly comparable to events which had taken place many years before. During the 'troubled times'.

Such as Altnavogue, of course, when things had been 'off-centre', demons released on a scale that had never been experienced before in the district. Although there were those who continued to insist that, even on that occasion, there had been no express intention of

harming people. And that the only intention had been to give the family concerned a severe and final warning. After all, they were well known to be bigots who had relatives in the security forces. Most certainly had been no intention to harm Wee Boab, to send the infant to his eternal reward – good God, how could there be?

Which Dog White on the night had made abundantly clear to everyone present. Just as they were putting on their masks. They had just come to fire 'a shot across the bows', he explained – in effect, to caution this family who had been 'marked' for some time.

—Yes, continued Dog, to make it clear to these enemies of the Catholic people that if they didn't get their house in order next time they would be taught a lesson for good.

With the only problem being, as I well knew at the time, and as did the others, that there never would be a next time.

Because one of the occupants had been impertinent to Dog White. Yes, one of the teenage boys present had stood up for his mother and brazenly defied the intruders.

—We'll have to raze the place to the ground, decided Dog, every stick in the place, we'll burn it. But as well as that, we'll teach this fellow a lesson.

And it was then that I stepped forward – for the young fellow's impertinence – I'm afraid I have to say that it really had annoyed me.

—I wonder is he fond of Wee Boab? I suggested. You know, somehow, I think that he is.

And that soon changed things, as I dropped the bomb into the cradle – blowing the baby into the fireplace. Not so much impertinence then, I'm afraid. With its little helpless arm raised upwards

like a snowdrop. Sad, of course. But, like I'd explained to Beni – that's war.

---

*Manikin Banikin under the sun*
*Manikin Banikin she ain't any fun!*

That was what the children of Goshen used to chant on those Indiana afternoons whenever they'd see little Bethany approach. Jostling against her to spill her pails of water and calling after her:

—Manikin Banikin, why are you dumb?

Which was nasty and unfair but also quite untrue. For Bethany Banikin could, in fact, speak. It was just that only recently she had decided she didn't want to, not long after finding her dead father in a barn.

—From now on I'll never talk to anyone, she resolved, I'll just fetch my water and stare at the wall.

And that was exactly what she did – until the elders summoned her mother. There were lots of these old men – with not so much as a single woman in their ranks. Which was wrong, and Bethany knew it. But she also knew it was unwise to challenge them publicly, and certainly not like Fannie Banikin had done. Her mother had actually sworn at the elders. And no one in Goshen, absolutely no one, ever swore.

The men stood in the kitchen and demanded that her mother take the oath, with her hand on the Bible, before admitting to the fact that it was hers, and hers only, the blame for her husband having taken his own life.

—Because of your various adulteries, they said, and your licentious dalliance with the disgraced Cooper Kemble.

—Ha ha, she laughed, is that what you say?

—Yes, that's what we say but not only that, but also that you are a Jezebel, a red temptress who has brought disgrace upon our village.

—Fuck!, hissed Fannie. To have to listen to this!

Then what happened – didn't Pa Larsson strike her? Which wasn't good because after that Fannie used her nails. Her red nails. Drawing blood from Pa Larsson's face. The elders said that she would pay for that. So now her child would be taken away forever.

Which was indeed what eventually happened. But not in Goshen – in faraway Louisiana. Where she and her mother had been tenanted in a brothel – until, finally, they came to take Bethany to Maria Coeli Orphanage in New Orleans – where the rotund shadow of Dr Karsten lay waiting.

---

In a place every bit as sterile and inhospitable as the hospital ward in which Beni Banikin now was to find herself lying, in the aftermath of the 'accident', being ferried at high speed from Mickey's Bar in an ambulance.

—I'm afraid the news isn't good, the consultant was explaining to a truly ghastly-looking Esther McCaul. Who had just arrived, as she subsequently would on an almost daily basis, in the company of an equally traumatised Walter Reilly.

—The facts are that the cerebral cortex is significantly contused, and she appears to have haemorrhaged. There has also been severe sudden twisting and there is evidence of concomitant diffuse axonal injury. It's looking, I'm sorry to have to say, that your friend may well end up being permanently brain-damaged.

—It's all my fault! Please forgive me, Oh God, I'm so sorry! wept Esther helplessly, before collapsing in a flood of tears – which this time weren't put on but were genuine – before being led away by Walter Reilly, like a vulnerable foal with a broken leg.

---

A truly stupefying denouement, I suppose – hardly elevated, and certainly not in the Yeatsian league – to an adventure which had begun as nothing if not a form of sacred pilgrimage, for the purposes of the interment of what remained of my somewhat undistinguished mortal remains. And in some ways, too, what can only be described as a quite heartbreaking conclusion, one which sees that sad broken party of heretofore loyal friends arriving at the door of their Long Island apartment. Lifting Beni's wheelchair across the threshold, bitterly choked up but trying their best not to show it, for William's sake. As he stands here, absently, in his black denim jacket. Looking like a dazed and out-of-sorts little Elvis, I can't help but thinking.

A little ashamed – for this is not the time for frivolity.

Even if TJ is hitting the whiskey. Something which he has always forsworn. He certainly gave me enough lectures about it.

—It's all about discipline, I remember him saying – before waddling off to the library in those stupid glasses.

---

The specialist, Soheb Bowry, had detained Beni in Beaumont Hospital in Dublin for seventeen days, with three further weeks scheduled in New York for aftercare and intensive observation. Subsequent to which it had been decided that she be discharged.

—There is little further advantage in her remaining here, the consultant neurologist had, apparently, informed 'Teej'.

And so now, in the days that were to follow, Mia could only marvel as His Majesty Dr Gartland – *saintly* was a word that Mia often used to describe him – continued to go out of his way to feed and clothe the patient. But, privately, although of course he would never confess it, he was finding it so damn difficult to think of Beni in this way – such a vital and lovely, abundantly creative person, whose writing career had effectively only just begun, with the artistic world falling at her feet when the tragedy had occurred.

The truth being that, without His Majesty, Mia didn't know what on earth she would have done – for he laboured quite selflessly. And if his efforts with Beni herself weren't enough, as well as that, didn't he agree to collect William from school every day, keeping the boy's spirits up magnificently, telling him endless jokes and driving him to football games? Trying to convince him that one day, miraculously, they would arrive home from one of these tournaments and find his mother, not in her wheelchair as might have been expected, but coming running towards them across the floor with her arms outstretched. With that same loving light, as of old, in her eyes.

---

Sadly, however, a most unlikely scenario indeed, one is compelled to observe. About as plausible, perhaps, as the boisterous arrival of a party of theatregoers fresh from the premises of Mickey's Bar for the purposes of viewing the first night of Beni Banikin's reinvention and updating of Yeats's dance-drama *The Dreaming of The Bones*, now

rechristened *The Night Visitor*, which had recently been lauded by the *Village Voice*, among many others, including the *New York Times*.

And a spontaneous, eccentric and certainly more extravagant production of which might be said to have been staged in the early morning hours of 25 July 2011, behind the locked doors of Mickey's Bar in Iron Valley, where already the patrons were stomping their boots with impunity on a carpet of the finest powdery dust which was all that remained of the contents of a certain receptacle – yes, *that* urn! – which they had only just, hilariously, retrieved from the privacy of Beni's room. After all, as Hushabye had observed, it wouldn't have been fair to exclude 'our Gabriel'.

—After all, we don't want him feeling lonely! And it's only right and proper that we give our old friend a proper send-off! Say goodbye to Mr Rat!

—Goodbye, Mr Rat! Hooray, everybody! Goodbye, fucker!

But by now the majority of the exercised imbibers – having done a more than acceptable job of tramping what was left of me into the carpet – were more than otherwise occupied, with their attentions unanimously focused on the spectacle of a semi-naked Beni Banikin on top of the bar, removing each item of clothing as she pirouetted, discarding them contemptuously as if casting rose petals upon the breeze. As, to their astonishment, they heard her declare:

—My housemistress used to dress up as a man and seduce me – yes! She brought me off to see the band in Baton Rouge! And guess what – *I loved her!* Every bit as much as Mia – don't you think that's strange?

Skipping with a surprising agility along the stainless steel counter with both her arms extended, endeavouring to balance herself with a drink in either hand. Before finishing one and casting away the other, as a pink striped sock went sailing into the air, and off she

stepped gaily once more, with a vigour and vitality that was almost preposterous.

Big Ulick, his tears dried at last, was lying prostrate underneath the belly of the mechanical bull. As Walter Reilly turned around in circles, chuckling hysterically but making no sense. Congressman Brewster was trying on a sombrero. As Beni, entirely naked, cried out gaily from the top of the counter:

—Yoo-hoo, everyone! I'm free of the bell jar! And I'm free, too, of that bastard, Johnny Roxbury! So the hell with you, spiders, with your fucking butch-waxed Elvis faces! For nothing at all can stop me now! I love you, Mia darling! Always remember that!

As the missile in question – a billiard ball, in fact – appeared to hang suspended in the air for almost a minute – which of course was illusory – before recovering its velocity and, in the course of striking her a glancing blow to the side of the face, caused Beni to fatally misjudge her balance, with the result that she slipped right off the edge of the counter.

—She made me do it! Esther McCaul was shrieking helplessly. I didn't want to – but she made me! She's been taunting me ever since she got here!

As Beni soared for a moment and then fell, arms flailing, cracking her head against the tiles, with her face and hair covered in the dust of my bones. About which what could you say?

Except maybe: The happy, fulfilled lovers – reunited at last!

---

But she was never to know that, was she, or how far-reaching the consequences of her misfortune were to be – for their dear friend,

the literary genius T.J. Gartland, every bit as much as for her long-term lover Mia Chiang. When, many long and sleepless nights after her return to Long Island, he would once more rise from his bed and start pacing, walking the floor in a state of absolute dread. As I stood there, motionless, directly behind him – whispering softly and laying my hand, ever so gently, on his shoulder.

—Did you dream about her again – your mother? Did you, TJ?

With his mounting feelings – in spite of Herculean efforts, he couldn't for the life of him seem to evict them – becoming close to unmanageable. And in no way alleviated by such sights as those of their little boy William handing Woody the pull-string cowboy doll from *Toy Story*, in a gesture of affection to his mother. An act responded to by a cry of appallingly abject terror. As the wheel-chair-bound woman tore wildly at the string, before flinging the brightly coloured object across the room – trembling uncontrollably, believing herself to be possessed by the spirit of Dr Karsten.

—Finally she has claimed me! she was trying to say.

I knew that, of course – but they didn't.

Because the only sound that left Beni's lips was:

—*Mmnngh!*

No, none of this helped poor *Teej* at all, and in the end he started visiting Belle Vue again. Complaining of 'troubles' which he, surprisingly, couldn't accurately seem to name.

—Strange, I remember thinking, for someone with such a disciplined mind. For someone who, as we all know, was such a 'scholar'.

Why, I mean, even an autodidact could describe a hallucination. Which was what he had experienced the first night of his ultimate 'breakdown'.

As I stood, without speaking – without even breathing, in fact, to be honest. Which was where I remained until he opened his eyes.

After which – it's true – he started looking like death. With his hair, in fact, actually standing upright.

In spite of everything, the head consultant psychiatrist at Belle Vue had concluded that the symptoms TJ manifested represented nothing more than the instinctive watchfulness of an already overtaxed imagination. But had, in any case, agreed to the drained lecturer's voluntary readmission to the hospital, for an initial period of six weeks. After which he was pronounced 'cured'. Which, unfortunately, as he was to discover, was a mistake – and quite premature.

When, in the aftermath of the consumption of a considerable amount of whiskey late one night, he became aware of my presence once again. Or what he quite unkindly had described as *that thing* in the corner. Whose gaze continued to fix him with a perfectly human expression of malice, which had somehow become transfused into the visage of a bloated, grey, heavy vermin, teasing through a missing incisor:

—Please don't worry – it's gonna be OK, Teej – you'll see.

But it wasn't.

No, I'm afraid it wasn't at all.

---

None of which makes anyone feel good – how could it? And for which I deserve every retribution. As, once more on the hillside, I find myself waiting . . . for Esther McCaul – who else! In my allotted role of The Night Visitor, I suppose you might say, tediously re-enacting my old life on the mountain.

Where very soon I know she'll be arriving, decked out in that infuriating leather coat, bawling her eyes out about how good it used to be.

—When Gabriel loved me.

That's what she always says.

*As if!* like the kids today say. Pulling what's left of me out of her plastic handbag – whatever little bit she's managed to scrape off Mickey's carpet. Opening the tin and casting a few fistfuls out across the water, like Beni Banikin was supposed to have done, before she went and made a bollocks of it – no, that's not fair, for we all have our troubles. And maybe it was too much of a tall order in the first place.

But anyway, now out it comes and off comes the lid, with the first handful of her former partner borne aloft on the wind, across the water.

—*Goodbye, Gabriel*, she starts to howl, launching into another dirge:

—*Step softly, stranger, for a dream lies buried here.*

Whatever prayerbook she got that out of, still bawling her eyes out as she fires fistful after fistful in a flurry.

But she's not a bad sort, Esther – even if she did bore me to tears, in the few sad years the pair of us spent together. As off she goes now on her little spindly legs, weeping and muttering about this life's heartless brevity. Or whatever her simplified version of such sentiments might be.

And I begin to sense the old familiar dread, already commencing my journey along the line of dripping firs, pushing back the branches, making my way into the clearing in the direction of the old stone cabin.

Where, as always, I'll sit, gazing fixedly into the fireplace, at the ash and what remains of a dead infant's bones. As the soft rains of April begin to drift across the valley, gently glazing the first snowdrops of spring.

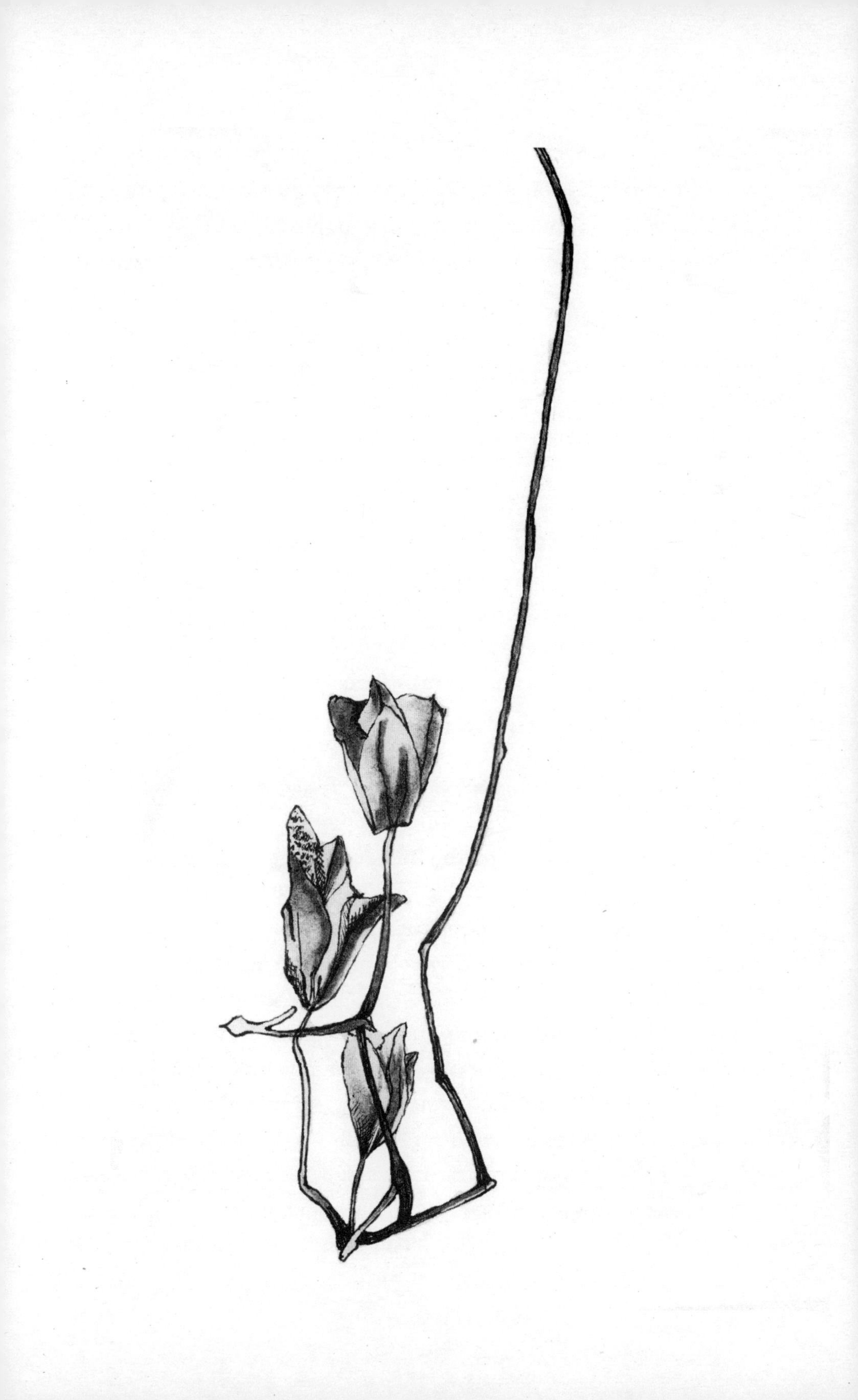